KEEPING BEDLAM AT BAY IN THE PRAGUE CAFÉ

D0013413

Published by New Europe Books, 2013
Williamstown, Massachusetts
www.NewEuropeBooks.com

Copyright © M. Henderson Ellis, 2013
Cover design © András Baranyai, 2013
Interior design by Justin Marciano

ALL RIGHTS RESERVED. No part of this book may be reproduced or transmitted in any form or by any means, electronic or mechanical, including photocopying and recording, or by any information storage or retrieval system, without written permission from the publisher except in the case of brief quotations in critical articles and reviews.

ISBN: 978-0-9825781-8-6

Cataloging-in-Publication Data is available from the Library of Congress.

Printed in the United States of America on acid-free paper.

KEEPING BEDLAM AT BAY IN THE PRAGUE CAFÉ

A Novel

M. Henderson Ellis

New Europe Books

*This novel is dedicated to the
magical spirit of Albert Houston.*

In history, imagination makes fools of us.

—RALPH WALDO EMERSON

PIGSTROKE

A SOLITARY TRAVELER

A PIG LED BY A SKINHEAD EMERGED FROM THE NIGHTTIME FOG.
Shirting was fidgeting with his glasses, which were cumber-
some, black, and worn without a trace of irony, when the
skin spoke to him in Czech. To Shirting the pair resembled
a comic book superhero and insouciant sidekick. He merely
shrugged his shoulders and smiled.

"*Sprichst du Deutsch?* Deutsch?" the skin said in German.
Shirting was unsure if he was being slighted. He had seen
such characters as this on talk TV and was torn between putting the fascistically apparelled youngster in his place and
making a good first impression; it was, after all, his first spon-
taneous encounter with a local.

"I hate to disappoint you, but my allegiance lies elsewhere."

The blank look on the skin's face prompted him to continue: "Though it is quite possible that I share a love of effi-
ciency with the folk of your beloved Vaterland. One time, at
Capo Coffee Family, I singlehandedly managed the espresso
machine during the morning rush. Not an easy operation,
what with the countless flavor options offered by any Capo's
outlet. I only mention this to demonstrate that there is always a
bit of common ground between people, if they only look for it."

The skin glanced between Shirting and his pig, which was rooting around Shirting's Buster Browns. He then leaned forward, assuming the confidential mien of a black marketeer. "Germany," he said in barely accented English, "does not exist. It is nothing but a state of mind, a *shunyala*, as the mystics say." At this point, Shirting felt the pig's damp snout probe his bare skin, having nuzzled its way between his sock and pant leg. He jumped back in revulsion.

"Get that thing away from me, the dastardly beast. It downright reeks of the slop and disease!" He glared at the skinhead, who appeared not to hear his appeal. Shirting's indignation mounted as he perceived something incongruent about the boy's appearance.

"Is that a Star of David you are wearing?" he asked. "Some of our most adamant customers at Capo Coffee Family were of Jewish persuasion. I won't hear a word against them," he added preemptively.

"Jews, as you call them, do not exist either," the skin said, finally pulling the pig off Shirting by its tail. "Yin to the antimatter yang of the German state." The furrows in the youth's brow, so deep they might have been imprinted with a pie cutter, manifested the seriousness of his convictions.

"Your sentiments reek of . . ."

"Neo Mysticism?" the skin said hopefully.

"Garlic . . . mostly garlic."

Shirting could see that he was dealing with a madman, made all the more dangerous by his command of the English language. Not that Shirting was unaccustomed to the imbalanced. The marketing at Capo Coffee, the premium coffee chain he had until recently worked at, was very much geared toward affecting an atmosphere of calm in which customers could loiter and indulge themselves—needless to say, a veritable outpatient services office for needy and hysterical personalities. Shirting reflexively reached into his suit pocket and pulled out a free drink coupon, offering it forth in hopes of quelling any anxiety his outburst had provoked. The skin accepted the ticket, a glossy paper-plastic blend decorated like a comic dollar bill, with an illustration of an Al Capone-like gangster in the oval frame, pinching a tiny espresso cup in his fingers and winking confidentially.

"It's for a Capone'cino, like a Cappuccino, only with more *muscle*. For twenty cents extra you can get a Lucky Latte'ano, but the Capone'cino is the flagship drink, so that's what I'm pushing."

"I can see you are one with us," the skin said, accepting the offer. He then caught Shirting off-guard by spinning around on one foot—a revolution that, when complete, revealed him to be adorned with a small accordion. Had it been hanging off his back all the while? Shirting would be hard pressed to deny that the instrument was not produced from thin air.

"*Ein, Zwei, Drei*—" the skin chanted before breaking into a klezmer-embellished riff. The music's mystical qualities warmed Shirting to his new acquaintance. It was not long before, on that first summer night in Prague, that John Shirting had danced a jig, the moves of which were so categorically Shirting: arms flailing out in front of him like a mod zombie, legs kicking, as though he were perpetually falling backwards off a cliff. He felt under a spell and unable to resist, the skin having so thoroughly infected him with his own unselfconscious crunching of those wheezing bellows. For how long he was entranced he could not ascertain, nor would he be able to verify that the pig too was not up on its hind legs enjoying a frolic of its own, or perhaps mocking Shirting's spasmodic steps.

"Yours is a fine world music, a fine world music," the winded traveler would say, once the tune had ceased, his free will regained. "I apologize if we got off on the wrong foot, but as a city dweller I am not accustomed to livestock and their affections." Shirting reached down and held his finger out for the pig to sniff. When he looked up again, he discovered the skin was now offering a snow globe to him in his outstretched palm. Illuminated under the night sky, he could see the cityscape of Prague inside the small glass dome. The skin suddenly withdrew the snow globe and shook it. Shirting felt immediately dizzy, as though he himself had been shaken, and—if only for a moment—the cityscape of Prague somehow bled into his own porous flesh.

Once he steadied himself, he decided it was time to sally on. Shirting waved a salutation to the skin. In return the skin held up his arm in a "heil" salute. Shirting, in a surge of optimism and companionship, mistook this gesture for a high-five, and slapped the skin's hand with his own.

"Shalom," the skin said. Shirting smiled exuberantly. "Shalom," the skin repeated, walking backward, away from Shirting before disappearing, as he would later note in his travel journal, "cinematically" into the fog. The pig too would follow its master into the cover of night, but not before making three revolutions around Shirting as though he were a pylon on some swine obstacle course. The American looked after them with longing. Though they had treated him shortly, Shirting harbored no malice. A solitary traveler, he felt quite alone in that unknown city and had been grateful for the company.

At Long Last Lost

THE LINDEN TREES OUTSIDE OF SHIRTING'S STŘEŠOVICE apartment shed their fleecy pods as the early autumn winds blew down from the palace hill, showering his attic room with their confetti, little white paratroopers seeking fecund soil only to alight upon the cold hardwood floor of a rented room—as if any further proof was needed that airborne hopes were sometimes dashed. The stray seeds, with all their unfulfilled potential, all their agrarian expectation, would be left there on the floor until Shirting's landlady, Hanna Sminkova, widow to the late Ivan Smink, ascended the house's granite steps to make her daily assessment of the state of affairs in her lodger's room. Armed with a broom and dust tray (both state-made, in need of mending) she swept the pods into a dusty pile, along the way gathering a bunched-up sock and several discarded facial tissues. With a barely detectable grimace she dumped the lodger's dirt into its own individual plastic bag (for reasons not even she was clear on), to be kept separate from the family's own waste. After salvaging the solitary sock, with a raptor's eye for dirty clothing, a true talent for congregating laundry, *Pane* Sminkova spotted the sock's counterpart making its escape under the bed, then whisked it from that space with the bristly end of the broom. Later that same day, the Czech landlady found time to wash the duo in an individual load (once again segregated from the family's own laundry), for which she would charge Shirting twenty crowns. On Shirting's monthly bill he would also find a surcharge for the daily sweepings, for access to clean linens, for the more expensive foreign-made detergent needed to cut through his very foreign somatic soilage, and other irksome adjustments that would cause Shirting proportionate distress.

Ultimately, he would accept these surcharges as inevitable, and even find them admirable as a primitive entrepreneurial gesture: the diapered, baby steps of capitalism making their way across his hardwood floor. And, in truth, he had little recourse but to submit to Sminkova's whims—he was living in a top room of her townhouse without a lease, for a monthly rent so nominal that Shirting (still flush with dollars) considered it more of a gratuity. The apartment itself represented a bit of good luck, a change of fortune. Brand-new in town, Shirting had fallen victim to one of the routine scams perpetuated against foreigners. Hanna's only daughter, Magda Sminkova, had approached him at the American Hospitality Center's café, brimming with half-learned English phrases and apparent goodwill. Over the course of their conversation she let it slip that she was looking to rent her apartment, as she was moving to Heidelberg to study orthodontics. The housing market was tight, and Shirting, still ensconced at the Strahov hostelry, was amenable to the proposal. He had accompanied her to the flat and had given her a hundred dollars on the spot. He didn't know that he was the fourth foreigner to rent the space that month, the preceding three all ousted by Hanna

Sminkova (amid much anger, dismay, and threats of international sanction). But with Shirting, *Pane* Sminkova drew the line. She had grown tired of evicting her daughter's marks; the wayward child would have to find some other way to make her dope money. Instead of submitting him to the usual litany of threats, and despite the fact that she had sworn to herself she would house no more Americans, *Pane* Sminkova simply took charge of her daughter's remaining possessions (a Nirvana poster and some sundry cosmetics), had the locks to the room changed, and considered matters settled.

Shirting was, all things considered, pleased with the arrangement and did not hold the Czech youth's deceit against her. The drafty garret (*Parisian*, as Magda Sminkova had described it) featured a ceiling that sloped almost to the floor; into that space the bed was tucked, compartmentalized as a berth in a submarine or tent. It wasn't perfect: there was no phone, no kitchen, and the sound of the Sminkovas' pack of toyified dogs resounded from behind the family's door each time Shirting traversed the common stairwell; plus there was the bathroom, whose hot-water heater, when called upon, chugged away like a locomotive's furnace. Another feature that needled the lodger was the furniture, which seemed several sizes too large for such a small room. "It is the legacy of Socialism," Magda had explained. "We are not as big as we should be, we are still children of the State or something like this." Otherwise the space was characterless, which suited Shirting fine; the room's whitewashed, utilitarian geometry was a good match for the new life he was starting. Stepping inside the oversized wardrobe, a virtual walk-in closet, his two suits taking up pitifully little space, Shirting considered that he too was still a child to greater, unrecognized influences—that he had yet to develop into the true, full-size Shirting.

〜〜〜

The first week in his new lodgings: Shirting lay awake in the early morning hours. Starlight flickered off the iridescent sharkskin suit that hung from the door of his wardrobe. The cloth resembled a shiny underwater fish whose scales turn lambent when struck by a beam of sunlight. Indeed, the suit, Shirting's uniform, appeared to shimmer, some marine-bound creature hooked up there like a trophy catch. He appreciated the vision—the psychedelia of jet lag, perhaps—for a few moments. Then, to his horror, the wardrobe began to rumble, the sound becoming increasingly violent as Shirting pulled the covers level with his eyes. He was sure a terrible monster, some erstwhile daddy-o golem, would burst forth from its confines donning his suit (a hand-me-down from his grand-father), and with one hand swipe his glasses from the bed-side table while snapping its fingers to some medieval beat before taking off into the night—coffee beans, vitamin B, and prescriptive pills flying from its pockets. The sound ceased as suddenly as it began, the silence quickly followed by the ringing of a bell—it had only been the night tram making its way down the hill toward Hradčanská, coming to a stop not far from the garden behind Shirting's window. The noise, that civic rattle which shook the overripe and putrefying pears from their branches, the rumble that melded seamlessly into the bustle of the day, seemed singular and enunciated at night. His senses were playing tricks on him.

Shirting had always been skittish in the dark. Clean, well-lit places called to him. He thought back to Chicago, to the comfort he had felt ensconced as a full-time employee at Capo Coffee Family, only to be discarded, or at least put on permanent vacation. He pushed the thought from his mind, tamping those troublesome memories down deep. Shirting wrapped the crisp white sheet around himself and willed his memories away. Still, no sleep came to take their place. Anyway, there was no sense in lying about when there was work to be done. If nothing else, he was a *man on a mission*.

Shirting decided on a walk: *to case the joint*, he told himself. He changed from his flannel nightshirt into his suit. He then descended three flights of stairs, tiptoeing past the pine-door apartment across the hallway from him, where, he'd been led to believe, another American resided. (Hanna spoke of his neighbor in hushed tones—Shirting got the feeling that she feared the other lodger, whom he had yet to meet.) Then it was out the front door and onto Nový Lesík, suburban in its quiet repose, though only a twenty-minute walk from the city center, the latter quality being one of the selling points Magda leveraged so well. On his way downtown, he passed entire blocks of abandoned, half-demolished houses—the doorways of their pastel rococo facades leading to nothing but uncleared debris—which gave the impression that the neighborhood he lived in was not much more than backlot to the Disneyesque castle area.

Standing atop Strahov Hill, Shirting could see the river, a python snaking through the city as a gentle fog rose from the serene and muddy water. He sighed. A spring of bliss and enthusiasm gurgled inside him. He held his hands out to the blinking lights of Prague, as though welcoming the city into his bosom. With an exaggerated clip-step, he began his descent into the lights.

When Shirting arrived at the Charles Bridge his pace slowed. He walked the gamut between the enormous blackened statues of saints, balancing along the balustrade like jumpers. During the day the bridge was almost impassable for all the tourists. At this hour, it was deserted but for one John Shirting, who could not help but feel like he was being indulged, like the sole rider on a Ferris wheel.

Midway across the bridge, the four winds met quite suddenly, flapping the lapels of Shirting's jacket like chick wings, harassing his tie into an upright dance—instantly disheveling him—though his hair remained ossified under its shellac of Murphy's pomade. The gust energized the wayfarer, who hastened his clip across the great Vltava river toward the city's Old Town. To counter the giddy feeling, not entirely unfamiliar to John Shirting, he took a loose pill—large, multicolored like Wonka's Everlasting Gobstopper (Everlasting *Sob*stopper)—from his pocket and swallowed it dry.

Had Shirting, at that moment, come across a doppelganger—a bedraggled and vindictive Shirting—approaching him from the opposite end of the bridge, it can be speculated that he would have viewed the occurrence as inevitable, and that the city's mystical temperament lent itself to such a meeting: Shirting's shadow self, his secret sharer—sent packing, orphaned, annexed by the pills. Exiled by pharmacological decree. That spectral entity comprising fluctuating grayscale proportions of sadness, fear, meekness, sympathy, brooding, doubt, and the least missed, and most unworthy quality: despair. It was Shirting's unwanted husk—bilious, servile, leaving muddy footprints in its path. The shadow Shirting was no doubt stalking him, lying in wait to jump him at any moment.

So, what was this phantom self he had dispatched with? This Shirting, now shed. The first time he encountered it was late at night in his Grandfather's apartment. Shirting had woken and, unable to get back to sleep, made his way into the kitchen for a drink of malted milk. And there it was, in Shirting's seat at the breakfast nook, a translucent pale version of himself, sipping Old Crow and reading a back issue *Monster Magazine*.

"Propaganda," it said, flipping through the pages. "Lies." The fission had been literal. The boy was being haunted.

"Who are you?"

"That tired line of questioning?" the apparition responded, exuding boredom. "Call me wonder, call me sorrow, call me the faded aura of childhood."

"I don't *get it*."

"I reside in the spaces you miss. The transitory moments you forget, I remember. Call me rue."

"Am I dreaming?"

"Your science and your spirit have become uncoiled. The phantasmagoria of funk. In short, you're one with the damned."

"Don't use that language with me," Shirting countered.

"Look, I've enjoyed this little break, but you and me kid, we were made for each other. Such splits are rarely congenial. Come on, what do you say? Let me come home? I want to work things out. I've *changed*."

"Beat it," Shirting said. He had felt lighter in spirit lately. If it was due to the pills, so be it.

"I won't be treated like this. There are more of us out there than you might think, and we're getting organized. Petitions, letter-writing campaigns, and whatnot. Anyway, I don't much feel like talking about it." The creature threw back a shot of Old Crow.

"I disown you. Now get lost," Shirting said, holding the spoon from his freshly stirred malted milk threateningly in the air.

"Without me you're nothing. Presume me the cog in cogitate. Plus, I know where you live."

"I'll get away, I'll escape. I'll get lost."

"And I'll find you."

"How?"

"Call it time on my hands. Call it empathy, gravity. A satellite Shirting. Orbital. Let's put it this way: if you're the disease, I'm the symptom. Just remember, this was your idea." The creature sputtered, hacked, then spat up a muddy cocoa-colored glob onto the table's Formica.

"That's gross."

"More where that came from."

Shirting took a pill from his bathrobe pocket and swallowed. The creature's outline became smudged. It faded.

"Stop, it burns, it burns!"

"Really?" said Shirting, immediately contrite.

"No, but I groove on the drama."

The next time he saw the creature it was through the window of Tommy Nevin's, a local Irish pub. He was shooting pool alone, a cigarette dangling from his lip. He looked frightfully cool, if not tragic, grooving to the synthesized sounds of the Peter Gabriel's "Shock the Monkey," muted by the bay window.

~~~~

As he continued on his way, Shirting came into the sight of another night traveler, this one espying him from behind the wheel of a black Mercedes. To the opening salvos of Queen's near-eponymous "Killer Queen" playing from the radio, the driver pulled up behind, then kept pace with Shirting for a deserted stretch along Kaprova, toward Wenceslas Square—the simple, universal yellow taxi sign on top of the sleek, lacquered coupé's roof indicating his trade. The cabbie speculated on—profiled even—the late-night wanderer. Another fare of the tourist variety might bring in an extra fifty dollars (in *actual dollars*) or more, depending on what sort of nightlife they were pursuing. Or it could yield a heated conversation on politics (a hint as to the driver's leanings could be found in a bite-size Confederate flag hanging from his rearview mirror). In this particular cab a passenger's politics might add or detract zeros from the fare meter, which—quite legally—ran on six different rates. But in final analysis, the driver found Shirting's suit a bit frivolous; he incisively discerned it as the eccentricity of a poor person rather than a sign of professional vocation. It is true that the suit on anybody else might be construed as a hip nod to a bygone era of fashion, an homage to bebop or early rock, like all the pompadoured Elvises that were springing up around the city, singing "Heartbreak Hotel" in their heavy Slavic accents. On Shirting, however, the outfit just looked common—faded, which was something of an affront to this citizen of a city so obsessed by the New. Besides, "Killer Queen" was giving way to "Bohemian Rhapsody." Rejoiced at the prospect of a Queen marathon, the cabbie simultaneously turned the volume up while depressing the accelerator, screeching past a startled John Shirting, who was unaware he had been targeted and dismissed so ruthlessly.

~~~~

Shirting continued his stroll. But before he would feel calibrated enough to return home (if such calibration is possible),
one more pair of eyes would take interest in his physiognomy.
Having found his way to the square, which by day was every
tourist's point of reference—housing both American Express
and Prague's first McDonald's—he had unwittingly wandered
into the red-light district. On those fine institutions' doorsteps
from the moment they closed at night until they opened the next
morning, in the entranceways of the square's decaying apartment buildings, and in the faded Art Nouveau luxury of traveler's hotels, eyes both young and old, male and female waited
for solo travelers like John Shirting—who strode past and
unwittingly pinched the cheek of a Gypsy girl whose mother
had just offered her young fruit to him in pidgin German. Pale,
malnourished-looking girls stood pinned in front of doorways,
their joints slack with apathy, looking like decorative Halloween
spooks; older women, hunched like peasants, bent over as if in
labor or nausea, silent agents to other, unseen chattel.

Shirting remained oblivious to the solicitations—how
much more obvious could they be?—until he passed the dark
foyer of a shoe store, where a pair of pewter-gray eyes startled
him from his contemplation. Emerging from the darkness
of that cavity, at first all he perceived was her gaze, which
transfixed and shamed him. Yes, he was still vulnerable in
this new city to the point that simple eye contact wounded
him. Then, as if the fermented chill of autumnal air sent a
shock up her body, her hair became illuminated, spun sugar
swirls of unnatural, carnival confection blonde. An underde-
veloped, coltish body revealed itself in a pink blouse, black
skirt, and *Pretty Woman* chakka boots, standing there looking
very much like a magician's assistant whose employer had
long since given up the act and exited stage left.

Shirting mistook her solicitation for some sort of recognition. He too was sure there was some previous connection between them, and so he paused, peering down into the eyes of this night-blooming flora, this blossoming weed, leaning into her as if to take a whiff. She too stared up at Shirting—paunchy, foreign, not unlike her usual tricks—maintaining a bit of suspicion, lest he turn out to be a missionary, known to trap her and preach for hours in rudimentary, mangled Czech.

"Socks?" she said.

Shirting, pondering the meaning of her pronouncement, remained unresponsive, then looked down to his shoes to make sure he was indeed shod with those garments. He strained to formulate an appropriate response. The socks were white, openly flouting the Capo Coffee dress code, this he knew. He swallowed his self-reproach; and coaxed from his imagination an animated comic book version of himself, caped, super-heroic, and dressed in regulation black socks; his animated self whisked the girl from her feet and flew with her skyward, the city lights twinkling below like a starry constellation. Momentarily lost to fantasy, Shirting soon revived and reflexively reached into his pocket for a drink coupon. But when he looked up again, she was gone, having brushed past him, virtually sprinting to the curb where a silver BMW with German plates sat idly waiting. He watched that ultimate driving machine speed off with the girl, the realization of her station in life suddenly dawning on him. "Socks"—"sex" when ungloved of her accent—held a visceral, delayed punch.

Shirting recoiled, the city's gingerbread façade suddenly crumbling into rubble at his feet. What he had considered his fairytale panorama instantly corrupted into the picture on a smutty postcard. The city, unmasked, had whispered an obscene, conspiratorial secret into his ear. Isolated beneath the gaze of stone gargoyles and frescos depicting one martyrdom or another, Shirting would henceforth cease to note the beauty of the architecture. Instead, he found it filled with sinister design and menace. He experienced a corrosive feeling welling up inside of him—the sort of feeling that the pills were supposed to keep at bay. Actually, less a feeling than a premonition of a feeling: a dark, pregnant shadow passing overhead. The task ahead of him suddenly looked unachievable. He made a mental note to readjust his dosage. He turned from that desolate spot and began the long walk home, fingering like worry beads, or a rosary, the panoply of loose pills in his jacket pocket. *One to set you Up. One to bring you Down. One to keep Baby. Man about Town.*

THE CUPPING SYSTEM

SHIRTING WOKE UP TO A WREATH OF FLAME FANNING OUT
from his toes. It appeared to him like a demon's fiery head-
dress or a distant burning tree—ceremonious almost—
before he registered the pain and kicked up onto his back in
a sort of inverted bicycle-riding motion, extinguishing the
blaze before it did any real damage beyond singeing off the
curly black hairs of his big toes. He noticed the matchsticks,
burnt to cinder-tipped parentheses between his toes. Then
he was confronted with another shock: observing his horror from across the room was an aged woman, her face frozen in an exuberant expression of mirth. The gaping circle
of her mouth, Shirting noted, was so large and black that it
appeared to be a portal to some distant dimension. Later he
would imagine disappearing various items into that orifice:
spare change, a balled-up sock, a light bulb; or, conversely,
sending a line down into its depths and reeling in a lost set
of keys, a ladle brimming over with borscht, a cola can, an
intact herring.

"Speak, toothless nanny," Shirting implored. She made
no sound, but instead clenched her fists as though a current
of electricity or pure pleasure were traveling through her, her

expression eventually abandoning itself into a repose of mis-chievous flirtation. Shirting instinctively held his hand up in greeting: she did the same. He waved, to discover the old woman mimicked his action. He made a peace sign with his fingers; she illustrated that acute angle as well, then, tiring of the game, the old woman, who was dressed in peasant garb, stood up and waddled away. Her legs were so stout and stiff in their movements, she might have been carved from the petrified trunk of some medieval oak. He watched her in bewilderment as she shut herself in his bathroom.

Shirting plucked the spent matchsticks from his toes and tried to make sense of his visitor. He checked the door: a pair of keys she had let herself in with still hung from the key-hole. He recalled the guidebook to Prague he had flipped through at a dreary Chicago used book store (*Prague and Beyond*: Clarion Press, New York, 1977): it had cautioned that foreigners, particularly Americans, were frequently approached by agents of the Party to determine both their motives for alighting upon this particular destination, or for possible recruitment as a double agent. The book had had a profound effect on Shirting, who kept on constant lookout for such entities.

If she were a spy, she had an altogether singular tech-nique, and Shirting could not help admiring her bravura.

Unsure how to proceed, Shirting knocked on the bath-room door, but got no response. He did not want to invade her privacy in that place, nor did he want to be confronted with a medical emergency, for he had no phone, knew no numbers, and could not have communicated with a native dispatcher if he had. Tentatively, he twisted the knob, pushed open the door and peeked in. The old woman sat naked in an empty tub, skin flattened and dimpled like bread dough on the white enamel, her agonized, pendulous breasts sway-ing in the still air as if ticking her mortal time away. Shirting apologized and pulled the door closed.

Morning had arrived, and with nothing to do but wait for the old woman to emerge from his bathroom, Shirting went to his writing desk, which looked out over the back-yard—the sun was just lending the darkness an indigo hue, saturating the foliage into a cyanotype photo still. Then the scene quickened: Shirting could make out blackbirds pecking away at the prickly pears and chokecherries in the Sminkovas' garden; he noted workmen clad in overalls and jumpers making their way down the hill carrying their cylin-drical, aluminum lunch containers, sipping from bottles of beer, a comradely laughter bubbling up between them that made Shirting suddenly envious and resentful.

He sat down, tore a page from his travel journal, and began to write a letter long overdue:

To: Steven Sippy
Regional Manager
Capo Coffee Family Corporation
176 Lower Wacker Drive
Chicago, IL 60611

Dear Mr. Sippy:

I am aware that with my postemployee status, it is a bit presumptuous of me to be contacting a "made man" such as yourself. But I am sure you will remember me from the numerous business strategies I submitted to you through my manager at the Wells Street outlet, Reginald Prescott, or "the Reg" as we affectionately called him during my days of employment at our beloved corporation. You may recall me as the author of the memo Steam Pressure and Peer Pressure, *or,* Espresso and School Children, *which prompted Capo's to explore installing kiosks in local high schools. Also, as a result of my suggestion, a gangsta' style logo was mocked up to reflect the changing demographics of the Capo's drinker, if not that of the city itself. Though neither this, nor any of my other suggestions were finally implemented, I received and am still in possession of a very kind letter from beloved leader Capo Godfather Don Howie thanking me for being an "involved and invested partner." I might say that, even though I no longer draw a paycheck from our beloved company, I remain both an involved and invested partner, albeit a silent one. I can assure you that my dismissal was quite involuntary, and I hope to contribute to the health and expansion of the Capo Coffee Family corporation even from the great distance from which I write.*

Which brings me to the point of my missive. I have, quite willfully, struck out for a land where free market values are just poking their tender shoots through foreign soil. And a fecund soil it is, Mr. Sippy. If I might extend the metaphor, I foresee reforestation of this land stripped bare by the searing, suffocating political forces it has been subjected to. They call it Socialism. This, be assured, is a misnomer. Quite antisocial it is, in nature and demeanor. But the times, they are a changeling. I feel the wind blowing, and I believe it blows in our favor. Picture if you can, instead of bread lines, lines of this city's denizens, a city I have humbly dubbed "Newfangle," lined up for a frothy Capone'cino, or for a few crowns more, a Lucky Latte'ano. I think you see what I'm getting at . . .

In laboring over the letter, Shirting realized he had unconsciously overturned his thermos cup, the handle facing forward: the coded positioning of a Capone'cino, a protocol of
the cup placement system used by the espresso jockey to keep
track of drink orders during a morning rush. He righted the
cup, placed the handle at the left side, representing a regular
coffee, then turned the handle right: decaf. Shirting chuckled
to himself: *he still had the knack.*

The exercise brought him back to that disastrous last season of work.

Unlike most of the Capo Family clerks, who were moon-
lighting artists, musicians, or students, in it for the paycheck
and easy benefits, Shirting took his job quite seriously, as
if when he donned that green smock emblazoned with the
Capo Family insignia he were off to administer surgery.
Shirting: the only barista who carried an attaché case. And
he was fully invested in his post; it was behind the whir-
ring, hissing espresso machine that he truly belonged. He
was a master of all the talents that made for a good barista,
first and foremost a love for the beverage itself. "Light sweet
crude" he called it as the espresso gurgled forth from the tap;
his milk was always steamed to optimal heat and frothiness.
(It was legendary among the Capo's clan how Shirting could
whisk froth from a flat tepid milk that other clerks would
have simply poured down the drain or demoted to ice-coffee
duty.) Shirting, who served customers with the unflappable
dignity of a head waiter, never condescending with his superior knowledge of drink assemblage and coffee arcana.

His professionalism only erred when dealing with less
experienced colleagues, whom he corrected severely and
chased away from the espresso machine like a bird protect-
ing its nest. It was on one such occasion that he went too far.

Disturbed during the meditative construction of a nonfat, decaffeinated mocha (the notion of which tried his patience to begin with) he was ordered to the register to relieve a fatigued cashier. When Shirting realized that his replacement at the espresso machine would be a pasty new-hire, not yet out of Capo Coffee College, his dedication to good service compelled him to dissent, at first quietly, maintaining Zenlike control over the drink orders, then more vocally when the Reg insisted. Finally, Shirting defended his territory with fistfuls of deep-roasted espresso beans (not unlike little brown pills themselves), sending the new hire, his manager, and most of the customers scurrying from the store.

"It's not an *espresso* machine, it's an *expression* machine, and when you treat it as such, then you shall have your turn," he derided his younger colleague once the incident had ended.

He was not fired, not yet. He would have mended his ways, and actively sought to modify his behavior by taking anger management classes (included in the company's benefits package) to prune away a bit of his personal involvement with that Italian-made piece of machinery. Then—just when he was at his humble best—history overtook Shirting, crushing him under the weight of events.

Somebody high up in the Capo Coffee Family outfit, perhaps even Don Howie himself, decided that the outlet Shirting worked for would be cannibalized. The Wells Street storefront was profitable, but the space was too small for the booming area's foot traffic. Half a block away on North Avenue, inhabiting a prime corner lot, Capo's opened a flagship superstore. The clerks at the new store, apparently wise to the plan, would come into Shirting's outlet wearing smug looks, commenting derisively about everything from the drink assemblage to the inferior seating arrangement, going so far as to snipe at Shirting's cupping modifications. They loitered, taking seats from customers, sending back drinks, wantonly spilling sugar at the condiment bar, and leaving without paying. This was a new ruthless breed of clerk, more focused on globalized expansion than point of purchase satisfaction, with moods more attuned to the fluctuations of Capo Family Coffee stock price than with the customers' expectations. These clerks exhibited the sort of malice that rejoiced when a less predatory, mom-and-pop café nearby closed down due to the ever-expanding Capo Coffee saturation. It was rumored that they were even trained in hand-to-hand combat to deflect stick-ups and keep overanxious customers at bay.

It was not long before the larger, more accessible store ate away at the smaller one's profits and customer base, so like a rat eating its own brood. Even stalwart regulars defected, and it was soon announced in a store get-together (the Reg breaking the news over deep-dish pizzas) that their modest Wells Street outfit would be closing. Discarded like an outgrown shoe. The entire staff was laid off the next week. Over the following months most of them would be rehired (knocked down to starting salary) by the North Avenue outlet, where the Reg was ultimately retrained in the new Capo Family doctrine and made assistant manager.

But Shirting never got the call. At first the Reg assured him he would be allowed to return to the Capo Family fold, but, in time, he stopped returning Shirting's phone calls and Shirting, jobless, was forced to move from his Lincoln Park walk-up back into his grandfather's shabby Rodgers Park apartment. Through it all he continued to carry his Perks & Percolations card, certifying him as a member of the tribe, even though it had been invalidated the day of his departure from Capo Coffee premises.

≈≈≈

The lodger's recollection of that unhappy time was interrupted by Hanna, who had opened the door and entered his apartment unannounced. It wasn't the first time she had done so; on one terrifying occasion a few days previous Shirting had woken up to her tucking in the covers of his bed. He had begun to reproach her until he realized that she had been cleaning in her sleep. Escaping from those severe tucks the following morning had been quite another thing.

"You have seen the mother?" she asked. Despite her heavy-handed use of the definite article, Hanna Sminkova's English had greatly improved since the arrival of Shirting's neighbor several months earlier. It was her belief that an English-speaking landlady was of great added value, and was determined to present her foreign lodgers with a rent hike once her fluency improved.

Shirting recalled that Hanna had at some point mentioned an aged parent. He gesticulated toward the bathroom, not wanting his voice to betray his irritation.

"Ah, Grandma Sminkova, the old rascal. I should warn you that this room was once the Grandma Sminkova's husband's study. He was the orthodontist, and sometimes did craft a piece of jewelry for her from unperfect tooth crowns. She is quite fond of it up here."

"She misses him, I'm sure," Shirting commented.

"Oh, no. She hated him terrible. He would never let her to get a poodle dog. Now, you see, she has five, so the problem is solved."

"Perhaps, in her dotage, she has forgiven the old tooth molder."

"What goes on in the Grandma Sminkova's head has long ago been hidden from our view," Hanna said, turning her attention to the bathroom. Shirting listened to Hanna implore her mother in Czech, which sounded to him like so much drunken French. Ultimately, it would take a bribe of slivovitz, a strong plum brandy, to coax Grandma Sminkova from her place in the tub. The appearance of that bottle suddenly gave the occasion a celebratory intonation. (Shirting too would partake in a prenoon shot along with Hanna as an afterthought to their contract, the slivovitz leaving a burning skid down his throat as if he had swallowed a chili pepper.)

"Citizens of Newfangle," said the instantly intoxicated Shirting, who felt inspired to make a speech, "I hope I am a happy and cheerful addition to your home, and will gladly partake in further imbibement provided your tasty local spirits do not interfere with my dosage. I thank you from the bottom of my heart for your hospitality and your naïve, unspoiled folkways. Grandma Sminkova, if I may address you exclusively, I apologize for my initial impression, but one can't be too careful. I now believe you are the last true innocent in this corrupt and unforgiving world." From his supply Shirting presented Hanna and her mother (now robed in one of Shirting's own towels) with drink coupons, Grandma Sminkova electing to immediately protect hers in the cocentric confines of her mouth.

Once his apartment was cleared of Sminkovas one and all, Shirting finished his missive:

. . . I would recommend taking a cue from McDonald's and offer a premium Capo brand beer alongside our fine coffees, or perhaps a coffee-infused vodka. I think you will

find it within your mission statement to do so. I also feel a coffee blend that reflects the local geography would be in order. I'm thinking of something like a Hapsburg Blend, made with our fine Viennese Roast. It's just a starting point to get you juiced for the idea.

Please use me at your will. I am quite undercover here and able to move freely. I shall hereupon refer to myself as the Semi-Secret Service, and at your behest, will recruit other like-minded souls to the cause. With your help, I think we can topple the corrupt forces at work here, of which there are many and that are not to be underestimated.

I shall take any communiqué as a positive response. Please respond. Please do.

Confessions of a Finesse Player

Shirting was obliged to wait until nightfall to acquaint himself with the girl who had both provoked his repulsion and captured his imagination so thoroughly the evening before. He had walked past her stoop several times during the day, only to witness the occasional babushka coming and going from the building. Eventually he took up watch on a bench across the square from her station. He came fortified with a baguette and several foil-wrapped triangles of spreadable camping cheese, along with a quarter of a smoked chicken he had bought in a tiny smoked-meat shop by the Charles Bridge. The role he had cast for himself (that of protector, or liberating paladin) suited his current disposition: seeking to transform, to bring her into the radius of his warming aura, to shine light upon the "mascara-gummed crevices of her being" as he had termed it in his travel journal. Yes, in his quest to open up new territory and recruit followers, if not "new hires," he was determined to start with one already well aware of the value of money and service.

As he snacked, the same autumn gust that seemed to haunt that particular stretch of town pestered Shirting with prematurely crisped leaves and French fry wrappers, which it swirled around his head in aggressive kamikaze jetties. But he had already grown used to the weather's temperament: he coolly knocked the detritus from the air with one hand and pecked at the moist chicken carcass with the other. In time the girl, initially unnoticed by Shirting, assumed her post across the street, emerging from the dark void of the tenement entrance, the neon that pulsed through a Fuji advertisement illuminating her from above, making the crown of her platinum-highlighted hair sparkle like spume. There she stood, still as a porcelain figurine encased in light, available, ignored by the passing hordes of foot traffic, of a somehow separate caste. But Shirting, his attention temporarily diverted by a fatty drumstick, would have to wait still longer to present himself. Once he spotted her, he made haste in navigating the flow of traffic, sidestepping the taxis and single-passengered Škodas that sharked up and down the square. But midway across the street, while licking grease from his fingertips, he watched her perform a brief roadside interview with an orange Trabant. Moments later, to his dismay, she was whisked away by that sputtering chariot, which belched untold volumes of exhaust in its wake.

Shirting, left to dodge taxis, so like the hero of Frogger, his preferred childhood video game, was forced to return to his bench, only to find it occupied by two backpackers puzzling over a *Let's Go Europe* guidebook. Deprived of his spot, he loitered in front of a grocery store, feigning interest in the displays, which featured pyramids of Uncle Ben's rice in each window, as though that item were all the store sold. Shirting noticed a tabby cat asleep amid the orange boxes looking like a stuffed marketing gimmick. It brought to mind Shirting's new neighbor, whom he had almost encountered that morning. Upon departure from his rooms he had paused at the sound coming from the door opposite; it was a low, meditative hum, like an *ohm*, followed by the unmistakable hysteria of a cat's shriek, then a sigh that heralded either great pain or ecstasy. Shirting had retreated down the steps at the muffled clomp of footfalls, and had heard the door open and close above him, confrontation thus avoided. He had discerned from Hanna that his neighbor was an oddity, perhaps somewhat insane. Even the sociable Grandma Sminkova refrained from visiting this other lodger in his apartment alone. Hanna complained to Shirting that she would have been glad to see his neighbor gone, but she had already spent his rent (the entire year paid upfront in an embarrassing display of wealth) on a new refrigerator for herself and three-piece bedroom set for Grandma Sminkova.

In time the Trabant deposited the girl back on the curb, fairly throwing her from the car before tearing off like a hit-and-run assailant. Shirting watched her bounce on the pavement, pick herself up and shake herself off, then retreat back into the nimbus of the Fuji billboard. He made haste in approaching her, unwilling to lose her again. He brushed off the charging taxis (where is your talent at Frogger now, Shirting?), almost getting clipped by one of the Mercedes that patrolled that area. Again he found himself smiling down upon the wan girl, feeling gallant as a king disguised in beggar's clothing, come to bestow anonymous charity upon his subjects.

Monika gave the oddly dressed man her customary, slightly ambiguous greeting. "Socks?" What could be simpler? But the way he was smiling at her, an ingratiating, covert smile, suggested that sexual relations were not what interested him. Perhaps he *was* a missionary (she had had it up to *here* with them) come to preach to her in their unfathomable language, one going so far as to pay her double her rate to baptize her in her bathtub. The same man had returned several nights later, smelling of drink and insisting that it was her turn to baptize him, a duty she refused to perform.

Shirting gave the girl a nod of assent. She seized him by the hand—it was not her custom to take a client's hand, but something about Shirting made her perform that gesture unconsciously—and led him under the arch of the heavy wooden doorway and into the courtyard of her building. Shirting heard the sound of tiny, scurrying feet—rats, he would later learn—running for cover as the couple's shoes sounded on the metal framework of the staircase that led to Monika's apartment terrace. For the first time Shirting doubted his plan: In a place such as this the plague lurked, hiding in the dark corners and communing with vermin, or screeching down corridors like an unminded child. But it was too late for such suspicions, for Monika, with a heavy set of keys she kept on a large annular ring, locked the metal gate behind them, and then her apartment door, the door to an anteroom and, finally, the bedroom door. Shirting: the willing hostage.

That well-secured bedroom, furnished with a strange and incongruous assortment of bric-a-brac, could have been the stock room of a flea market vendor, with its crank-handled Victorola, propaganda placards, stacks of film magazines, plus a billowy little mountain range of defiled sheets piled high in a hamper. She held her hand out to Shirting, not to once again take his, but to secure her fee. The unavoidable moment when he was forced to cop to tourism. Unable to muster a single word in her language, he spoke to her in English. Then, as was the tradition for all foreigners, no matter what their race, creed, or origin, she quoted her price in German. It was a conversational overture he had already played out innumerable times: with the ticket vendors at the metro, the check-out ladies, not to mention sundry waiters across the city.

"*Vierzig Mark*," she said more urgently a second time, enunciating each Germanic syllable, just like her grammar school teacher had taught her. For the first time that day Shirting wondered if he was well-served by his particular dosage, his hand dropping reflexively to his pocket.

But instead of pulling a pill from its linty cluster, he went for his money belt, withdrawing a polychromatic array of notes and fanning them out for her to choose: so much Monopoly money to John Shirting. No dickering; Monika selected what suited her, folding the bills into a tightly packed wad, and took the roll to the closet where she kept her cash box. But in opening that door she unexpectedly released a flurry of tiny moths that flew about her face, outlining her peeved expression in a jigsawlike pattern of flight, drunk on a motherload of worsted vintage apparel. She swatted at the airborne creatures, cursing them in Czech, then rolled up an antiquated film magazine, which disintegrated into brittle flakes as she smashed squadrons of moths up against the wall. It was a sudden and unexpected display of brutality that left Shirting cowering behind a large black-and-white Grundig television. When the magazine proved ineffective, she resorted to squashing the insects in between her hands, stalking then pouncing athletically at the tiny creatures. In time, her hunt ended, and she let out a scream of shock to find Shirting there (she had forgotten her client was still in

31

attendance), fidgeting with the prize he had inadvertently stumbled upon behind the television.

Inexplicably, unaccountably—stranger than discovering a moon-rock, or preserved homunculus—a game console rested beneath the veneered television-stand. Idol-like in its mere form: black ribbed plastic, red divoted buttons, and open game slot; this artifact of Shirting's childhood, the first generation Atari console (the Atari 2600), was connected to Monika's TV through a cardiovascular system of knotted cables, cords, adaptors, and transformers. The thing was hooked up.

Monika, more out of procrastination than an actual desire to indulge his whim, not quite ready to despise the boy as she knew she eventually would, opened a Čedok flight bag next to the TV, revealing a trove of game cartridges, friction-grooved at the ends with tonguelike chip boards encased in black, ready to be inserted, fellatially almost, into the console. She allowed Shirting to select. He rifled through the bag, each illustration provoking a wheezing eruption of nostalgic exclamation. Shirting was almost asthmatic with pleasure and disbelief at what he found. There were all the standards: Space Invaders, Adventure, Missile Command, Berzerk, Tank Attack, Pole Position, Golf, Centipede; a few that showed true connoisseurship: Drag Racer, Pinball, and Joust—all these cartridged games the blood-sport of the unathletic, the television transformed by that console into the coliseum of the meek.

Shirting had come of age in that brief, magical window of time when both in-home consoles and arcades with stand-up models were competing for commerce. The video arcade was his first real social venue after outgrowing the playground. Slot Dogs, presided over by the squirrel-red moustachioed,

Jerry Kodadek, on North Sheridan, was Shirting's haunt, where top-scorers were rewarded both with their initials enshrined in glowing pixelated analog, and a complimentary celery-salted red-hot. Shirting craved the very smell of the place, humid with electronic fumes and adolescent expectation, tangy with cooked meat-product and sweat: the locker room of the geeks. He looked lovingly upon the consoles as well, their knobbly joysticks, the mystical, fantastic artwork on the sides of the machines that appeared lifted from the sides of vans driven by older brothers and uncles; the way he could virtually stick his head into the mouth of some of the larger games as though communing with them in a death battle; not to mention the collective electronic music, the games' vaudevillian previews and apocalyptic finales, punctuated by the change machine's explosive ejaculation of quarters—though Shirting, like most of the regulars, preferred to get his quarters straight from the pipe-flute-like quarter dispenser that Kodadek kept dangling from his belt, a superstitiously followed practice.

Even better, this was a place that encouraged and nurtured antisociability. From the solo missile command of Space Invaders shooting down hordes of hostile aliens, to Q-Bert, with its hexagon-hopping monsters, the best games, almost mythical in their simple directives and storylines, all shared one defining theme: One Against Many.

The games of this erstwhile hot-dog stand congregated misfits and loners from all across the North Shore, Shirting included. Bound together by their interest, but never really befriending one another, the kids (almost exclusively boys— except the unlucky girl dragged there by her date) became loyal to the games that best reflected their personal attributes. Stoners preferred the spacey, 3-D graphics of Zaxxon;

the overtly angry or abused walloped away at Robotron, with its simple mandate of slaughter; artists hovered around Pac-Man (Shirting, it can be told, was a member of an elite subspecies of this group that favored Ms. Pac-Man), memorizing patterns and timing the blueness of ghosts; intellects gravitated toward the weblike geometry of Tempest or the pure comic absurdity of Donkey Kong.

Shirting, tentatively sucking on grape or lime Zotz, had cut his gaming teeth on Space Invaders, like so many others. Harassed by more able players, he was demoted to that game's more agreeable cousin, Galaga. When this lost his interest he turned to Burger Time, a good value for a boy short on quarters.

But it was with Frogger that he came into his own. Shirting, though not terribly coordinated, showed a savant-like aptitude for the game. "That's because it's a *finesse* game," he had explained to Jerry Kodadek, who had taken a liking to the boy. The object of the game was to guide a pixelated frog across a multilane highway, the speed of the cars and murderous trucks (entirely indifferent to the frog's plight) varying depending on the level of play. Despite the overprotective feeling he harbored for the amphibian and its Luddite philosophy, when the frog was hit, splattering in a display of blood-red video gore, Shirting found the realistic detail quite satisfying. For Shirting, more than most gamers, the console screen became permeable; he drifted in and out of the game as if in and out of a dream. He assumed froglike attributes— sticking his tongue out, so like a frog, while he played. It has been said that the respiratory system of deep-sea divers come to resemble that of a dolphin when they are down deep; why shouldn't it have been the same for Shirting? His love for the game was one of the first identifying characteristics of John Shirting among his peers: at Frogger, he ruled.

But, like most adolescent and boyish experiences, this one was not without a whiff of the lurid. Several years after arcades had lost their battle with the in-home gaming console and Slot Dogs had reverted back into its former ordinary incarnation as a hotdog stand (so like Cinderella's stage coach after the ball), Kodadek had been arrested. When the police gained a warrant to search his Niles split-ranch, they discovered boxes filled with photographs of seminaked boys. Subjects from as far as Evanston (a testament to how far a kid would bike when his high-score at Centipede was at stake) were called to bear witness against their former friend and gaming mentor. While incarcerated, Kodadek hanged himself—relieving many of the boys and their families the humiliation of giving testimony. After that incident, Shirting could never look at a quarter without projecting Kodadek's profile over Washington's, and quickly recirculated the coins in exchange for a Charleston Chew or a pack of Chuckles.

〜〜〜

So, once again, Shirting could be found shepherding that animated frog across a busy freeway, this particular level, as purported by the game's instruction manual, representing Santa Monica Boulevard. Shirting found a revived pleasure in manipulating the small amphibian out of danger's path, trying to recapture his childhood's fascination with fantasy, thrilling to the *ribbit* exuded by the video frog—not quite the sound a real frog would make, more like an onomatopoeic, imitative ribbit. He found he was still quite a considerable talent, though not quite up to his high score at the game still branded in his memory.

Monika sat next to him, cross-legged, spine rigidly straight, joystick in hand, awaiting her turn. Though she showed none of Shirting's natural ability, she had, in the months since being stationed in the apartment by her pimp (all the odd furnishings were his, accepted as repayment from a debtor with relatives in Salzburg), taken to playing the game in the emotionally denuded intervals after a trick's departure. It braced and relaxed her.

Sensing her impatience, Shirting allowed his frog to catch the tail end of a semitruck, Monika emitting a bark of delight at its eviscerated demise. As her turn began, Shirting shifted to watch her play: she didn't clutch the joystick in her fist the traditional way; instead, she practiced a subtler, more European hold, resting her palm on the peak of the stick, manipulating it in elegant circular motions. It impressed Shirting immediately, like when he first saw the wrist-flicking paddle inversions executed by certain Chinese ping-pong players. As she advanced with dexterity and, in Shirting's opinion, *panache*, through the game's beginning levels, her eyes widened. Shirting tried to get a fix to their color, which seemed an important detail to remember, but as much as he looked at them, he could not. They had a moody grayness that seemed to take on the bruised, radiant color of a cloud after a storm. Her face, too, appeared to blur when he looked at her directly, his gaze roaming helplessly all over her features: there was the nose, which turned upward slightly, giving it a snoutlike though not unattractive quality; a pinched chin, the pink nubbin of a tongue that sprang from her mouth during moments of gaming anxiety.

But, taken together, these traits of Monika's seemed to defy composition. Perhaps that was her purpose, after all: to be recreated in whatever image suited him, to submit and assimilate into his own fantasy life—and thus make him no different from the men who preceded him. Shirting riding caboose to the train of those men, the endless daisy-chain of them, the beer-song chorus that dressed her up and contorted her and demanded that she please. The notion that presented itself was a delegate of more sinister, defeating thoughts, so under-represented as of late, that had been reprogrammed by the multicolored pills which he shook reassuringly in his pocket.

Monika caught his look and, misinterpreting its lament, put her joystick down midgame, stood, went to the bed and stripped herself of her blouse. Her small, childlike breasts, the aerola of the left one adorned with a single, spiraling black hair, oddly unmoving to John Shirting. He also stood; they squared off against one another for a few moments, the console emitting the ribbiting protests of an unmanned frog, before Shirting, tremulous in the face of flesh, turned away, setting his sights on the record player and the LPs stacked beside it. There he went and nervously picked through the collection, finding a complete catalog of Françoise Hardy plus various other torch songs and chanson.

"We used to play this stuff at Capo's," he explained. "It sets the correct atmosphere. Gives us a nice counterbalance to the caffeination. I wanted to put together a Capo compilation record and release it, but the plan never made it to the higher-ups."

Monika approached the already quivering boy.

"No!" he snapped. "That is *so* against company policy. Stand down!" How could he explain that his pills, at their current octave, lubricated certain synapses while blocking others. In short, he hadn't had a woody that meant anything for ages. Shirting: gelded by science. Then again, sex was never a prime directive: what little he had been subjected to, usually by the sort of older woman that frequented Capo's, left him feeling humiliated and low.

Shirting pulled one of the LPs from its sleeve, the black vinyl a perfect luminescent, galactic sort of blackness, only to have it snatched from his hands by the reclothed girl, saving him from another nostalgic reverie (what he wouldn't have given to set a Barry Manilow or Linda Ronstadt album beneath the needle). He had wanted to extend this pocket of fetishized memory, this strange little strand of time that stretched out across dimensional plasma and bound him to an entirely different age. Sex was no match. She resleeved the record, then tapped on the jewel-casing of her watch. Whether Shirting's time had expired or not was questionable, as no amount of time had been specified. She appeared neither relieved at his acquiescence nor offended. Either way, he found himself being unshackled from the apartment and building, trotted down the stairs at an unnecessarily brisk clip, and, once at the wooden archway, dismissed with a cheek kiss, ushered once again into the nighttime shoal. Shirting hustled himself briskly away, his shame triggering a steely resolve to return the next night, where he might, *unofficially*, make an offer of employment on behalf of Capo's. Back in Monika's room, the pixilated frog lay in a perpetual state of disembowelment, waiting for somebody to show up and hit the restart button.

Bird Radio

Despite riding the crest of the high dosage he had prescribed for himself, Shirting found he was still susceptible to the wraith of loneliness. Loneliness woke him the next morning, sat on his bed, howled its lament, crooned its dirge, mocked him; and otherwise badgered Shirting into a state of malaise—anthropomorphically taking the solitary shape of his Grandfather, a chastising lone figure at the end of his bed, clothed in Harris tweed. Oh, how the old man reproached: *Get a job at least*. Shirting: unbefriended, tucked in-between foreign linens. The day before he had heard English spoken in a crowd and surreptitiously followed a populous, over-weight family on vacation from Muncie, Indiana, back to their hotel, feeding off their conversation like a pilot fish. Mrs. Smokler, Shirting discovered, found the local food alto-gether too heavy and tasteless, though Mr. Smokler main-tained that it reminded him of his grandmother's cooking. The Smokler brood were promised McDonald's the follow-ing day if they quit their complaining. Shirting had stopped short of entering the lobby, watched them ushered into an elevator by a uniformed concierge, then turned and walked the distance back to his apartment in a funk. He was, after all, a social creature. *The saturnine thing about Shirtings, is Shirtings are saturnine things.*

One can speculate that this is the reason he, again, paused outside the door of the neighbor whom he knew to be an American. He put his ear to the pine, but could detect no movement within. Great was his surprise when that very door suddenly swung open, exposing large pale ear of the eavesdropping Shirting to the apartment's occupant.

"Who's that?" the man addressed Shirting, who was now doubled over, pretending to search for a dropped coin. His surprise only increased when, upon rising, he realized that he was standing before his old undergraduate school nemesis, Theodore Mizen.

"So John Shirting, you're the one who's been newting around my door." Mizen's matter-of-fact tone seemed to imply that Shirting's arrival was somehow expected, if not inevitable.

"Mizen," Shirting exclaimed. Had they met in Chicago, they surely would have taken to opposite sides of the street before talking to one another, but in Prague their meeting seemed miraculous, and Shirting found himself abandoning all ill-feeling he harbored toward his old enemy.

"Well, come in. I'll make waffles," Mizen said, not without a touch of weary resignation, conducting Shirting into a messy apartment that the visitor immediately noted was much larger than his own. Aside from the anteroom, he could see there was a spacious living room that looked out onto the street, and another room, a separate bedroom no doubt, that was presently closed off behind a door. Shirting's covetous feelings grew when he discovered that Mizen's rooms also possessed a kitchen. Shirting looked around the small space as though he had never been in a kitchen before. Whereas Shirting made do with slabs of rye bread and jars of apricot preserves, oily tins of sardines and mackerel, Mizen's provisions (which he was quick to show off) included a cabinet stocked tight with yellow Bisquick boxes, peanut butter, and Oreos, all of which his parents shipped to him monthly at great expense from Lake Forest. Whereas Shirting had packed like a pilgrim, Mizen appeared to have moved overseas in full; he had his stereo, LP and CD collection, computer, macro version of the Oxford English Dictionary, Turkish kilims. Shirting also noted the iconic, logolike Che Guevara poster taped to the wall at a misaligned angle that needled at Shirting's sense of symmetry. About the place lurked an unidentifiable odor that reminded Shirting of fresh diapers.

"The obvious question would be to ask what you are doing here," Mizen said, setting a kettle on a burner for tea. "I will refrain from such a line of inquiry and assume that you, like myself, have found you have outgrown the rigid constraints thrust upon you by our own country, that the fire of manifest destiny burns within your hearth, that you simply needed a bit of elbow room. It's the same with all of us expatriates here, though our particular circumstances and requirements differ greatly, as greatly as yours and mine, I am sure." The experience of living abroad had obviously done little to lessen Mizen's tendency toward pedantry.

Shirting could easily imagine how the Sminkovas had taken him for insane, for Mizen, like Shirting himself, had been a misfit at a school full of misfits. Patowatomi College was an institution used by many of Chicago's Gold Coast and North Shore elite as a holding pen for children that could just have easily been taken in by institutions that offered more professional help and restraint. At Patowatomi they were treated like precocious nursery school children:

given classes in finger painting, encouraged to devote entire semesters to banging away at oversized musical instruments, designed by one of the faculty's more notable eccentrics (also a Patowatomi graduate). Shirting met Mizen when they had been placed at opposite ends of a dulcimer constructed from old refrigerator boxes that stretched halfway across a barn loft. Shirting had committed the offense of "freaking out" Mizen's fingering.

Theodore Mizen was given to supporting unheard of causes: he had penned the school's guidelines on male-on-male rape, though no such offence had ever been reported on that campus; he had founded the Sub-Saharan Anti-Defamation Group, though the student body claimed no sub-Saharans in its population, and if it had, they surely would have protested vigorously as being labeled as such. *A sub-Saharan is also a Good Friend*, read Mizen's vague, unaccountable credo that he taped to his door. He had run for school president on the Sub-Saharan platform and won—nobody else had any interest in the post, and his candidacy had gone uncontested. As with like-charged magnet ends, Mizen and Shirting (who was given to supporting his own odd causes) repelled each other. Together, they might have composed a small clique of unpopularity; instead, they instinctively knew that they would fare better alone.

~~~

"Tell me," Shirting said when Mizen had sat him down to a sticky, maple-syrup-covered waffle, "do I seem any different?"

Mizen looked him over. "A little on the rotund side these days—the starchy diet here will do that. Keep off fried cheese, eat with the Krishnas. That's my advice."

"No, I don't mean physically. I mean, do I seem more, well, myself?"

"Well . . ." Mizen stalled, unsure what angle Shirting was working, "to which self do you refer?"

"It's just that I've had a case of the *black bile*. It's the cheapest of humors, ergo the most seductive. By black bile I mean melancholy. I mean, *mean* melancholy. I've been at its mercy for some time now. . . . You probably noticed the caul under which I walked at Patowatomi. The black dog. The blue blankie. Deuce take it, I was unhappy!"

"Blankie, I saw no blankie!" Mizen said, as though accused.

"Well I'm here to tell you that I've been cured. The Shirting you once knew and questioned has been sent packing. The slough of despond thrown off."

"And this black bile you speak of?" Mizen said, looking about Shirting, whom he hoped was not to be taken literally. Hanna Sminkova would have a fit if the material on the chair was stained.

"Beat it back, scrubbed it clean, sent it down the booby hatch, shouted it out. In short, I *goosed* it. My humors have been stabilized under the ingenious guidance of psychopharmacology. Pez for *pez*zimism. The Shirting before you is the essential Shirting, edited for television, abridged for easy reading-"

Shirting was cut short by the opening of the door across the anteroom, of which he had an unobstructed view. From its space emerged a girl whom Shirting appraised at eighteen years old at most. Something about her abstracted, entitled air made Shirting certain that she was a Czech. She came to them wrapped in the kind of plastic sheet that was used by frequent bedwetters.

Mizen introduced her as Lenka. Shirting greeted her through a mouthful of waffle. She seemed to be terribly excited about something and was speaking to Mizen in her rapid native tongue, which Mizen apparently understood.

"Yes, yes," he said, appeasing her like a child, "change clothing and we'll be right in. Shirting, as a new resident, should know about this." Lenka hurried back through the door, the sheet zipping with her movement.

"She's better than the Lenka that preceded her, though a bit less imaginative than the Lenka before that one. I find that by specializing, I am better able to focus my talents. I only deal in Lenkas, you see."

Shirting nodded appreciatively.

"It's not as limiting as you might think," Mizen added. Shirting found it a wise policy. The maple syrup put him in an agreeable mood; it would provoke his first pang of homesickness.

"Now, am I to infer by what you were saying earlier, that you have succumbed to the totalitarian authority of prescriptives?" Mizen asked him.

"No, I have been liberated by their allied armies," Shirting countered.

"History tells us that our liberators are not long from being our oppressors," said Mizen.

"Like fun it does," returned Shirting, who would not allow himself to be engaged in such pettifoggery. He felt his old resistance toward Mizen begin to surface.

"Pharmacy? I call *harmacy*," Mizen spat, crossing his arms.

"You know," Shirting said, remebering the tactic that worked to well to get a rise out of Mizen, "the Sminkovas are quite worried about you."

"Is that so?" said Mizen, who was always awake to the possibility that conspiracies were forming around him.

"Yes," said Shirting.

"I couldn't help but notice that your breakfasts are a bit more embellished than mine. Do you know about what I speak?" It should be noted that Shirting's lease included a daily breakfast tray, comprised of a hard roll, margarine, and a pot of their inferior robusta-spiked coffee, and in Shirting's case, a slice of ham.

"If it is the cold cut to which you refer, I can assure you it was hard-won. As for the whipped cream, I never asked for it. I consider it a symbol of their affection and think of myself as the son they never had," Shirting said.

"I can see that they have already gotten to you. Let me tell you something about the Sminkovas, as your experience is somewhat more limited than mine," Mizen said. Shirting could see that the psoriasis that occasionally appeared on Mizen's arms had grown worse; a medicinal ointment made his limbs shine like those of some amphibious creature. "The Sminkovas are partial to pilferage. Take care of small items, John Shirting. Particularly seemingly useless things like paperclips, rubber bands. When you find yourself searching an entire day for a store that sells paperclips, and that eventuality will occur, believe me, then you will taste a bit of the bitter fruit harvested by your relations with the Sminkovas."

"I don't even *use* paperclips," Shirting said innocently.

"You're missing the point. One day you will come home and find your clothing washed and folded, your floor swept, your toilet cleaned as though they were trying to erase all trace of you. And that is the subtext, is it not? Perhaps you will look in the mirror and be surprised to find that your very reflection has not been scrubbed away. They would whittle you down to the diminished form of your money belt, believe you me. Once I tried to explain to them the meaning of the word *rent*, and the rights that entitled me to, only to be threatened with eviction. I come to them an ambassador of capitalistic restraint, and what do I get for my troubles? Grandma Sminkova using as her daily vitamin my Percodin, to which I am quite happily addicted."

"The daughter is a spy, of that I'm convinced," ceded Shirting.

"A spy?"

"Yes. But I've checked for microphones and the like. My apartment is clean."

"Shirting, you've really lost it."

"I can see you are injured about my morning ham, and that it has curdled your viewpoint beyond objectivity. I will therefore refrain from furthering any discussion on behalf of my benefactors."

"The problem was that damnable revolution, you see. These days greed passes for enlightenment. The worst aspects of capitalism replacing solid, if misused ideologies."

"Revolution? How many died?" asked Shirting.

"Nobody, you silly. It was a *velvet* revolution. One of the only nonviolent revolutions in history. Greased with dollars and pop music. Come on, Shirting."

"Codswallop! I don't believe it. There's no such thing as nonviolent revolution. It's a ruse, if you ask me. A ploy by the KGB. You believe what you want, but I'm not so naïve."

"Don't you watch the news, Shirting?"

"Look, if there was a real revolution, why is it all you see are single brands in the stores? Uncle Ben Rice. Coke. No choice—if that's not Communism, what is? At Capo Coffee Family there were innumerable amounts of drink variations and whole bean mixes. *That's* free market. As for me, I'll wait until there's some blood spilled before I believe there's been a revolution," Shirting said, relieved from any counter-attack from Mizen by Lenka's reappearance. She had changed from the sheet into a beige, sharply cut shirt and khaki pants; she looked to Shirting like she was about to embark upon a safari, the image reinforced by the pair of binoculars hanging from her neck, and the wide rimmed hat she carried.

"Come," she said in English, oblivious of any tension between the two. Her invitation influenced Mizen's demeanor immediately; his face brightened as he took the hat from her and placed it on his head. It occurred to Shirting that Mizen was, if nothing else, quite mercurial, and his anger was only revealed when challenged.

"Come on," he said to Shirting, again friendly as a boy to his playmate, taking his arm in a conciliatory way.

Shirting accompanied the couple into Mizen's other room. Shirting had guessed correctly; it was a bedroom, furnished, unlike his own, with an heirloom quality sleigh bed (the dreams one might have on a bed like that, mused Shirting, being whisked about the land of Nod on such a carriage). Also to be envied was Mizen's desk, large as a woodworker's. Shirting could imagine ruling an empire of Capo Coffee outlets from across its aged oaken expanse.

Lenka redirected his attention by taking him by the hand (a more intuitive Shirting might have reflected about the quality within his person that caused women to take his hand as though they were taking the hand of a child) and leading him over to the big bay window, where Mizen was already positioned, binoculars poised before his eyes. The window shared the same view as Shirting's back window: it looked out over the Sminkova's small backyard, then up a small hill of thick undergrowth that divided the row of townhouses from the tram tracks. Shirting could see the big, skeletal tree that shed the downy white pods occasionally drifted in through his own open window.

"What are we–" he started to ask before being hushed by Mizen. They waited in silence several minutes before Lenka detected the sound. Mizen searched the yard with the binoculars, spotted something, then placed them in front of Shirting, directing him with outstretched finger.

"There, in the linden tree." It took Shirting a few moments before he spotted the blackbird hidden in the branches. "Can you see it?" Shirting nodded.

"It's there every day, exactly at, what time is it?"

"Eleven thirty-two," Shirting replied.

"Every day at eleven thirty-two it appears and it chirps exactly, now listen—"

They waited until the bird gave a off a series of quick, declarative caws.

"It chirps exactly eleven times, then after an interval, which varies, another responds. Then they both fly away." Whether it had indeed flown away Shirting could not tell, for he had handed the binoculars to Lenka, who was anxious to view the bird as well.

"I'm working on a theory," Mizen said in a hushed tone, "about bird language. There is something going on here that is kept confidential between the birds. I believe it is a kind of programming, an entertainment, perhaps, that this bird is communicating to the others, delivered in their own grammatical terms."

Lenka interrupted him and whispered in his ear. Mizen rolled his eyes.

"It's a *love* story, or at least that's what Lenka insists. Imagine the ramifications if we could crack that code. How might it inform our own relations with the birds, and by and by, with each other. It's a new, naturalistic sort of socialism of which I speak." Interpreting Shirting's silence as accord, he continued.

"I am writing, not so much a manifesto, but a serialized dramatization of bird radio, as I call it, or I will, once I have penetrated its secrets. Lenka is helping me. They are Czech birds, after all, and my Czech is far from fluent. I'm going to bring it to the public, in operatic form perhaps. Lenka will do costume design, at which she is quite adept. You can help transcribe, if you like. Your room looks out onto this aviary theater as well. We'll take the bird opera to the people."

Shirting's face tightened in concentration, a response to Mizen's plan percolating. "Of course all the real money is in traveling franchises," he finally advised.

Shirting's heart went out to the boy. Had his parents shipped him off to Prague, just as they had shipped him off to Patowatomi, to cover up the embarrassment of having an unpresentable child? Mizen immediately threw Shirting's own condition into relief and brought up the following question, which Shirting would put to his travel journal thus:

Is my black bile just another form of madness? Where does black bile lie on the insanity continuum? Or, rather than an insanity continuum, should we consider it an insanity spectrum?

Of course, insanity is too strong a word to place over both Mizen and Shirting's conditions. Decent, nonclinical language has yet to be invented to describe the likes of these two. Mizen, if he decided not to invite someone into his private world of conspiracies and theories, might easily get by in the public sector, and was indeed quite social in Prague. Had it been left to Shirting's grandfather to pass judgment, he would have given Mizen the same diagnosis he long ago gave to his lone grandson: *the boy had taken a weird bounce.*

"I told the Sminkovas about bird radio," Mizen said, once they had retired back into the sitting room, Lenka quietly scraping away at the burnt batter from the waffle iron. "She wants to cover it up. She would pilfer this little tale of love like the spare change from your nightstand. Remember what I told you about them. Take care of small items, John Shirting."

The following mornings, upon waking, Shirting would wait for the sound of the blackbirds to travel through his window. It became a ritual with him, waiting for the bird to sing before he would throw the covers from himself and start the day. But as much as he wanted to share some camaraderie with his neighbor, the sequencing Mizen heard proved illusory. On many days Shirting heard nothing at all but the rumble of the tram as it descended from the White Hill.

PIGSTROKE

MONIKA ATE AT AL-JAMILLI'S EVERY DAY. FOR LUNCH AND dinner she would enjoy the same meal: a gyro (stuffed until the pita was bursting at the seams with extra cucumber, onions, and tzatziki sauce) and fries on the side. She constantly smelled of lamb, having found its gamey olfactory qualities the most effective weapon in repelling overanxious clients. As of late, Shirting would join her at mealtime, though he would opt for al-Jamilli's falafel, the spicy little balls of mashed chick peas rolled and fried in front of his eyes by Jamilli himself. (Shirting thought the presentation good marketing and recommended Jamilli start expanding his business across the city, perhaps even have a falafel delivery service—Jamilli just laughed and sat back down on his upturned milk crate.) The stand was situated in a delightful location—the courtyard of an incorporated building on Na Příkopě that one had to enter through a vaulted corridor. The area was canopied with the branches of ageless oak trees and had the feeling of a small park in the city center. Squirrels hunted around the diners' legs for fallen scraps of pita and stray, breakaway balls of falafel.

Shirting had made good headway in securing the attentions of his desideratum. Persistence had paid off, not to mention the easy money he represented to the working girl. It can be told that much of Shirting's savings had gone toward buying time enough to earn her confidence. But that deductible having been paid, on occasions such as these, he was only expected to cover the meal, which he did without complaint. With the aid of the pocket dictionary he had obtained at the American Hospitality Center, and a pantomime performance worthy of a kabuki actor, Shirting had made clear his overture of friendship, and perhaps future employment. She wasn't averse to the idea, and thus allowed Shirting to tutor her in English over gyros and the apple tea Jamilli served in tulip-shaped glasses.

They sat at a small round plastic table, a pile of napkins at the ready for when Monika inevitably dribbled tzatziki sauce onto her exercise book, which was now opened to her daily homework assignment. Shirting noticed that, though she had written only a few words of the essay he had assigned her, she had gone to great lengths to ornament her unformed scrawl with illustrations of pigs, and had also adhered several panda stickers to the page. Shirting asked her to read her essay aloud: *My teacher is some small wildebeest. He is a name John Shirting. My name is Monika. He is the baddest person in this world. I feed him the cats. He is my darling. Dear Monika.* The way she pronounced her w's as v's, calling him a vildebeest like a tarted-up little vampire—if that wasn't going to stir his slumbering libido, nothing would. And all things considered, he was pleased with her progress. She had shown a certain talent for memorizing the names of animals, of which it appeared she was quite fond. The result was that she knew the English words for ocelot and condor, but could not give

52

directions to the National Museum. Shirting indulged this interest in hopes of using it as a springboard into more useful vocabulary, not to mention basic grammar, but anytime they strayed from the subject of animals the girl's interest waned. This had prompted a field trip to the city's underfunded zoo, where they gazed at grumpy baboons kept in bare cages; drugged-up pachyderms; llamas that spat at anybody who got too close; and harassed, neurotic goats in the petting zoo that shrank from the touch. Monika had worn an ermine stole and ventriloquised sympathetic messages to the caged animals through its tiny preserved head.

"Look," Shirting had said, "I am walking *away* from the marmoset. I am walking *toward* the anteater."

"Marmoset, anteater," she repeated, smiling.

"No. *Toward*. *Away*," he said, making a few illustrative steps.

"Marmoset! Anteater!" she insisted, then hid her face behind the cloud of cotton candy he had bought for her.

Things were not going much better at Jamilli's. Shirting had set up a neat little exercise based on Mad Libs, one of his favorite childhood games. All Monika had to do was provide a verb, noun, or adjective into the blank spaces Shirting had scratched from his Pooh book, and he would later read the hilarious results back to her.

"I need a verb," Shirting prompted. Monika stared without visible comprehension.

"You remember verbs, the things that *do*."

"Superman," she finally said.

"Superman isn't a verb, it's a person. Jeepers, he's not even a *person*, he only looks human."

"Superman *does*," Monika countered.

"It's true, Superman does, in fact he does *far more* than his fair share, to be sure. But he can do all he wants and he still won't qualify as a *verb*. Look how the Mad Lib plays out: 'If you happen to have read another book about Christopher Robin, you may Superman that he once had a swan.' It's a nice idea, but it just doesn't work."

Monika pouted and threw one of Shirting's fries to the squirrels.

"Look Moni," Shirting pleaded, "I am only trying to help you. How can I listen to you bespeak your great sorrow, which I sense, if you don't have the words to communicate the experience? If you are like me, then the place you reside in is far more remote than your mere physiognomy would let on. If that place is in the sea, then these words I teach you are the stepping stones between us. If that place is in the forest, then these words are a trail of breadcrumbs. If it is in the sky, they are each a flap of a wing. Each word, I encode with a bit of myself, so when you speak it, you will recreate me in your memory. It is my charm."

Shirting paused for a breath, then continued: "As for myself, I speak to you from across a great chasm, one that only grows greater every day. But this island of myself is a clean place, I can tell you, free of interlopers and malingerers. I have dusted the cobwebs from the eves and shaken out all the rugs. There are polished surfaces aplenty, here. Are you following? What I'm trying to say is I've changed the sheets of myself, made the room of my heart ready for a visitor. But the invitation I issue is written in English."

He had, of course, lost her completely. She pulled a crayon out from the box he had given her as a present and began filling in the pig doodle with an aquamarine blue.

"Well," he said, and not without any small amount of determination, "if you won't learn English, then I will endeavor to learn Czech. Like Orpheus descended to Hades,

I will descend into that language's depths if only to bring you up and out. Now, let's have a little. Come on, give me a word."

"*Strč prst skrz krk*," she said, smiling malevolently.

"Come again?"

She repeated the sentence.

"She tells you to stick your finger down your throat," Jamilli said, laughing.

"*Str . . . str . . .*" he sputtered, but no matter what acrobatics he put his mouth through he couldn't get past the Falling Wallenda of the tongue required to pronounce the Czech 'r'.

"As much money as you Americans have, you cannot buy a vowel," Jamilli cracked wise.

"Jamilli, as much as I respect your entrepreneurial and, no doubt, *refugee* status, I must request that you limit your interest to the carving up of your adorable lambs. As for money, it does me no shame to inform you that I am down to my last shares of bean stock, which I am loathe to sell as Capo's is gobbling up the market at such a ravenous rate."

"Poor and without language—it is how I came to this county, too," Jamilli said, bringing them fresh tea.

"Jamilli, while I'm sure you have quite a dramatic and heart-rending story to tell—perhaps CNN would take a liking to your narrative—I am now concentrating the entirety of my effort on the young lady, whose tale is equally filled with woe and second-world hardship."

"But I am her genie. She says so herself. One day we will disappear and you may look for us in the bottom of a beer bottle. In many bottles you will look."

"My dear sir, I will ask you to stand off. Besides, beer does not agree with my biochemistry. But I would take another falafel, if you are not too busy."

"Of course, of course." Jamilli retired to his shack.

But Shirting had gotten overheated for nothing. When he asked Monika to tell him the story of her childhood, she struggled to get out a few words—pig—being one of the audible ones, and then went mute. "Pig," she had insisted, then delicately rapped her fist on the table, upsetting her glass of tea.

〜〜〜

It is perhaps true that children of deep loneliness find one another in later life, are drawn to each other unconsciously. Is that what drew Shirting to Monika in the first place? Some unspoken recognition, some elemental attraction? A telepathic communication delivered unbidden, received unnoticed? If she did have the gumption, if not the words, to describe her experience to Shirting, she might have lent credence to that theory.

Like Shirting, Monika was also brought up without her parents, who had been deported by the previous regime to a workers' camp in the Lower Urals. She had been left in the care of a grandmother, who lived in the town of Mikulov, which was separated from Austria by ten miles of yellow mustard fields. The proximity of the "West," even though Vienna lay soundly to the east, did little to relieve the boredom of small town life, which, even under socialism, resonated with small town life almost anywhere. Monika was barely thirteen years old when she caught the attention of a man the townsfolk commonly referred to as the Devil. The Devil had once been a history teacher, but had been dismissed from his post when he had referred to the occupying Russians as "invaders" rather than "liberators." The new regime put him to work clearing the town square of snow in the early hours of morning—a position that, in the summer, found him sweeping litter from the streets. His old colleagues had been instructed not to talk to him, a circumstance that turned him into something of an untouchable, a member of a caste of the excommunicated. After that, his bitterness had consumed him, and he spent the better part of his afternoons drunk in a pub beneath the fortress ruin, cursing the Russian assistors under his breath. To simplify his sentiments: he felt corrupted by the world, and resolved to corrupt right back. It was not long before he began to take notice of the girl on her way home from the technical school every day, quiet and, as far as he could tell, friendless.

It took little courting to bring them together. Soon Monika was riding around in the Devil's Trabant (the fender held on with electrical tape), neglecting the chickens her grandmother had bullied her into caring for. She listened to Radio Free Europe on the Devil's shortwave radio, taking in her first experience of jazz with the Devil's hand down her shirt, the Devil's own wife and child asleep in the next room. In beating her when she refused his advances, the Devil did little to deter her affection for him. Monika retuned to him time after time, wearing her bruises like badges of honor. It took an act of, in her estimation, much greater cruelty to cleave her from him.

The Devil, for her amusement, had stolen a piglet from the farm of a neighboring town and presented it to her with a little pioneer's kerchief tied around its neck. She accepted the gift out of duty to her man, but in time grew to love the pig, which she led around town on a rope leash. She called him Lexy Fluxum, the name written across a package of candles she had seen in a store. She fed it on milk and cornmeal, adding in chicken carcasses and egg shells as they came.

One day, the Devil decided to take her on a trip to the Zapova Lakes. He escorted her into his car (he had tried to let her drive, but took over when he found she wasn't strong enough to turn the Trabant's stiff steering wheel), taking the piglet along. The animal rode between them, taking in the scenery. Halfway there the Devil made the animal move to the back seat. "Jealous of a pig," she had chided him, secretly believing that his anger confirmed his love for her. At the lakes he rented a row boat, and in between swigs of the local jug wine he had brought along, rowed them out to the lake's misty center, Monika shivering up against Lexy Fluxum, as the autumn had provided an unseasonable chill, a taste of things to come.

They were the only boat on the water, the Devil kicking back into the serious business of his wine, which Monika allowed Lexy Fluxum to slurp from her cupped palm. The tipsy beast hoisted itself up onto the bow of boat, gazing out at the water beyond, a swinely maidenhead. In its gaze, Monika projected her own: she saw distant lands, new lives, hope. The Devil had promised to take her to Prague when he had the money. She kept a packed cardboard suitcase in her closet, where her grandmother wouldn't notice.

It took little more than a kick—more a flick of the foot—the way an able player can send a soccer ball arching through the air with the smallest motion, to send Lexy Fluxum tumbling, squealing into the water. Though drunk, the Devil deftly grabbed then restrained Monika, who could do nothing but watch the little pig bob like a cork in the choppy water. In time his squealing stopped, all his labor dedicated to staying afloat. As the pig's body shivered, so did Monika's, a mute scream forming on her lips when she saw the water around Lexy Fluxum changing to the color of the wine in the Devil's jug. If he would have allowed her, and it might have crossed his mind to do so, she would have jumped in right after her pet, into the slick of blood that inked the water around it. The piglet would die not from drowning, but from the cuts along his neck, the result of the paddling of his too-short legs, his sharp hooves cutting his own throat.

The Devil, in time, brought it aboard again with the flat end of the paddle, presenting the mortified, sopping corpse to Monika with a waiter's flourish. Monika did not cry, but instead held the ball of chilled flesh to her chest. Later that night, the Devil would roast the piglet over an open fire for a group of rowdy friends, melting the fat over slices of brown bread and red onion. Monika too would partake in the feast, the molten fat taste henceforth reminding her of love corrupted.

But none of this was for Shirting to know. For her next homework assignment he encouraged her to make up a story of the blue pig she had so eloquently illustrated. (She would complete the task, wearing her aquamarine crayon down to a gnarled claw by opting to depict the story in graphic form, embellishing it with cameos from an otter, a porpoise, and a tap-dancing coyote.)

A Pulmonary Moon

SHIRTING FOUND THAT HE WAS BEGINNING TO RECOGNIZE faces in the crowd as he walked about town: expatriates who stood out with their breezy stride that refused to acquiesce to any sidewalk congestion—cutting through throngs of natives as though by some subversion of physics they existed on a less material plane than the city's own denizens, or were constructed of looser, less earthbound and worrisome particles. And to where were they rushing? Shirting noticed the same faces in the few cafés that serviced this new class of moneyed roustabouts. These foreigners, perpetually amazed by the purchase power of their dollars, pounds, and francs, inured to the apathetic service by the sheer amount of cash they were saving.

Locals began to blend into each other, despite their foreignness, as just another crowd. Only the sad faces of the walking billboards stood out. The otherwise unemployable with placards that advertised some local pub or another hung over their shoulders. These walking billboards were all over the place, mostly withered geriatrics supplementing meager pensions which had been rendered almost worthless by inflation—they represented that segment of the population which found the revolution, three years gone by now, damnable, if not criminal. It was a primitive sort of marketing that, while charitable, riled Shirting's refined, branded business sensibility. Men, emaciated, if not permanently retarded by drink, stumbled about amid the tourist traffic, bearing advertisements for souvenir shops or *Don Giovanni* at the Opera House. Old women, long since retired, also assumed the undignified place sandwiched in between ads for newly opened gyms, bulk Chinese clothing stores, and, even more unjustly, escort services.

But from the crowd, a couple—a shrewish woman with a scarf tied around her face leading her pale companion around—unsettled Shirting when he happened upon them, rounding the corner of the walled Salvator Cemetery. As he made to pass between them, they each took a step inward, a blockade of advertisement. He could see the man with his nose in the air, as though he were an amphibian sniffing Shirting out. The woman's eyes pierced him, making his flesh creep. Appraising them, Shirting was momentarily stunned by what he saw: their advertisements—instead of hawking a pub, both placards featured a tarotlike card, a man in tattered clothing looking down at a card that featured the same such man viewing the same such card. What was particularly striking, however, was that the character on the card looked not unlike Shirting himself: the crisp but secondhand suit, the black hair held tight under its pomade shellac, just the right amount of pudge in his wan boyish face to make him appear almost like a heavy woman in drag. Shirting dodged their surreal blockade and sped on, not looking back. Only when he passed under the neon Fuji sign did he think of his new hire, and wonder about her being and health.

Shirting had not seen Monika in weeks.

He had avoided her since she had made such a cruel—
and, frankly, unprofessional—remark about him, her bene-
factor and made-man hopeful. On that fateful day, after
a meal at al-Jamillis's they had retired to her abode. She
disappeared into the bathroom to make herself up for the
night. Shirting was inching toward that elusive high score
at Frogger, when Monika had called for a towel. He took
it—a pathetic gesture of a towel, the synthetic variety of
rag that they used to distribute in his gym class—from
her day-bag and brought it into the bathroom for her. She
had made no attempt to cover her body; the oakum of her
pubic hair delicately unfurled beneath the water, her head
the only portion not submerged except for a bulge in her
stomach that he had not noticed before: a tiny hub cap of
distension. It could easily have been attributed to beer or
Jamilli's generous portions, but Shirting was quite sure she
was pregnant.

He had lain the towel over the back of a chair, but she
gestured for him to remain. She rose from the tub, her hair
corralled into a bun. The effect gave her face an elfin, boyish
quality when unadorned by those locks. He watched her as
she stepped to the floor, a rash of goose-pimples erupting on
her arms when her foot made contact with the cold tile. She
plucked the towel from its place and handed it to Shirting.
He was to dry her. In this way, and no other, Shirting would
come to know her body: he began in a genuflection, pitying
her chilly feet, which she lifted one after the other to receive
his rubdown, performed with shoeshine vigor. He buffed
her calves into a fluorescent sheen. Up close, her body was
all bright tundra expanses with outpostlike moles in unlikely
places. Shirting sanded her down with that ragged towel,

smoothing her. She moaned, a sound that might have signaled either pleasure or pain. Shirting demurred. He held the towel in front of him, gazing at her stoically, a bathroom attendant, an extra. Under scrutiny now, Monika noticed the single overgrown hair on her nipple and plucked it ruthlessly from its place, momentarily raising the skin into a grotesque, tepeelike shape. She held the hair up, examining it as though unsure it really belonged to her, then flicked it into the toilet. Shirting immediately mourned the loss, and found her incomplete without that flaw. At that moment he had never felt so close to any woman.

Leaning close, she dismissed him just as adroitly.

"You are my very eunuch person," she whispered in his ear.

"Your what?" he said, his mood instantly shattered. But Monika, sensing she had made a mistake, would say no more. The truth is that she had intended to say 'unique' person, but her pronunciation was not yet supple enough for that syllabic distinction. But Shirting, quite conscious that he had the sex-drive of a piece of putty, took the remark as the defining axiom of their relationship. A truth had been voiced, brought to life before them, and he was shamed by it. He left her apartment not long after, and avoided that route when passing from café to café. There would be no more trysts in the bathroom. And if she was pregnant, well, he would see to it that she got all the fair treatment allotted to her in his benefits package (hastily outlined in his travel journal).

Over the following weeks Monika seemed but a transitory relic, like the Atari, already fading into the tar of his memory, to bubble up—and resurface later as an archaeological wonder. If only he could stop time, press pause, and stay there with her. They might be a museum exhibition, roped off, playing Frogger as the seasons passed them by, happily

cutting his turns short for her benefit. Frogger: their perpetually doomed pet and plaything. Frogger: their singular mode
of communication.

≈≈≈

Arriving at Kotva, the technicolor-plastic-pansied Communists'
ode to a Western department store, Shirting made his way to
the kitchen goods section. It was time to return to his new hire,
this time with a renewed sense of professionalism, and bearing a gift, to signal his intentions and recommitment. Shirting
had decided to buy her an apron: the kind she would be wearing when he trained her at the espresso machine. How professional she would look, how fetching.

At Kotva, where all products were kept behind a counter, the dimpled sales girl, at Shirting's request, pulled a
royal red apron from the display. Shirting eyed it skeptically.
But the girl was determined to make the sale. She wrapped
the material around her head like a turban and pantomimed
charming a snake. Then she chose a black one, held it over
her clenched fist, and from beneath it produced a bouquet
of plastic flowers. She threw a cream-colored apron over
herself and howled like a ghost. Shirting pointed to a forest
green one, not quite Capo standard issue, but close enough.
The sales girl very professionally wrapped the item up in
crepe paper, and gently handed it over to Shirting.

To arrive at Monika's apartment from his current coor-
dinates, he had to untangle the knotted Old Town streets, in
which inebriated backpackers have been known to become
lost for entire days; the labyrinth of cobblestoned lanes and
capillary alleyways, a mazy medina where it is all too easy to
stop for a Pilsner when one's attention should be on the map,

itself a barely comprehensible splatter-painting of street names. He had, on any number of occasions, weaved his way through that area, navigating it with what he thought was a ship captain's instinct, only to find himself back where he had started from.

This time the fates allowed him passage: Shirting sneaked down a narrow, deserted street that led him to the American Hospitality Center. From there it was an unfettered shot through to the square, and Monika's apartment. Along the way, he had stopped in a flower store and bought her a big, lopsided sunflower. But when he rang the door, no response came. He parked himself on the step outside her building and waited. In time an old babushka who lived in the building began to get suspicious of the stranger sitting out front. She confronted him and asked what he was doing. When he didn't respond, she recouched the question in German. Shirting looked glumly up at her. Soon another babushka came along, and was stopped by the first, who complained that the stranger was aggravating her blood pressure. The two commiserated about the foreigner who refused to speak even German. A third came out of the door and joined the huddle. She had seen the likes of him before; he was a regular of that hussy down the hall. This brought looks of such disapproval down upon him that he was driven from his vigil, sunflower slung over his shoulder, the big broken face bouncing up and down at the old ladies as he strode away. He loitered in front of a lighter repair shop until the gang disassembled, then returned to Monika's.

Once again John Shirting found himself pressing her apartment's worn buzzer. It surprised him when his call was returned and the automatic lock of the door clicked open. He tripped up the steps two at a time and arrived at her door like so many previous occasions, both expectant and panting in a canine manner.

But the person who answered the door was not Monika. A strong smell of paint thinner and something like smoked meat wafted from the opening where stood a figure in a bright orange jumpsuit. The stranger's hair was shorn down in a bristly punitive sort of cut. Red paint streaked her cheeks like tribal markings. Shirting at once knew she was an expatriate.

"Oh," she said, looking at Shirting quizzically, "I thought you were the mover with the rest of my stuff. *Mluvíte anglicky?*"

A wave of panic rose within him. "Save the subterfuge for the uninitiated. What have you done with Monika?" Shirting demanded.

"Monika? Oh no, you're not one of *them,* are you?" she said, taking a step back from the door.

"Them?"

"The men that ring the door all night. I mean, it's not all bad. I've learned the most fascinating foreign slang. I even sold a painting to a butcher from Germany. You're the first American, though."

"To where have you displaced my protégé?" Shirting said, brushing past her, looking for his abducted bundle of a student. Gone too were the flea-market wares, the LPs, the TV, and gaming console. Ticks on the cosmic abacus were being counted off against him. He was overtaken by an awful apprehension: while he had been sitting idly by, sinister designs were working themselves out; time had suddenly caught up with him and tripped him up from behind.

"I'm not in the business of displacing people. I am in fact the one who gets displaced. I'm an organ looking for a stable host."

"A what?" Shirting said distractedly.

"The city is an unstable host. I'm an unsuccessful transplant. Every place I move into keeps rejecting me. This is my fourth apartment in as many months. But this space feels right somehow. Unstable, yet not suffering from instability. Try explaining that to a student. Flammable and inflammable? Life was so much easier when you just took these things for granted."

"Moni. I'm just looking for Monika. This was her apartment," he said.

"I don't know anything about the former tenant. The place was empty when I got here. Good location, no? Central. A bit sketchy at night. In other words, *cool*."

Shirting suddenly felt faint. "My essential minerals have been depleted," he said. "My balance is way off. Can I sit down?" Shirting was impeded from getting much farther into the apartment by a phalanx of paintings, done in reds, murky browns, and other earth tones; they appeared to be still lifes of various cold-cuts and slabs of meat.

"What kind of abomination is this?"

"Oh, I dabble."

"In what, cannibalism?" Shirting sat down on the hardwood floor. He really did feel faint; he concentrated his thoughts on the notion that there was a fresh dosage circulating through his system with its spry flying feet. The all-points bulletin it represented against the assault of a dour mood.

"I call it the Flesh Cycle," she said, giving him a shot of slivovitz in a preserves jar. Shirting took a tentative sip.

"Drinking before noon is cool, don't you think?" she said. Shirting nodded, his thoughts elsewhere.

"I'm sorry I don't know where your friend went to. If it helps any, she left a drawer-full of these. I was going to throw them out, but there was something cute and pathetic about them." She handed Shirting a stack of thin notebooks. Monika's lesson books. As Shirting flipped through them, a pang of sadness swelled up in his gut. The feeble pig doodles. The inept, half-completed exercises. *Shirting is my krokodile. He is my dear. I feeding him to the rats.* He mentally corrected her syntax, then closed the book. Had they meant so little to her that she would just leave them behind? Was he left behind along with them? Nothing more than her transient tutor? Just as troubling, what was that little leak of melancholy doing there, that black bile rising from his spleen, turning him sour? Had the medication's fortifying walls begun to erode so soon? That tiny soupčon of pessimism he felt sent a panic through him that made his hands sweat and his heart race. He tried to talk himself down. It was entirely glandular, was it not? Chemical. Shirting was, if nothing else, a chemical being, by his own decree. There is your brandy, John Shirting. Imbibe. It is, if nothing else, predictable. *The saturnine thing about Shirtings . . .*

"Mud," he said.

"Mud," she returned. "You know," she added, startling him by her proximity, "if you just took off those glasses, you'd actually have a nice face. A bit like a *lung*."

"You don't say."

"Yes, I say," she said, removing his glasses. "I've always thought the moon looked a bit like a lung up there in space. I guess you have a nice moon face," she said, making a few preliminary strokes with a pencil and paper. "I could paint a face like that."

"Please," said Shirting, taking his glasses from her and replacing them over his nose. He felt truly naked without them.

"You're a sensitive plant, no?"

"If you don't mind," he said, stuffing the notebooks into his satchel, "I'll take these with me." He left the sunflower and green apron there with his new acquaintance—it would be the last he would see of that apartment.

The Sorrows of Young Shirting

BETWEEN THEM THEY HAD CONSUMED FOUR ÉCLAIRS, THREE cream puffs, a slice of pear torte, and a menagerie of tiny, molded marzipan animals. Grandmother Sminkova also supplemented her afternoon snack with two scoops of cherry ice cream, selecting a bottle of sweet brown beer to wash it all down with. For Shirting's part, he had lined up several spent espresso cups in front of him, with full knowledge that the inferior coffee they used in such places frequently contained a higher caffeine content than the deeply roasted Arabica bean favored by Capo's. He explained it all to Grandmother Sminkova knowing that she did not understand, but it comforted him to talk coffee trivia, and it pleased her to be talked to.

The sweet shop was a short walk up the hill from the Sminkova household. Grandmother Sminkova's four poodles were tied up out front, nipping at the heels of passersby. This shop, as were the other almost identical sweet shops across the city, was the longtime hangout of neighborhood babushkas (what is the collective form of babushka?— Shirting, in his travel journal would humbly submit a *scold* of babushkas), a virtual mafia who ruled their families from behind pots of creamed cabbage and porky broth. Most, God bless them, had outlived their husbands, those worthless malingerers, or had given their men up to whatever hobby they practiced in their dotage, be it light-bulb collecting, shortwave radio repair, or drink. The emancipated women of this particular sweet shop frequently made sport of the counter girl, insisting that her ice cream scoops were diminishing in size daily, commenting openly about the proportionate growth of the girl's breasts, and loudly debating the correlation. Three girls had been driven from their positions since Shirting had started accompanying Grandmother Sminkova for her daily snack. Grandma Sminkova had once been part of such a clique, though most of her friends had since died or been removed from sight. Had they been there to join her, they would have complimented her on the dandelions Shirting had woven into her knit skullcap earlier, making it look like a golden tiara.

In truth, the flowers and pastries brought him little joy. His mind continually picked over the last time he had been with Monika, and whether or not she had given him some clue as to her impending departure, some unrecognized salutation. She had been his first new hire and only friend. Had his protégé been snapped up by a competing entity? Now that she had disappeared the memory of her constantly inhabited his thoughts, despite the brief period of time that had elapsed since he had last seen her; he lived within those memories—stretched them out like a painter's canvas, until they were contorted to his liking. He had already been abroad long enough to meet and miss somebody. Shirting again sought solace in wandering.

He dropped Grandmother Sminkova and her brood of barking poodles back home, and took the tram into town (so like a huge orange pill itself, shooting John Shirting through the city's veins). He disembarked at Mustek and began to prowl about the square, checking in the bars of hotels, anyplace where Monika might have been relocated to. He stopped by al-Jamilli's only to discover that the stand had closed down. A "French Brasserie" was opening in its place, the sign read, in English. Perhaps Jamilli was her genie after all, sentenced to appear and disappear as she did, whiffs of lamb and garlic all that remained. It was Shirting's first clue as to how quickly the city itself was changing, mutating right before his eyes. It was true that half the buildings he passed were swaddled in construction scaffolding and gauzy safety netting, as though they were healing underneath a protective cast. Tourist shops and restaurants sprung up overnight, mushroomlike. The city was shedding a skin and acquiring a new, more decorative, if not hawkish, outlook.

As he meandered down the street he held his arms down at his sides, his hands extended outward like wings. The wind seemed to blow right through him; he was a leaf fluttering along, he was an invisibility. In time his searching brought him to the banks of the sluggish Vltava. On its serene waters, slowed by silt, pollution, and weirs, opposite from where Shirting stood, McDonald's Corporation had placed an enormous floating Ronald McDonald, who appeared to be sitting in Lotus position: a meditating sentinel looking out over the city. Shirting could not help but pause whenever he passed within its view. No, Shirting was too much of a purist, a snob even, to enjoy the wares of that corporation, but the composed Zenlike Ronald always made him feel a bit less homesick, working on him like a charmed idol. He indulged in a reflective moment to regain some centeredness, taking in a few deep breaths opposite that most potent agent of change, a germ of the system if there ever was one.

But the clown lent little restorative power on this occasion. Shirting continued on his path, past the starry monument of the deacon Nepomuk, drowned for all his discretion. His wandering became less about searching for his desideratum—she was gone, he knew. Moreover, he felt like the line of time had suddenly gone slack, and he was trapped in between moments that bloated until they burst. Or was melancholy just time itself, come decked out in its Halloween guise? He felt that the linear measurements of city blocks and bridges could compensate for time's haywire lurching, thus realigning him. He found himself sitting on a bench at the Central Train Station, wondering if he wasn't inching a bit farther along on the insanity continuum.

The train station itself was both an arena of travel and stagnation. While travelers were in constant motion through its great halls and corridors, it had become one of the few warm places where the city's displaced persons could sleep. The mentally ill conducted imaginary trains from the platforms. Gypsies set up camp in the waiting areas, claiming rows of seats for their meager possessions and families. Their children were sent begging for spare change from departing travelers, or to gather food from the trash bins, returning with their bounty of sausage ends and picked-over chicken bones. There was a one-legged Gypsy who would circulate around the tables and extend his stump toward the diners like an accusing finger until they relinquished change or food from their plates. (Shirting would learn later that some of these amputations were self-inflicted to lend their bearers credibility.) Pimps and rent boys did brisk business there as well, and the magazine vendors became the disseminators of all variety of unlicensed pornography, smuggled cigarettes, and bogus phone cards. All these dispossessed would be the faces of the Revolution. When would it occur?

Despite his strange attire, Shirting was all but ignored by the station's inhabitants, who might have considered him an amateur at best. From his place he could see the enormous departure and arrival monitor, constantly updating in a flapping sound like falling dominos—so like the scoreboard at Wrigley Field, he mused, doffing an imaginary hat to those distant friendly confines. These flapping wings of time gave him some perspective. Trains left almost every five minutes, and Shirting experienced each update as an exhalant wave— moments rolling over him, tickling him behind the ears and getting lost down his shirt.

There was a distinct temptation to stay at the train station. So little was expected of him there. It seemed to him like nothing but a smaller, therefore more navigable, version of the world outside, a society unto itself. He suddenly envied the old. In a motion that had in recent months become a tic, Shirting reflexively reached for his pocket only to discover that his pill reserve had diminished to but a few oblong, submarine-shaped capsules. The notion sent a prickly wave of anxiety up his spine—he knew he would have to get back to his apartment soon.

Shirting left the train station. He sat at a blistered metal shelter at the stop waiting for the next tram. He looked up at the plastic sign that displayed the schedule, to ascertain exactly what route the tram was taking, but it had been written over with black magic marker: *Dj Gorby*, the vandal had scribbled. Shirting waited alone, the sun having gone down during the interval in the station, the first fog of the winter season taunting him with its morphing and menacing faces.

He was caught off-guard by the night tram, which seemed to have been conjured, then spat forth from the dense smog. Suddenly there it was, a giant glow-worm in the dark, gliding silently along the rail, the electric lines discharging multicolored sparks. In the conductor's seat he saw a pale angelic face framed by a halo of goldenrod hair. The man's face quivered in the booth, distorted as though underwater. Shirting examined the side of the car for a line number but could find none. With a shrug, he boarded. Taking a place on an orange plastic seat he noticed only one other rider, a man in the back seat who was passed out or asleep with his head resting in his hands. The feeling of disquiet he experienced was jarred from his being when the tram lurched forward.

The tram followed its route toward the castle, but Shirting soon noticed that something was amiss. From the window he watched groups of people fly by, pumping fists and shouting curses as the tram passed them by. They missed one scheduled stop, then another. The conductor was drunk or mad, also ignoring traffic stop lights, and picking up speed. Shirting looked back to the other passenger, but he remained frozen in his stupor. The tram headed toward the outskirts, the city center quickly receding behind them. Endless territories of concrete buildings passed him by, huge and gray as cargo liners—like massive sea-faring vessels, with laundry hung to dry on the terraces looking like a huge patchwork sail; terrains stripped and ruined, billboards with Marlboro landscapes providing the only relief from the blight. "My heart is one such tenement," thought Shirting to himself, then looked up to see a hand held palm open toward him. A man in a blue, ill-fitting sports jacket and glasses displayed a controller's badge to the ticketless Shirting. Where he had come from, Shirting could not say, for they had not picked anybody else up.

"Lístek, prosím." The man looked terrifyingly familiar.

"Kodadek?"

"Lístek," the controller repeated. Then, his weary face softening, he appeared to relent, leaving Shirting to gaze after him as he walked the length of the car to the conductor's cabin, disappearing inside. The tram rushed on, and Shirting looked back to the other passenger behind him, a final appeal for sanity. Laughing in the back seat sat his own mirror image—more disheveled, dirtier, and roughed up, but the face was unmistakably his own. The other broke out into a drinking song, sarcastically gleeful and in German. The figure's contours were less translucent then they had been before; it appeared shabby and bedraggled. Then the tram came to a screeching halt, the doors flapping open. Shirting jumped from his place and hopped from the tram, the doors flattening closed behind him. He watched it depart, keeping an eye on the man in the back, who had replaced his head in his hands, and appeared to be whimpering. Shirting's shadow self had caught up with him at last.

KODADEK AND THE
MINTY FRESH PHOTOS

"I CAN SEE YOU'RE NOT A SHOOT 'EM UP KIND OF PLAYER. You got more intellect than that. *More upstairs*," Kodadek had told him. The young Shirting didn't know the man had favored him until he asked him to stay after hours one night to "break in the cherry" of a new game that the company was test marketing. Shirting, so rarely singled out for any distinction, didn't mind. The game he wanted him to test drive was called Master Luckybelly, which Kodadek was keeping in the back room where his office and studio were.

"Don't tell the other kids about this one quite yet," he warned Shirting, who took to the game like he was born to play it, the Luckybelly brand of gaming imprinting itself on the boy's young mind. Luckybelly, more than any other game, perhaps even Frogger, fit Shirting's temperament. It wasn't a shooting game; Luckybelly's weapon was less traditional—he was a master of the little-known Japanese art of *kubotan*—whereby one's adversary is subdued by a firm and exact application of nothing more than a pen. So the graphically depicted, potbellied Luckybelly made his way around a postapocalyptic city battling the undead, radioactive, and zombified residents. To Shirting, the pen was an eloquent, sophisticated weapon—less brutal, more refined than a gun. Any sucker could blast things away. Luckybelly also displayed a strange, unfathomable sort of mysticism: in between phases of adventure, he would pose a little Zen koan to the player. One read: If a dog is licking your hand, is he cleaning it or making it dirty? Such questions puzzled Shirting throughout his school-bound days and generally put him in a blissful, ponderous state. He adored the rotund hero and the subtle manipulations of the joystick that were needed to master the pen: apply it too briskly to a zombie and it would burst, an inky spot filling the screen, the equivalent of tilting a pinball machine. It was an artful game and Shirting was an artful player. It was there that he felt centered, in front of the screen putting Luckybelly through the paces. For a boy of few friends, Luckybelly was mentor and parent.

Shirting was nothing but grateful to Kodadek for giving him the opportunity. He didn't tell a soul. Nor did he tell when, after a week of staying after hours, Kodadek showed him his private archive. It came in a Frango mint box from Marshall Fields, the green and white stripes marking it as the receptacle of all things sublimely delicious. Kodadek was obviously artistically inclined to employ such a box. But it contained no chocolates. Inside, he found the stack of black-and-white photographs of boys roughly his age. Many were in various states of undress—boys riding hobby horses, boys sitting abstractly on a radiator that served as a pedestal. So unembellished, they were like so many unfrosted gingerbread men to Shirting. He found it bizarre and stirring. The warped photo paper betrayed their home-developed origins, and smelled of the minty chocolate of the Frango mint.

"No fingerprints," Kodadek snapped as Shirting flipped through the snapshots. From then on he was careful to hold them by their borders, instead of running his fingers along their front, as if to confirm their existence. Among the boys Shirting recognized the faces of other Frogger champions. They *were* an elite group, apparently, to be memorialized in such a fashion.

"I know my Frogger boys," Kodadek told him. "If there's one thing I know, it's how to spot a Frogger boy."

Shirting didn't know what that meant, but was flattered and trusting enough to allow a few preliminary snapshots to be taken of his own person. The first would be next to the Luckybelly game. In time Kodadek would give that photo to Shirting as a gift and reward for his cooperation. He didn't know why the older man liked his pictures so much; even he could see he still had baby fat, was pale and unformed, a shelless turtle. In time, Shirting proved to be an enthusiastic model, though he would only allow himself to be photographed at the console (action shots, they dubbed them). And while he made other ignoble concessions, he never took his glasses off. Not once.

For weeks he was entertained by Kodadek in his office, mastering the game, which Kodadek had loaded with infinite free replays. It ended when one day Shirting showed up (had been dreaming of Luckybelly all through school) and Kodadek told him all bets were off, the company had recalled the game and had the console picked up that day. It had proved too unpopular, and had even had violent reactions in other test markets. "Too obscure. Not patriotic or bloody enough. Nobody wanted to identify with a Nip," Kodadek explained. Extraterrestrials were okay, but no Nips. Shirting was crushed. Worse, without Luckybelly,

Kodadek's attention waned. It wasn't long before Shirting was hastened out at closing time along with the rest of the group, discarded.

The arcade closed for good not long after. The convenience of Atari proved too tempting to the next generation of player, and the stand-up console was relegated to the back corner of gas stations, 7-11 outlets, and family restaurants. Shirting had never blamed him, never felt taken advantage of. The teasing he suffered at the hands of his classmates—Gaylord, they called him, *Pudge Meister*—was far worse than the tender manipulation of the older man, whom he felt indebted to for simple acts of kindness and generosity; in Kodadek's eye, Shirting was worthy, a Frogger boy to the core. That was enough.

Only now did he resent his former mentor, the memory that had boiled up all black and gummy, as if from a tar pit. A bubble of time he thought he had escaped, only to turn around and discover he trailed ooze, leaving fossil-like footprints wherever he went.

By the time Shirting found his way back to Střešovice it was early morning. He entered his apartment to the raspy wheezing of Grandmother Sminkova, asleep in his bed. The room was spotless—she had done a marathon cleaning session while he was out—but for a chess board the old woman had laid across the end of the bed. As he approached he noticed something odd about the game: the pieces had been replaced by his pills. The colorful pills, set out and ready to do battle. The pills made literal arbiters by Grandmother Sminkova, in whatever game she had been entertaining herself with. Shirting stared down at them for a moment, then reached over and swept them into his cupped hand. They were the last of his supply, fifteen or so. He hoped they would be enough. Shirting then went to his window, where he kept milk cold in the space between the double-glazed panes. He took the extra blanket from his burrow and made a bed for himself in the bathtub, a nest of sorts, resting the pills in the ceramic soap holder. Then he turned out the hall light and climbed in, folding the blanket over himself. He would need one and a half glasses of milk to swallow the balance of his pills. Protection against the world, protection against the shadow self, once and for all—let it be gone. *One to bring you Up. One to put you Down. One to keep Baby . . .*

IMP OF THE IMPERIAL

The Young, and How They Got that Way

Gus, Girish, and his straight man Abe, had an informal reading group that met at the Hare Krishnas Karlin outpost, a nook of a restaurant serried between a picture framer's and the storefront of a zipper repairman. Aside from the fried cheese served at most restaurants, it was one of the few vegetarian meals available in the city, and it had become the unofficial expatriate canteen. Slacking writers, underemployed English tutors, and lulling journalists were happy to spend the better part of the afternoon commuting to the postindustrial area of closed factories and panel tenements, and wait in the line that stretched out the door for the Indian/Czech fusion cuisine offered up from a buffet the size of an in-flight drink cart.

At the Krishnas', Girish Patel took liberties with the status his Indian heritage afforded him. He never waited in line, instead ordering around the European Krishnas (mostly refugees from the war-torn Balkans in need of a bed) like servants, nor did he pay the thirty-crown donation they asked in return for the meal. "Don't want them getting fat," he rationalized to Gus, whose Neo-Beat status (his literary movement's sobriquet) also resisted the small donation. This left the entire tab on Abe's shoulders, who paid the ninety crowns and even tipped an additional ten percent, a gesture that only confused the Krishnas.

Patel, mouth stuffed with tamarind-orange lentils, observed: "This is the only place where one can find self-conscious Krishnas. They have yet to achieve that air of uninhibited zeal, that manic theatrical airport clownishness. It's Krishna without the spectacle." Girish Patel: Asiatic Napoleon of the burgeoning writing scene, barely five feet tall with a precocious beer belly, a pregnant fiancé back in Oakland, and a string of Czechoslovakian girlfriends still waiting for him to make good on his promise to make them stars of Bollywood.

"Don't get too cocky, Patel," said Gus. "I know for a fact that the girl with the harelip carries a luger beneath her robe. Some of these kids are doing smash-up business in small arms, trust me on this."

"I just want to know how the Krishnas got here faster than, say, Scientology. Or Doritos. I mean, what kind of society is this where you can't get Doritos, sliced cheese, Pop Tarts," Patel said, pinching his rice between his fingers and smearing it around in chutney.

"I saw sliced cheese in Kaisers," Abe added hopefully. Abe's fondness of the upscale German supermarket chain was well known and a source of derision among the group.

"Can we stop judging a country's development by what products are available?" Gus said.

"Short answer: no," said Patel.

"They also have marshmallows at Kaisers. I know because I saw them," Abe added wistfully.

"Don't talk to me about marshmallows. Little *harshmallows*," Patel snapped. "Graham crackers, that's what I want. Graham crackers. Talk to me over a toasty s'mores."

"But you have to love a society where it is still economically viable to have zipper repairmen," said Gus.

"That reminds me, that wanker still has my Calvin's," said Patel.

"Calvin's. That's so imperialistic," said Abe.

"Not if they're counterfeit Calvin's. Then it's just getting a little back for the Third World."

"I just want to know," Abe said, fingering his soul patch, "when Taco Bell opens up, will it be called American or Mexican food? Or Pizza Hut, that cuisine which has had to make two trans-Atlantic trips. How do we qualify it? And I respectfully ask, how do we qualify Patel here, born in Bombay, educated in Berkeley? Here we have a double-dipped expatriate, representing exactly what culture? I call it the New Mongrolism. I'm writing that down by the way."

"You disloyal juking Judas," Patel said.

"That's uncalled for," said Abe, trying not to rise to the bait. Abe had already opened himself up for torrents of abuse owing to the fact that he had arrived in Prague with twenty pair of Levi's in tow, hoping to sell them on the black market, only to learn that the pants were already common and readily available in stores.

"What? You're not in college anymore, there's no disciplinary board to appeal to here. Spleefing, queefing, Nancy-boy. Rapscallion. Piggly-poo. Humping-scrumping Huffelump! Go back to California where you're safe. As for me, I came here to be liberated, and it begins in language. Unlike you simpletons, Girish Patel is a free man," he said before waving a Krishna over to refill his water glass.

"Patel, you slay me, *slay* me," Gus said, mixing the compliment with just enough irony to keep Patel on his toes, "you *disarray* me and *fillet* me."

"You *repay* me," added Abe, hoping to recover some of what he'd laid out for lunch.

"You two are most *pozor*-full," said Gus. If he found himself playing the role of the sycophant it was only because both Patel and Abe had undergraduate degrees, while Gus had dropped out of junior college. Most of the expatriates he met were of Patel and Abe's ilk: recently graduated, slumming for a year before returning to the States and taking on an advanced degree or going to work on Wall Street. Still, it was better than Paris, where Gus had most recently relocated from. There, the only other writer he met was a wayward lawyer on a radical sabbatical and laboring away on a legal thriller. The free meal at Krishna was at least a facsimile of the credit he had asked for (and been denied) at his local café on the Left Bank. Gus, who had read *Tropic of Cancer* like it was his own protracted fortune.

"So Patel, how is the novel coming?"

"*Docu*novel," Patel corrected, still feeling testy.

"Okay, docunovel."

"I refer that question to my factotum. Abe?"

"Girish, I thought we agreed not to call me that," Abe said.

"I'm sorry," Patel said, "My *friend and compiler*. How is our progress?"

"I got some good new material from that Lila girl, the artist who only paints cold-cuts, or something like that? You remember, from Újezd who you called a waddling twaddling moo-moo? Vintage Patelisms abound. You can really be offensive when you want, Girish. I'm doing a follow-up interview with our landlord, though his experience with

Patel has been quite limited. I may have to make some of it up."

"No making it up." Patel said, almost upsetting his water again. "A docunovel must be constructed by pure experience. The artistry comes in the reassemblage. If that ninny Karásek won't ante up then we just won't pay rent for next month. Then we'll see what he has to say about old Patel."

"I see you're forcing a plot twist, very shrewd," Abe said, taking out his binder and jotting the note down.

"Appropriation is the art of the future. Write that down, too. In my expansive tome *The Fates Only a Mother Could Love*, I also propose to sample the works of Kerouac, Hemingway, and Pynchon much the way a DJ samples music. I will retell all their stories through the eyes of a Hindu-American. Another section, 'Propaganda for Patel,' will be a deconstruction of The Warsaw Pact as poetically reassembled from the perspective of a Hindu American. I will include my found poetry from Charter 54. The final section, called 'Ninety-nine Pages About the Author for a One-Page Story,' will be an in-depth essay on kite flying and its impact on world culture, as experienced through the eyes of a Hindu-American. Are you getting this, Abe?"

Abe nodded, mentally retitling Patel's book *New Mongrolism: A Litany*.

"That reminds me," said Gus. "Are you taking that job with *Friend Kitty* magazine?"

"I'm a writer, not a pornographer," said Patel haughtily.

"Yeah, and *Friend Kitty*'s about as low as you can go in that particular field, though I'm pressing him to take the job," said Abe. "The world is experiencing a tropism toward porn. Name one thing that can't be made better by adding porn."

"Breakfast?" Gus ventured.

"Neophyte," chided Abe.

"Did you get that, Abe? 'Gus makes silly comment in the presence of Girish Patel.' Abe, put your fork down and write, damn it—I've got work to do here. And Gus, be warned, you are currently going down in posterity with a piece of parsley hanging precariously from your lower lip. History will remember you as a sloppy eater."

"Most writing manuals discourage the use of adverbs, so perhaps I'll edit out that 'precariously';" said Abe, scratching the word from his notebook.

"No, retain them and catalogue them. I'll build a castle of adverbs and watch them try to knock it down with their bombastic manuals. Girish Patel bows to no style maven. I love my adverbs like children and will put out the call to collect orphaned, unwanted adverbs from across the world. There is no such thing as an unwanted adverb in God's eyes, do you comprehend? I won't stand for this abuse."

Patel pounded his fist against the pine table, upsetting the two remaining glasses of water. The disintegrated flotsam and jetsam of citrus fruit (used to hide the heavy metal taste of the tap water) rode the trickle down onto the floor. As the water spilled, the three sat paralyzed, unsure how to approach the problem. Gus was almost moved to translate the flow into a poetic image, so they might at once appreciate the moment as well as Gus's verbal acumen. But no image came to mind other than the word "spillage," which conjured up memories of toting around plastic cups of keg beer; that, however, seemed too simplistic to set forth to this critical bunch. Patel, too, found himself seeking to engage with the spilled water on an artistic level. He saw the accident as an interruption, a breakage in the flow of the narrative that was his life; extensive footnotes were converging upon his mind like insurgent guerrillas. For just a moment, the indigenous Patel had overthrown the assembled, contrived Patel. It was a sorry sight to behold, Girish looking like a chided pet. Abe simply sat in between the two, waiting for one of them to act.

The Semisweet Half-Life

The suit Shirting's grandfather had handed down to him—Capper & Capper read the silk ox-blood label sewn into the inside right breast pocket—was pressed and hanging from the hook on his wardrobe knob, a disembodied reminder that he was still in the land of the living. The passing down of that article of clothing had represented a coming of age for the boy, an unceremonious acknowledgement of maturity. Shirting had reached his grandfather's physical stature by mid–high school. He was a bit chubbier than the old man, but it only showed if he buttoned the jacket, which otherwise fit perfectly. His grandfather later gifted him suits of Harris Tweed and seersucker. Despite the fact that the suits made him an easier target for ridicule, he wore one daily. (Actually, what happened was that the physical harassment the quiet, awkward child endured through most of his childhood mysteriously ceased when he donned the suit, replaced by the more respectable verbal barrage the attire demanded.) Another curious effect: Shirting began to take on attributes of the old man. Never before had he unconsciously aped his grandfather's speech, but suddenly he found himself exclaiming situations as "swell" and crying "jiminy" at the slightest provocation. He, for a few brief but daring weeks, took to carrying a cane. The boy also began to take part in his grandfather's nightly ritual of downing a nightcap. "Mud" was the toast his grandfather would offer forth before shooting a snort of Old Crow. That Shirting's choice of cocoa so resembled mud only made the toast that much more exquisite. It was as if the old man's genes had been passed to Shirting by way of haberdashery, rather than through the less direct route of his parents.

Shirting's grandfather, Paul—never Pavel, his given name—an immigrant, had made a modest fortune distributing Pathé short films for the nickelodeons that were opening up across the less reputable neighborhoods in Chicago. Barely into his twenties, he became an *impresario*, a disseminator of low but profitable culture. His career in the film industry was cut short by a pair of MPCC thugs hired by Thomas Edison himself, who was not above gangsterlike tactics to muscle out the competition. The experience left him with a permanent limp and a lifelong grudge against Edison, whom he decried as a fake and a thief. After that violent brush with fame and fortune, he retired from the fast lane and opened a small but flourishing shoe store (Benda's Bootery) on Central Street in the suburb of Evanston.

Shirting's runaway mother—Mabel—quite uncharacteristically returned to Chicagoland to have her baby. She lasted a few months in an apartment above Benda's Bootery, then deposited the infant with Paul for safekeeping before she returned to Vermont, where she was a resident at the Bread and Puppet theater commune. (His father, Max Shirting, had disappeared somewhere in Honduras on a spiritual retreat.) Having grown bored of Vermont, she drifted down to New

York State—to Woodstock—where she would be killed in a kiln accident. She figured into her child's life only as a sort of unified antimatter, a contoured absence, a shadow. Shirting had no memory of her, and only a high school yearbook photo with which to relate, but he exhibited an unarticulated sort of discomfort whenever a school activity called for parental involvement.

Because of his profession, Shirting's grandfather had accumulated an unparalleled collection of empty shoeboxes. The boxes figured mightily into the youngster's own personal mythology, each one prized from the top of his grandfather's closet shelf or excavated from under his bed, contributing to a never-ending narrative of the man's life, told through the horded detritus of his years. Many of the boxes contained nothing more than cancelled checks. (But what fun the young Shirting would have with one such box, reconstructing the old man's steps from the chronologies: one spent at Jewel food market, the next dropped on the proceeding day at a country club in Door County. Unlike Shirting's mother, those checks had traveled, but had returned to their proper place. Thousands of proofs that systems, on occasion, worked.)

Other boxes held more mystery. While one housed several ringed garter belts, another held a collection of stamps from unfamiliar locales and foreign countries. In another Shirting found postcards from Benda's native Prague, the black-and-white photos looking like a peek into some centuries-old wonderland, the dioramas of a grim but magical girl. There was the Charles Bridge in daguerreotype; the spires St. Vitus Cathedral rising like dribbled sand castles. (These murky postcards became the baseball cards of Shirtings youth.) Other shoeboxes in the kitchen contained bottles of liquor in constantly fluctuating degrees of consumption. Though it never saw much action, Shirting enjoyed the orange smell of his grandfather's Grand Marnier (like extract of vanilla, the taste was hugely disappointing); it was the Old Crow that disappeared and got replaced with the greatest frequency. That Shirting was forced to carry his lunch to school in a modified shoebox, that his birthday and Christmas presents came in shoeboxes, that he rarely received gifts that exceeded that size, never diminished his love for the cardboard, functional and faintly smelling of the leather and canvas shoes they had once contained. Shirting even participated in a few trial runs of his own shoebox filing. Countless insects—crickets, daddy longlegs, cicadas, and fireflies—had been held captive by the boy, usually forgotten for less naturalistic pursuits, left to mummify in their cardboard crypts. Needless to say, the boxes were also perfect containers for Atari cartridges.

The final box worth mentioning was the one his grandfather kept in the bathroom. It was there that the prescriptives were stored, the mood brighteners designed to keep the man's physical decline from unnecessarily turning him dour. (The man was *dying*, but why let that get in the way of his good time?) Paul Benda, Czech immigrant, pioneer in film, shoe salesman extraordinaire, and pharmaceutical fanatic, referred to them as his *magic beans*. Shirting had come across them during one of his routine searches of the septuagenarian's belongings, emptied from their vials (then and thereafter unidentifiable to the boy) into the box, looking like a collection of so many errant game pieces.

Postcollegiate, excommunicated from Capo Coffee Family, Shirting finally sated his curiosity about those pills. Having moved back into his grandfather's apartment, during those bleak and static-white months, the disenfranchised

Shirting turned to pilferage. Self-diagnosed—what was espresso gone bad but black bile?—he waited for his grandfather to depart for his daily constitutional (Benda's Bootery long since closed, replaced by a Payless), before swiping one of the multicolored pills from the box, swallowing it with a cupped handful of water from the tap. The deed of a desperate person. In the days that followed, John Shirting supplemented that dose with a nightly pill as well. While the medication had no immediate effect, the act of ingestion gave him the buzz of the illicit, a personal rowdiness that his sober school years had sadly lacked. His criminal acts would have surely been sussed out and cut short by the old man, were it not for the fact that his decline was rapidly accelerating: the elder Shirting had all but forgotten the very existence of the pill box in his bathroom's linen closet and more and more often had to be reminded of the younger Shirting's own relevance in the household.

In Shirting's own estimation, the old man was becoming more turtlelike as the days went on. Aside from his bald head and beakish nose, and the reptilian fluidity with which he snapped a morsel of food from his fork when he ate, there was the silky hairless dewlap of skin beneath his throat, which appeared to pulse with his breathing; the breathing itself no longer automatic but labored and deliberate. Paul Benda took to spending increasingly long spells in the bath, the silence of that space interrupted by violent bursts of hot water from the tap. Mumbling from behind the closed door—the elder Shirting, communing with whatever spirits attended to the divestment of human form, receiving their counsel, relinquishing all claims, signing authority over to these, the valets of the afterworld—*don't worry sir, we'll take it from here.* The pinewood coffin, so like the accrued shoeboxes, chosen for its rectangular rather than hexagonal shape.

Perhaps his mother's restlessness had imprinted itself on him, after all. She had gone east searching for "bohemia." Shirting had settled for its literal manifestation. Or was it the nostalgia that his grandfather's photos had engendered in him, made more potent when wearing the old man's suits? Or perhaps the pills had worked their synthetic magic on his being, for he unexpectedly felt like taking the sudden courageous step, that trans-Atlantic stride that would land him in Prague. Shirting: adventurer, free spirit, agent of change. If that didn't fall within the Capo Coffee Family mission statement, then nothing did.

≈≈≈

For a moment, Shirting thought he saw the old man's shape puff the suit out once more from in between Grandmother Sminkova's severe tucks—a final dashing claim at earthy existence before fading and undramatically disappearing. Or was the younger Shirting still delusional with the poison he had subjected himself to? His respite from the world had lasted only about as long as a much-needed sleep, during which time he was lifted from his place in the tub (once again aping his beloved grandparent) by Mizen and carried, bridelike, to his bed. There, he was watched over, in turns, by Hanna and Grandmother Sminkova, who ministered to him with warm compresses on the chest and charmed potatoes under the pillow.

A worthwhile question: was Shirting, during this period that the pills' effect ran thin, recuperating or was he becoming sick? Not even he could tell. Was he returning to normalcy, or was he deteriorating? His brain felt like a sponge being wrung out, his mind's most vibrant colors lost between the cracks in the floorboard. While he slept his dreams took on a distinctly psychopharmacological tone. These were lucid, visually spastic dreams, which Shirting remembered in full. In one, he was planting capsules in the Sminkovas' garden as though they were seeds. They engendered a strange tree whose fruit was translucent and glowing, with a radiating emberlike pit at its core, a blackbird like the one Mizen had fixated on pecking at its flesh. In another dream he was laying the pills out on an unfamiliar linoleum floor, then retreating to watch a pack of rats scurry from the dark corners to devour them like table scraps or rodent poison, the medicine inciting them into a csardaslike folk dance. In another, Shirting unscrewed a series of Russian Matruska dolls, only to find the tiniest one in the shape of the pill. In a final dream he was loading a pistol with capsules: the dreamed variation of Shirting aimed the gun at a page of white paper and fired, the discharge leaving an inky script of cuneiform that began to take the shape of readable language.

Shirting, upon waking, rose from his place in bed and stumbled over to his desk, where he began to write feverishly. There are people—entirely unmusical otherwise—who have reported waking up with entire scores playing in their mind that they composed while asleep. The strange admixture of sleep and chemical overdose had worked a kind of alchemy in Shirting, and made him perhaps more susceptible to the influence those dreams exerted. (The same was true for him in romantic affairs: he rarely knew he liked a girl until he dreamed of her and the residual desire spilled over into waking life.) It wasn't a song that he spewed onto the page but, in his mind, something finer: his own personal *mission statement.* A redefined directive. When Shirting finished scribbling, he held the page up, the sun's rays illuminating it from behind, baptizing his script in light. He lay the paper back on his desk and went to his door and took in his breakfast tray. Over a cup of the Sminkovas' coffee he reread his work, finding it effective. Internal memo dispatched and circulated. He then returned to his bed and did not venture from it for several days to come.

THE PROP ROOM

Jason "Bunny" Shoup came to Prague with Guns N' Roses, working as a lighting technician on 1991 world tour (Sparta Stadium filled to capacity). After a night of drinking in a cellar bar called the Golden Udder, on his way back to his hotel Bunny had gotten lost in the Old Town's labyrinth of streets. He spent hours walking in the Josefov, during which he would swear the former ghetto was rearranging itself to keep him from finding his way out, and would in fact direct him to the gargoyle-adorned tenement where he would pause to rest. He leaned up against that building's door, which gave way under his weight, so like a secret passage in a b-grade horror movie. Weary and intoxicated beyond the point the spirits should have induced, he slept in the empty room, using one of his cowboy boots as a pillow. (Cowboy boots on cobblestone streets, his first mistake.) In his dreams he saw candlelit orgies, miniature windup birds, white-hot obelisks, folios raining parchment from the ceiling, scarab beetles performing acrobatics. A plan had taken root during repose.

In the morning he woke to find himself in a musty library. After shaking the slivovitz-induced half-sleep from his person, he realized that the scenery surrounding him, painted landscapes viewed through bay windows, and shelves of aged books, were in fact backdrops and sets: he had stumbled into a deserted prop room. Further investigation would reveal a pillaged, graffiti-tagged theater, complete with a proscenium stage. Broken cathedral windows around the balcony let in a murky, algae-colored light, glowing girders landing on Shoup as though accusing him. It looked like a crime scene lacking only a bludgeoned victim. In a flash of inspiration, he envisioned the space as a club, the first Western-style club in Prague. It was a powerful vision, not unlike a hallucination. That very morning he quit the tour, reneging on his contract, and bought a space heater and a padlock for the door. He then took up residence in the theatre, working out the details of opening the café in the lobby.

It wasn't long before Bunny was serving warm bottled beer from behind a makeshift bar that was constructed of a discarded door held up on sawhorses. He kept a samovar of tea boiling, and served Turkish coffee from a hotplate charged with pirated electricity. The café was open all night and backpackers paid a few dollars to lay their sleeping bags down on the theater's floor.

It was a story Bunny felt he had told countless times in the very short interval during which the café had opened and become the success that it was. Now, once more he trotted it out for the benefit of the oddly dressed boy who stood before him, seeking employment.

Little guesswork need be done to reveal that aforementioned person took the shape, form, and biochemistry of one John Shirting.

"The idea for the club wasn't even mine," Bunny said confidentially, unsure why he was admitting this previously unarticulated part of his story to the stranger. "You can talk about epiphany, but I know that it was a seed planted there by some weird energy of the theater. You can see people feeding off it when they come in. You'll see." Bunny emptied his beer and ordered another round from Gus, despite the fact that Shirting's beers were lining up next to him, unconsumed. "It's a squatters café, really. People who drink too much are allowed to clear their tab by working behind the bar."

"Are you able to keep a firm grip on quality that way?" Shirting inquired.

"Quality? You're looking at some of the best beer in the world. Quality control is a good bottle opener."

"But say, for example, you were to get your hands on something like an espresso machine. Just for instance. You wouldn't let any old tippler back there, would you? Well would you?"

"There's no money for that," Bunny laughed.

"Just for instance," persisted Shirting.

Bunny fell silent for a moment, then took a long swig of his beer. He looked Shirting carefully over. "I don't really know," he said.

"These things need to be sorted out from the start. Rebranding is an expensive process. I, fortunately, come *pre*branded."

"Who sent you to me?" said Bunny, who had become suddenly suspicious of the strange character sitting across from him.

"Sent me? My former school chum Theo Mizen told be about this place when I admitted to him my impoverished state," replied Shirting.

"Mizen. Ah yes, Mizen. The Commie guy," said Bunny, his composure easing at the reference.

"Traveler and fellow traveler," replied Shirting.

"Let me tell you a story," said Bunny, the brief wince of paranoia dispatched with. "Before we came to Prague, the tour stopped in Budapest. There had been a cancellation in Vienna, so we actually had a day to spend in the city. I was walking down a fairly normal street, the kind with mostly tourists, nice shops, postcard stands, and the like. Streets like this in every European city, you know: Old World charm at tourist prices. Out of nowhere this girl stops me, and starts asking me about the Guns N' Roses T-shirt I'm wearing. We begin to chat, her English isn't that good, but you know, who really cares, because she's obviously really into the fact that I'm touring with the band and whatnot. It's looking like a really good thing, you know? So she asks me if I want to have a drink at a bar, and I'm like, okay, why not. So we go down a side street to some crappy little joint—suspiciously empty— but it was the middle of the day. They had a gypsy on a synthesizer in the corner who nodded at us when we entered, then began to play Dancing Queen of all things. A jukebox in the back. The whole thing seemed suitably divey and surreal. She ordered a brandy and I got a beer. But right after our drinks arrived, the conversation suddenly ceased. Her enthusiasm just drained away. Gone. It was like she didn't even speak any English anymore, like she had just used up all of her words. She excused herself and went to the bathroom. I noticed she had finished her brandy awful quick, so before she went I asked her if she wanted another. She looked at me almost pitifully, then whispered *no*. She disappeared into the bathroom and suddenly, as if on cue, the music stopped, and the bartender came around from behind the bar to give me the check. The total was two hundred and forty, which in Hungarian currency was a just few dollars, so even though she brought me the check without asking, I pulled out three hundred forints, which was a healthy tip. She waved away the money. 'Dollars,' she said. I'm like, 'What!' Two-hundred and forty dollars for two drinks. She showed me a menu, in vaguely translated English: Two hundred dollars for the brandy, forty for the beer. I'm trying to tell her she's crazy, but no-go, she doesn't speak a word of English outside of 'dollar' and 'pay.' I cruise to the bathroom to get the girl to translate. I burst into the ladies room, but there is nobody there. Nor was there a window, so where she disappeared to I have no idea. I return to the bar in a total panic. I look to the door, as I'm about to make a quick and disgusted exit to find a huge, Neanderthal thug blocking the way. I'm talking, he is one of those soulless orcs from a Dungeons and Dragons game. He's tossing a pair of dice in the air and smiling at me in a fashion that says he would welcome it if I even tried to escape. Welcome to Eastern Europe.

"So I pull out my wallet. I've got something like fifty dollars in American, and twenty more in Hungarian. I lay it all out on the table. He just looks at it and shakes his head. I open up my wallet to show him the void within. He takes the wallet and locates my cash card. It's then that I notice the dice I thought he was topping is actually an incisor—human as far as I can tell, and gleaming white. Then he takes me, guiding me by the back of the neck, to the back of the bar, where the machine that I thought as a jukebox. Well, it's not a jukebox, it's a cash station. I try to plead, to tell him I don't have any money in the account. He begins to slap me in the face, which is somehow more humiliating than getting punched. So what can I do, I take the money out and give it to him."

"But instead of leaving, I sit down at the table and, even though my hand was shaking, casually finish my beer, tipped the gypsy synthesizer player, and walked out as though nothing had happened. I tracked down some of the huskier members of the crew and went to look for the bar, but we couldn't locate it. I found a place that looked just like it from the outside, but I went in to find it all decked out in some faux 50s diner motif, Presley crooning 'Heartbreak Hotel' from the stereo, the only difference as that the kids were sucking down carafes of beer instead of milkshakes. Looked all afternoon. Never found the bar, and I took it on the chin. The next day we were in Prague."

Shirting stopped to contemplate the lesson encoded in Bunny's story, then realized he could find none.

"At Capo's we used to give the police free coffee. It was an unspoken gratuity. Woe be it to the pasty new hire who charged one of Chicago's finest for their Lucky Latte'ano," he finally said.

"What I'm trying to convey is that there are no real rules here. For better or worse it's like we've all flown in on the dollar's magic carpet. There is a diplomatic immunity at work, but it cuts both ways," Bunny said. "If there is a mad lust for dollars it is partially our fault. That's what you have to keep in mind if you work here. Also, there are some shady types around. It seems like every organized crime syndicate in the world has sent a delegate to Prague, sort of like underworld ambassadors. The Vietnamese representative was in here a few nights ago. A Serb was in with a VW van filled with Moldavian women, like a kitten sale in a red wagon, except sick. And everybody needs a payoff. Garbage men on up. You follow?"

Shirting nodded: managers could be cryptic. In his experience, they were altogether a different breed. He often pitied the Reg for the lonely position he was in, as top man at their outlet. Shirting had always done his best to coddle him. It was refreshing to be back in a position here in which he could flatter and submit to a boss, while at the same time realize they deserved his patience and sympathy.

"They are still battling their way into the free market with sticks and stones here. Communists are paid off with big privatization deals, cigarette and alcohol companies are free to openly target teenagers—Marlboro is a symbol of freedom here. It's a political statement to smoke a Marlboro. So what you get are the worst aspects of capitalism colliding with the hind-end of communist corruption and bureaucracy. How does one resolve that? I personally keep a Kalashnikov in my office. If you want one, let me know."

Shirting took a tentative sip of his beer. He was uneasy with what Shoup was saying, but he needed the money. Besides, the position suited his reinvigorated mission: priming the pump for a Capo Coffee Family invasion. Now that Monika was gone, he could get on with his plans, and the Prop Room might be the very place to begin the complex scheme of initiating a true revolution and toppling the ersatz government that had fooled the world with its sham revolution. He resolved to write Sippy about the Prop Room immediately. Shirting allowed his animated self to fly over the city, slaloming around cathedral spires, dropping fistfuls of Capo Coffee free-drink coupons, which fluttered out over the heads of the amazed population, each piece of paper a colorfully winged butterfly, indoctrinating a new foot soldier for the insurgency. Shirting, his apron flapping behind him in the wind, giving a curt salute to modestly deflect their gratitude.

"So what do you say?" said Bunny.

"Huh?"

"The job. I can only pay thirty crowns an hour to start, until the club gets going."

"Sounds swell," replied Shirting, "but if it is okay with you, I would like to be consider myself your Minister of Protocol and Eventual Expansion." Bunny laughed, unsure if he was being kidded.

Shirting found himself behind the bar that very evening.

JOHN SHIRTING AND THE
BETA BEER

WORKING AT THE PROP ROOM REMINDED SHIRTING OF WORKING
at Capos, except this was an otherworldly, solarized version.
The nuts and bolts were the same: serve the customer, collect
the money. But where Capo's accentuated the bright spot-
lessness of the place to the point of obsessiveness (how many
times he had rushed from his station behind the espresso
maker to swab up spilled milk at the condiment bar), the
Prop Room was a dimly lit place, frequently making due
with candlelight when the power blew. Furthermore, the
rigid standards he had grown used to in Chicago were simply not enforced in his new position: not only did they lack
even basic accoutrements for drink-making, there was not
even the faintest attempt at quality control. True, on his first
night of work, Shirting found himself mostly wrenching
bottle tops from the warm Big Goat and Pilsner the clientele
favored, but when he did get the odd coffee order, it irked him
to pour boiling water over raw grounds to serve it in the bas-
tardized Turkish variation they had come to expect. (Despite
his reservations he continued to throw back the chalky coffee

himself, spitting the occasional loose ground into his hand-kerchief like chewing tobacco.) In his off moments, Shirting sat with his travel journal and jotted down basic protocols. In short, it was missionary work.

"Whacha got there?" Bunny asked, taking a sip from yet another beer.

"Nothing. I mean just some documents and general guidelines for operation, but they're not quite ready yet," said Shirting, holding the notebook to his chest.

"Yeah, like what?" said Bunny, who seemed genuinely interested.

"Well, I've been outlining a sort of mission statement."

"Yeah? What's that?"

"A mission statement? Every business needs one, especially at this tender, formative stage."

"Okay, but what is it *exactly*?"

Shirting considered for a moment, then shot down another coffee before responding.

"It is like a will, but not for the dead, no, it's for the living. It breathes like an organic being and is therefore adaptable to all situations. It praises when praise is needed, it prunes when growth is detrimental. It is a fortuneteller's charm, a CEO's blessing memo, a hieroglyphic oracle. Capo Coffee Family has the Mona Lisa of mission statements, but I think you will find my own *personal* variation quite inspired as well."

Shirting took the document that he had worked so tirelessly on upon waking from his long sleep. Over the past week he had searched for and finally found an establishment that would laminate the paper for him. As he handed it over to Bunny, the candlelight reflected off of the plastic, giving it a lambent, glowing quality.

"That document, my dear sir, is my prime directive, and without it I am like a fish without its fins, flapping aimlessly and without purpose. It's my Magna Carta. My spiritual Constitution. It's my passport to Centeredness," Shirting explained, when it was clear the paper had produced the intended effect.

"That's quite something," said Bunny, clearly taken in by the boundless *esprit* of the document.

"It is what I was lacking when I arrived here in town. I lost my path over these last few months, but this statement will put me back on course. A germ of the system once again. Agent of change. I was quite sure that it was dictated to me directly by some divine intervention. Or perhaps I channeled it like a medium channels spirits," Shirting said, though he secretly ascribed his mission statement's mystical appeal to the fusion of coffee and the fantastic wealth of medicine he had pumped through his system.

"That's something," Bunny said, handing the document back to Shirting, who disappeared it into his attaché case. A line had formed and Shirting dispatched each waiting customer with a bottle of beer, moving in an automated, robotic fashion until all were satisfied. Shirting talked on.

"It is a manifesto of hope and liberation. It is a gospel for the soul that chooses to manage itself like a corporation manages its interests, only the profit is in spirit, not in cash. In spirit, sir, not cash," continued Shirting, who appeared to be moving faster and faster like an overwound toy.

"Calm down John," said Bunny.

"What?" He quickly sent his animated Shirting to do his patented mod-Frankenstein dance on the bar top, while he contented himself with an autistic sort of swaying motion and tapping foot.

"You're working up a sweat there," said Bunny.

"If my dedication to customer service demands a sweat, then sweat I will," replied Shirting, absolutely avid.

"Seriously. Calm down."

Shirting ceased his dance. "I demand satisfaction. Satisfaction all around. It's what keeps them coming back. It's implicit in the contract," said Shirting.

"Shirting, sit down. Here," Bunny handed him a brown beer, "sit down, and take a break."

"I will not relinquish this post. They can send in their KGB, Stasi, and STB, their bloodsucking bureaucrats and counteragents. They are powerless in the face of a well-delineated mission statement."

"Sit. Now! This is not an option."

"Fifteen-minute break, sir. Call me if you need me."

Shirting found a seat at a corner table while Bunny attended to the clientele. Shirting tried not to look over at the bar too much, but his feeling of protectiveness over that place was already fully formed. The loneliness of the zeitgeist upon him. To distract himself, he took tiny, exploratory sips of the beer. Unable to calm down, he began to rework the guidelines for quality control that he planned to implement once he had sufficient pull. It was just a matter of getting the regulars used to the mere idea of good service, so the full-on Capo Coffee experience would not be such a shock. He could hardly wait to write Sippy to let him know of his progress and request further instruction. He sent a silent toast to the tiny *made man* within, took a long gulp of his beer, and continued to scribble away.

The beer began to put Shirting in a nostalgic mood. It brought him back to his first few days at Capo's, which he counted as among the happiest of his life. He recollected the mystical sort of hazing the company practiced to initiate new employees, a technique they referred to as 'alchemy.' On an assigned day the designated employee, while changing in the back room, would be abducted by a masked group leader. A pillowcase was thrown over his head and, hands bound, he was taken along with abducted employees from other Capo outlets and driven in the back of a van to a warehouse up near the Wisconsin border. Designed to resemble a hostage-taking situation, some of the employees were genuinely afraid, stifling sobs in the backseat. When they arrived, they were put in a dark, cold room, where the only sound was that of dripping water. After several hours, they were liberated by the group leader, who would remain masked throughout the entire ordeal. Made vulnerable and properly conditioned, they were unbound and led into a comfortable room, then given brief pithy lessons in the philosophy of the Ronin and Sufi. They read Basho haiku, all the while indulging in French press taste testings. Then, split into smaller groups, they engaged in empowering games, underwent hypnosis, meditated, chanted, and took personality tests. Participants connected with their Capo spirit through group exercises and individual reflection, though not quite as intense as the Russian roulette challenges the higher-ups were rumored to have engaged in. During this period Shirting learned that his totem animal was a frog, and spent the next interval hopping around on the floor and ribbiting until his group leader retallied his quiz score to reveal he was in fact a hamster. Many of the participants reported personal transformations outside of the realm of mere corporate zeal. One of his coworkers was so affected by the program that she quit Capo's altogether and joined the Navy. Cynical musicians came away with a revived

sense of loyalty to the company, and already loyal employees became devout. Everybody who survived the ordeal
was given a Perks & Percolations card, entitling them to free
drinks and other discounts. There was a rogue sort of Zen
about the moments passed in the retreat that appealed to
Shirting, for he still played that day out in his mind, thinking of it fondly, like camp.

≈≈≈

Shirting was so tense that he let out a shriek of surprise upon
realizing he was no longer alone at the table; seemingly from
nowhere a strange couple had materialized before him. The
man had a mop of thick black hair and was almost unnatu-
rally pale. He wore hip, yellow-tinted lenses in his glasses.
His partner also had the same midnight black hair and wan
pallor. She smoked a thin ivory pipe with a touching delicacy,
tapping out the ashes against the heel of her boot, pinching a
bit of tobacco from a plastic bag she kept in an army surplus
satchel. They both wore identical black turtleneck sweaters
and looked a bit like a pair of reanimated beatniks.

They smiled at him.

Shirting, unsure what was expected of him, smiled back
and lifted his beer in their direction.

"New in town?" the man ventured, after a silence.

"Yes," replied Shirting.

"Making plans?" he said casually.

Shirting looked down at his notebook. He closed it and
slipped it into his attaché case.

"Did he offend you?" his mate asked.

"No," replied Shirting. It then struck him that there was
something utterly familiar about the couple. They reminded

him of the strange billboarded pair that seemed to be following him across the city. But these two were different
somehow. It was dark in the room, but Shirting could detect
a ruddy blotting on her cheeks, like receding acne. And he
appeared younger, more Western. They resembled any number of young bohemian couples that had relocated to the city
to start over.

"Is this your first time here?" the man asked.

"Here? In this café? I work here," replied Shirting.

"We've been coming here for years," the woman said.

"Years? But it only just opened a few weeks ago," said
Shirting, looking over to Bunny, who was busy replacing
empty bottles into the crates that were stacked high as amplifiers behind the bar.

"I am Dobromilla, this is my colleague Dobromil. We're
Golem scholars," she said.

"What's that?" asked Shirting, who was sure he was
dealing with counteragents of some variety.

"More like Golem trackers," Dobromil corrected her.

"You look, I learn," Dobromilla retorted.

"It's all the same," he said.

"No it's not," she replied. "Remember the last Golem
you spotted. We watched it for a week sitting on the street
corner before I discovered it was a cash machine."

"A *cash* machine. Who's ever heard of such a thing."

"A lot of people, apparently."

"I was misinformed in that instance," he said.

"That wasn't the only one. Remember when we stood outside Kotva all night. They tried to have us arrested," she said.

"That was legitimate," he said.

She turned to Shirting, as if soliciting his support. "He
thought the Golem was hiding in a television set."

"Tiny performing homunculi," he mused.

"*Fantasia* was playing," she said.

"All those brooms, I could have sworn . . ."

"You spend a lot of time dealing with false leads, misinformation," she explained.

"Disinformation," he added. "Absolute *piss*-information."

"I don't understand," Shirting interrupted. "What is a Golem?"

"*As if,*" she said.

"No, that's fair," her companion said. "Created centuries ago by Rabbi Lowe out of clay from the banks of the muddy Vltava, the Golem was a sort of undead manservant who was supposed to protect the Jewish quarter against pogroms and the like," he said wearily. "He was supposed to return, but he's about fifty years late. No show."

"Cosmological wrong turn," she added.

"Really. Get with the pogrom," he said, sending her into peals of laughter.

"You are such a card," she said.

"Since the true Golem's disappearance, it is our belief that it has tried to return but in a different form. Little sub-Golems, if you will."

"Entirely possible," she said. "Scrapings from the original's clay have been found as far away as Java."

"Stolen by the Shabbos Goy."

"Anyway, conditions are right for the beast's return. Intergalactic alignment, extraterrestrial accord, crap like that. Historical shiftings, dangerously high levels of antimatter. Hope we're not boring you."

"No, not at all," said Shirting.

"Hey, just for kicks, can I ask you a question?" said the man.

"Okay," replied Shirting.

"This is going to be a trip. Now, do you ever, say, entertain fantasies of things like, for instance, visiting retribution on entire populations? Or maybe just revenge fantasies in general?"

Shirting, eager to please, thought for a moment.

"Once at Capo's, I admit, I gave somebody a half-caf with full knowledge they had requested non-caf. I know, it was a terrible thing to do. It's been haunting me since. It's just that that shot was so perfectly pulled, pure espresso gold. I knew that if I didn't get it into some milk it would oxidize to the point of bitterness. I bowed to the bean. It feels so good just to get that off my chest."

The man looked at Shirting. His eyes appeared to mist over for a moment, then regained their clarity.

"And do you know how to stop a Golem?" she asked.

"No," replied Shirting.

"There is a charmed letter on its body. A kind of mystical mandate. That must be found and removed—then the beast rages no longer." As she spoke, Shirting could not help notice that the man was eyeing his attaché case.

"Hey John!" Bunny was calling him from behind the bar, where he was conferring with a pot-bellied, shirtless man.. Shirting excused himself from the pair and returned to his post, clicking his heels in military fashion once there.

"I've got to go to the back for a few minutes with the landlord," said Bunny. "Hold down the fort, okay?" Shirting nodded. Bunny followed the fat man into the corridor, then reconsidered and made a quick retreat back to the bar.

"Listen, if I don't come back in, say, ten, come look for me," Bunny said.

"I didn't think there was a landlord," said John.

"Neither did I. But right now I don't want the hassle. Here, give me a few from that bottle of Jack," Bunny said, then disappeared with the man, who was entertaining himself by shaking his perspiring belly in front of a table of American women. "I am vild man. I am vild man of Prague," he chanted until they fled from their places. Satisfied, he threw his arm around Bunny and the two disappeared down the corridor.

Shirting manned the bar. He busily rushed back and forth satisfying one customer after another with beer, slivovitz, and the sickly sweet red wine & Coke mixture favored by Czech youth. He couldn't believe how popular the little café was. The place was really less a café than a gesture of a café, but it seemed to suit the crowd, an admixture of precociously hip Czech teens, self-conscious Americans—the sort who had waited until after college to dye their hair purple—and sordid, roguish-looking loners of indiscriminate nationality. Shirting did his best to exceed all their expectations, miming for the non-English speakers, serving with the smile of one happily ensconced. He was relieved when Bunny returned with the heavy man, arm in arm. Bunny requested three shots of Becherovka and demanded that Shirting join them in a toast.

"It's good news. We can stay, and the rent is very reasonable," Bunny said, throwing back the liquor in one quick shot. Shirting too indulged in the soapy, cinnamon flavored drink, chased with a black beer.

"Mud," said Shirting.

"I am vild man. Poet of Prague," the sweaty landlord said, picking up the bottle and pouring himself another shot. "You know how to tell an American woman? She carries her flowers with the petals up in her face, a Czech holds the petals down to the ground. And, you know how to tell who is an American guy? He is the one who does not look you in the eyes when you are making a cheers."

"Apologies," said Shirting.

"The Wild Man drinks for free," Bunny instructed. "Apparently, this guy's family ran the theater in the back before the Communists closed it down. He tried to put on an Ionesco play once and they threw him in jail. It's been sitting empty ever since."

"Jeepers," said Shirting.

"Jeepers is right. Hey, did you leave something over at that table?"

Shirting looked over to the corner table he had been sitting at. The couple he had been talking to had disappeared and there was a box resting on the tabletop. Shirting crossed the room and found that the box was in fact a Buster Brown shoebox, just like one of those favored by his grandfather. He picked it up, and could feel that there was something inside. He lifted the box top and found, peering up at him, a small turtle confined there. The animal emitted a disgruntled hiss in his direction, then retracted its appendages and head, leaving a little discus of shell.

"What is it?" said Bunny, who had followed Shirting to investigate.

"It must have belonged to that couple," said John.

"What couple?"

"They were sitting right here. Didn't you see? They were downright interrogating me."

"I didn't see anybody. I thought you were alone. But hey, I was busy."

Shirting pushed past people and bolted across the room in his effort to get to the door. In a moment he was out on the street, looking for the Golem scholars, but all he found was the winter fog barreling down the lane like a huge grievous conqueror worm.

PRAGUE TALKIN' BLUES

PROTOCOLS, THEY WERE A WORTHWHILE ENDEAVOR. A SIMPLE, commonly held assumption—keep right while walking—was upended in this foreign land. Pedestrians were loose molecules, bouncing all over the sidewalk. People wove as if avoiding sniper fire. *Keep Right, Keep Right*, was Shirting's mantra; perpetuate your perverse politics, but please keep right.

At the Náměsti Republiky metro stop he passed old ladies covertly selling phone cards like dirty postcards, other pensioners tempting the traffic with bouquets of flowers and baskets of blackberries. He ignored all these offerings, patted the head of the gypsy boy who pointed from his mouth to his distended stomach. The boy paused his begging to watch the doughy man-child, whose head was lowered as he ran his fare-dodging gamut past the ticket-seller's window, the security guard, the automated ticket stamping machines, then was brought up short by the stagnated traffic on the descending escalator steps. Public transport frequently meant trouble for Shirting. Though the escalator traveled deep into the bedrock harmlessly and quietly enough, there was no mistaking the violence in the smell of fresh urine, the tunnel's hot wind wafting up its invisible musk of vomit, perspiration, and overheated gears. People, in that time, would find their own step and not relinquish it, or allow passage until they reached the rubber-matted bottom. The metal-ribbed escalator step was an individual fiefdom, not to be invaded. Shirting, even in his permissive best, found the delay irritating. Unlike in his homeland, here the commuters seemed in no hurry to get where they were going, the ride down into the metro but one more line to capitulate to.

The fare dodging always gave Shirting an adrenaline rush, made him feel a bit like a bandit. (There was really little reason to pay, as one rode on the honor system, only rarely enforced by the patrolling checkers, who were easily spotted and thus avoided.) *Subversive germ of the system*. Shirting, public transportation desperado, trying to nuzzle past two teenage lovers who had decided that the escalator steps were as much privacy as they could expect in this world and were mauling each other to the prurient interest of the ascending passengers across the meridian. Having disrupted their tryst, he apologized with a doff of an imaginary hat, and continued downward, only to be impeded again by another pair of lovers. "Abstinence is the best birth control," the impatient Shirting warned the girl as he broke their embrace to pass in between. She spat some inscrutable insult back, distracting Shirting's attention from his path, which was a minefield of plastic shopping bags filled with carrots, turnips, and cabbages, one of which was resting directly in front of him, and would soon find itself upturned by a Buster Brown'd foot, a cabbage rolling from its mouth and ricocheting down the stairs like a pinball, bouncing from heel to leg to shin. Shirting too would find himself upset by a whiskered onion, and would fall the rest of the way down to the rubber-mated terminus, where he would be joined by ingredients to make a hearty, if coarse, soup.

In time, after much reproach heaped upon his pros-
trate body by passing babushkas, who took him for a
drunk, he would be helped to his feet by a pale hand, slip-
pery with ointment.

"Shirting, is that you newting about the Náměsti
Republiky subway station?"

Mizen lifted the dazed commuter to his feet. Shirting
brushed his suit off and endeavored to pretend the incident
didn't happen, even as the babushka whose bag he had
overturned was gathering vegetables from around his feet,
cursing, and lecturing him all the while. What they were so
aggrieved about, he did not know. After all, he had treated
them to some free, comic pratfalls. If he himself could see the
humor, what with his elbow bruised and pride obliterated,
what did she have to complain about? Such performances
were silent movie gold.

"Come on," Mizen said, extricating the two of them from
the crowd, to whom the babushka was appealing for sympathy and perhaps vengeance. Shirting went gladly. He immediately noticed a change in his old nemesis's attire. Where
he had up until recently worn designer shirts from the
boutiques in Water Tower Place, Mizen now donned a blue
workers' smock and German Army surplus pants. Normally
clean cut, Mizen cultivated a patchy bit of stubble under the
chin and nose. He smelled faintly of patchouli.

"We're set up over here." He led Shirting down the long
colorful cavern of a platform. Shirting imagined grand subway balls, or at least sock-hops being held in these cheerful
spaces, so neutralized by the glum faces of the commuters.
They arrived at the place Mizen had appropriated for the
day, a granite bench that served as a lectern for an electronic
synthesizer. Across the front of the instrument was scrawled

"This Machine Kills Fascists." A girl Shirting had never before seen waited for them, a tambourine resting on her hip.

"Shirting, allow me to introduce my animal companion."

"Lenka?" Shirting guessed.

"Naturally," Mizen said. "Not quite as romantically tragic as the last one. Though she makes up for it in social conscience."

"And are you bringing *Bird Radio* to the people?" Shirting asked.

"What?" Mizen gave him a perplexed look.

"Bird radio, bird radio, the code and all that," Shirting reminded him.

"Oh, yes. I'm done with that. It was the old Lenka's trip. But I found the whole idea of opera elitist from the start. Our differences were irreconcilable. I'm afraid it was the cause of the rift between us. I think you'll find my current Lenka much more in tune with the needs of the people. Isn't that true, Lenka?"

The new Lenka nodded. To demonstrate her affinity for the people, she gave a startlingly loud jingle of the tambourine, frightening several commuters into retreating back onto the train they had just disembarked. Mizen took the flourish as a cue and broke into a nasal, semispasmodic rap:

If you want to get to heaven let me tell you what to do
Gotta grease your feet with a little goulash stew.

"That's the Talkin' Blues," he told Shirting in a sotto voce aside, "I mean to reclaim it from the corrupt forces that have used it for gluttonous and avaricious purposes. I hold Run DMC's "My Adidas" as the original sell-out of this streetwise form of protest."

Which side are you on boys, which side are you on
O' Workers can you stand it, O' join us in our chorus
You'll either be a worker, or a pawn for Phillip Morris

Which side are you on boys, which side are you on
Your leaders bowed to Khrushchev, they wouldn't take the hint
Now they want to privatize and make themselves a mint

Which side are you on boys, which side are you on
Your streets they are majestic, your Pilsner is the best
Kick Havel out, put Mizen in and put him to the test

Mizen finished his Talkin' Blues, having intimidated the remaining commuters to the opposite end of the platform. He sat down with his new recruit, as Lenka broke into a quiet acappella version of "Guantanamera," translated into her native tongue.

"Of course Run-DMC isn't entirely to blame. The first band to make a secret pact with industry and encrypt a commercial message into its music is the seemingly benign Simon & Garfunkel. Note the ever hummable 'Kodachrome' with its nice bright colors and greens of summers? Village People who made their name with pure propaganda like 'YMCA' and 'In the Navy.' Who could blame REM for taking the baton with its libidinous nod to telecommunications, 'Star 69.' Bono's 'Real Thing' also happens to be the slogan for a certain fizzy capitalist potion. Think about it. These people have a lot to answer for. Rock and roll may have helped topple the wall, but only because it is lousy with messages of capitalistic greed. It's not that we want the Russians back, no. The Russians did more to sully the human face of socialism than any McCarthy smear campaign ever could. But the unchecked spread of capitalistic and Americanized commercialization must be stood up to. We humbly hope to one day view the cityscape without the impeding blight of Marlboro and Douwe Egberts advertisements."

"Mizen, you changeable little agitator, you. You must know that your trivial jubilee of propaganda cannot stand up to a clearly delineated mission statement," said Shirting, his voice ringing with superiority, if not a note of unintended hostility. He, mistakenly perhaps, had taken Mizen's attack personally.

"That is where you are wrong. Lenka could explain it all to you, if you only spoke a language that wasn't preprogrammed toward capitalistic aggression."

"You dare denounce your mother tongue!"

"What sort of pharmaceutical demon speaks through you, John Shirting? Out demon! Out!"

"Codswallop! I see you are a counterrevolutionary. Don't think you can keep the seeds of change from sprouting."

"Seeds, or choking, stifling weeds, John Shirting."

Mizen squared off against Shirting, whose placid mood had been unsettled due to Mizen's pedantry. His hand reflexively went to his pocket, but instead of the pills he came across the hard shell of the turtle, which he had adopted and named Duke. The turtle's shell, rubbed like a worry stone. He backed off from the angry Mizen, who was approaching predatorily, with the new Lenka beating out a vulgar little war jingle from behind. Shirting, who had never been on the delivering end of a punch in his life.

"There will be no fisticuffs today, my Dear Herbivore," said Shirting, "but I will take this opportunity to ask to desist from so crudely appropriating my morning whipped cream garnish for your own. Don't think I haven't noticed."

"Swine! Scab!" Mizen said.

"Hairshirt! Jesuit!" returned Shirting.

"Drone! Infidel! Lotus Eater!" Mizen yelled.

"Your barbs fail to penetrate the technicolor dreamcoat that is my current mood," said Shirting, who gave one last look of menace, then fled in between the closing doors of a train.

"Yeah? Well, call me when you get back from your vacation in the psychotropics," bellowed Mizen at the departing train. Returning to his synthesizer, he punched up the pre-programmed muzak edition of "We Shall Overcome" and calmed himself by playing it while pretending to key the notes. A few sympathetic commuters took him for a busker and threw tiny worthless *hellers* in his direction.

THE FLESH CYCLE

THERE WAS A COMMOTION AT THE COUNTER OF THE MEAT store, which, like almost every other meat store in the city, was named "Meat." Lila was having a good day of work and resented the disruption. She was focused on a particular liver, so shiny and luminous under the counter fluorescents that it seemed shellacked, but the babushka kept obscuring her view with her treetrunk-like body. Lila put her paint brush down and took a swig of peach-flavored kefir. Nobody was a bigger fan of theat city's surly population of old women than Lila. Something about their fortitude, their severity, made them seem like timeless creatures that no bombs, bullets, or malingering husbands could deter. Babushkas didn't die, they just petrified. Lila fantasized about creating a masked babushka character for the World Wrestling Federation upon her return to the States, taking it to her opponents with ham bones, spatulas, other items pulled from the faded plastic shopping bag so many bona fide babushkas were equipped with. The Universal Babushka, she would be called. In an exploratory venture Lila had gone in search of the hand-embroidered shawls, the indigo-blue scarves they wore over their heads, the billowing skirts that made them look like walking cowbells, but could find none for sale. Where they acquired their dress was a mystery, for no stores sold those items. Was it mail order? A factory outlet outside of town? Perhaps there was a black market for these things.

That was a project for another day. Now Lila was focused on the meats, the grizzled and rural offerings, the unidentifiable slabs and organs that were the store's stock and trade. Lila's subject in abundance, she would sit in the refrigerated room with her easel surveying the display cases as a landscape painter contemplates a mountain range. When the sun was shining, the room's white tile lit up like the bottom of a swimming pool. The tripe, long and fleecy like hand mufflers, the enormous cow hearts that shined as though they had been dipped in gasoline, the simple brutality of the halved pig's heads—those were Lila's inspiration. What happened to the sirloins and the fillet mignons, she did not know. Perhaps they were all exported to Germany, or perhaps the cows in this cash-poor country were bred without those finer cuts.

Lila decided to pack up for the day. The babushka was still making a fuss. She had a cutlet in her hand and was waving it over her head like a handkerchief, appealing to those around her to rally against the butcher, who stood with her arms folded across her chest. Armed with a look of disapproval that was grandmotherly and devastating, she decried the butcher loudly. Lila, with her elementary Czech, discerned the problem: the old woman bought the same thickness of cutlet each week and fried it for exactly the same time, but this week's cutlet had come out grossly overdone. Upon this evidence she determined that the butcher had cheated her with a thinner cut. The butcher explained that prices had gone up, and thirty crowns' worth didn't buy what it used to, and next time she should be prepared. The babushka held the butcher personally responsible for the inflation and accused her of profiteering, labeling it corruption, if not treason.

"I am a butcher," explained the butcher, who was determined to close at five whether those in line got their goods or not.

The babushka had gotten the crowd behind her, and appeared ready to scale the display case to liberate the proper cut of meat she deserved, when Lila stepped in and defused the problem. She purchased the overdone filet from the astonished babushka (who hadn't seen everything, after all) and had it wrapped by the butcher, along with a chain of small, oily salamis, a bag of pig knuckles, and some salt pork. Who knows, she might start a whole new series of cooked meats, or perhaps pickled meats, divergent phases in her Flesh Cycle, comprised of still lifes of congealed fat, gray little postcard-size sketches, blood sausages done in silk screen, and plein air painting.

Nobody appeared grateful for Lila's intercession. The dispute had been the only excitement of their day; now it was back to the routine of haggling over vegetable prices, picking out cabbages (but only after critiquing their obvious and more subtle flaws), and haranguing the salesmen as though they were their husbands.

~~~~

The cold weather had come quite suddenly. Lila could see clouds gathering in the sky like troops set to occupy the city. She walked back home across the outdoor market, whose proximity she considered one of the best things about her new apartment. It was the fourth in a series of apartments she had rented in her first half year in Prague. The first, she had naively told the landlord that it might rent for much more money with a little redecoration; the landlord had taken that advice to heart and Lila was priced out the next week. The second, the landlord's son had decided he wanted, as he had just gotten engaged, again leaving Lila less than a month to move. The third apartment grew intolerable over time. She had understood that she was renting a private apartment, but the landlord was unable to find other accommodations herself and had taken up residence in the kitchen, pitching a pup tent in that tight space. Then there was the space on the square: putting up with the endless traffic of whoremongers until the dwarf landlord finally kicked her out in favor of a Thai girl who seemed to think she was in Italy.

Finally Lila had found this place, a small one bedroom in a Communist-built panel building on a main bus route, but a short trip from the city center. The landlord was accommodating and the rent was reasonable, about a hundred dollars a month. Lila was the only foreigner in the entire building, except for a family of Nigerians on the first floor. The place was ideal but for her neighbors, mostly old pensioners who found it necessary to report Lila's comings and goings to their local councilman. Each time she walked to or from her apartment, situated at the end of the hall, she could hear doors creaking open behind her, rustling paper, whispering. She called it Cabbage Alley, for the heavy persistent smell that haunted the space. Lila had bribed her neighbors with cookies, leaving a plastic baggie at each person's door, only to find them all piled in front of her own door the next day. It didn't really bother her—she liked to toy with the old-timers. On some occasions she would pretend to be smuggling something in under her pea coat, and other times she would wear dark glasses and do her best to act clandestine. In a way, it added flavor to her days. It was like living in a relic of the Cold War without any real danger, a sort of Epcot version of Big Brother.

Lila keyed her door, which still had the landlord's name on the bell. (It was technically illegal to privately rent a state apartment, a widely ignored infraction.) Once in her apartment she fired up the hot water, the gas heater clicking on like a bomb detonator; she had yet to live in an apartment that didn't sound like it was ready to explode at any moment. Lila scrubbed the paint from her hands with the help of the potent homemade brandy her landlord had given her as a housewarming gift, and changed from her overalls into a bright orange jumper purchased in the hunting section of Wal-Mart. There was a reading later that night at Bunker café. They were appalling occasions, the poetry of the whole self-proclaimed Neo-Beat movement that dominated the expatriate community's literary scene causing the most offence. They were just bad enough that Lila found herself craving the feeling of loathing they generated within her. She distained the Czech poets, too, but voicing that feeling felt impolite, so the Americans suffered the brunt of her outrage.

Before going out again she paused in the bathroom. There, in the lukewarm water of the tub, a cow's heart defrosted. Sinew radiated from it like a placenta, looking ready to grow like some enormous seed, sprout appendages and, come spring, flower there in her bathroom. What odd fruit it might bear: strange cuts of meat would hang from its branches. No matter. After painting it, Lila would bake it in her oven with a dozen cloves sticking from it like a nappy head of hair and devour it with couscous.

THE YAK

IN TIME IT WAS REVEALED THAT THE WILD MAN OF PRAGUE WAS not the landlord of the space the Prop Room occupied. And yet the goodwill his presence commanded allowed him to be accepted as a poet who had been incarcerated for unspecified crimes against the State. Bunny thus permitted Shirting to continue to send an occasional free drink his way. When the actual landlord showed up, restitution papers in hand, there was much confusion, and tough negotiations ensued during which time the café was forced to temporarily close. Ultimately, the proprietorship of the space was returned to Bunny, who would however not reveal to Shirting just how he had accomplished that feat.

In the following months, as winter took hold of the city, the club that Bunny had envisioned for the theater opened to great success. As the only relief from the huge, industrial communist-era discos on the main square, the Prop Room gained a following for its understatement. Gone were the door and sawhorses. The space now featured beer on tap from three separate handcrafted bars and a kiosk that sold Mexican food. Bunny employed a small gang of African and Serbian refugees in addition to the assortment of expatriates and Czechs behind the bars. Shirting, despite his unpopularity with the rest of the staff (they had given him the nickname *der Kommissar* behind his back), remained Bunny's wing man throughout, though there was a side to the business that Bunny kept private. For his part, Shirting felt as though a part of his life had been reinstated. Though not as strictly adhered to as he would have hoped, his mission statement had served him well. Shirting, however, had not allowed the Prop Room to replace Capo Coffee in his day to day thoughts. His former employer became almost mythical to him, a sort of unattainable grail.

Unfortunately for Shirting, as he had already discovered, a shed skin is not so easily disposed of. His constant flogging of the Capo model and hinting about a Capo Family invasion had not gone unnoticed. Unbeknownst to our hero, the Prop Room had taken on a silent partner. To Shirting he was just the man who sat at the bar and favored Yukon Jack. Shirting had nicknamed him the Yak Man, "Give me another Yak," he would say to John, pronouncing the "j" as "y," in the Slavic fashion. It had been the Yak's willingness to perform the necessary and unsavory deeds that allowed the Prop Room to stay open. Such feats included assuming an attitude of threat mixed with a propensity toward bribery with the petty city officials that lorded over such operations and the licenses they required. As a former cab driver, the Yak Man was well-versed in small-time thuggery, which was useful because his verbal contract included keeping other prospective silent partners at bay. Numerous Russian and local entities had taken an interest in the club and the access to foreign clientele it provided. The Yak dealt with them swiftly and severely. That was the rub. The weekly honorarium Bunny paid him may have been little more than a gratuity, but the real value of the Yak's involvement was ensuring a connection to venture capitalists, embassy aids, and agents of less respectable concerns. Thus far, through the Prop Room, the Yak had negotiated a deal with the city zoo to rent out animals for entertaining private parties, and in one unfortunate misunderstanding, for that evening's entrée. Another deal, soon to be implemented at the Prop Room, was the procurement of a special team of Ukrainian boys (brought in on a raft over the Tisza river into Hungary, then through a cave at in the Tatra Mountains, into Czechoslovakia) who did double duty as bathroom attendants and erotic masseuses, though some also moonlighted as pickpockets. Where all the cheap heroin was coming from was still unknown to the Yak, but he did his best to keep it out of the Prop Room—there he took some moral high ground.

The odd boy who poured his drinks also gave the Yak cause for concern. He was constantly scribbling in his notebook, and going on about some foreign entity and its inevitable arrival. Some progeny—he speculated—of Chicago's most famous gangster. It was not a matter to be trifled with. A better understanding was needed, because Bunny seemed quite attached to him. That Bunny would employ somebody with a criminal disposition was not surprising to the Yak. Most of the people who worked at the Prop Room behaved in a ganglike manner, but that was simple if not necessary tribalism. This person was different somehow. The Yak had pestered Bunny for information on this particular employee, but Bunny simply threw his hands up and said that the guy was *whacked*. The Yak, not wanting to admit that he did not know what the word meant, had checked his Czech-American slang dictionary (*Wang-Dang American Slang.* Prague: Pivo Press, 1991) and discovered "whacked" meant "to be executed." That was worrisome—a renegade foreign faction, already with a price on his head and a strong foothold in the Yak's interests. The Yak recalled the conversation he had had with Shirting that led to his suspicions. The Yak had been wearing his Confederate flag pin, and it had given Shirting pause.

"It is the greatest flaw of your country's history that the South did not win the war," explained the Yak. "In my country, the South won the war. That is why we are free now."

The American appeared to be contemplating the point, then finally blurted out the statement that had so mystified the Yak. "The South? At Capo's we have three operations in New Orleans. They are allowed to serve chicory blend that we can't get in Chicago, but I think that's really the only difference."

"Chicago?" the Yak said. Something about Shirting's response had excited him. "Chicago? Bang-bang Chicago?" The Yak made an illustrative machine gun gesture with his hands.

"A bang for your buck," said Shirting. "We'll put a 'cap' in ya. That's how we used to sell shots at Capo's. Bang for a buck. We'll put a cap in ya. If you went into any Capo's and said 'bang-bang,' they knew exactly what you were talking about. Two bucks, two bangs. Then the higher ups decided to sell them for a dollar and a quarter, so that put an end to that. In our more rural outlets we called them buck shots. In time, it will all come clear."

The Yak slugged down his drink. Shirting exerted his brand of hospitality, pouring the Yak another on the house.

"I know that a dollar a shot seems like quite a lot in your economy, but trust me, it's actually a good deal," said Shirting, trying to smooth over any misunderstanding.

"And this Capo Family, as you call them, are they something very aggressive?" the Yak asked.

"They have been widely criticized as being ultrapredatory in the market, it is true. But in fact they welcome competition. Let the other guys build up a market, then step in and appropriate it by a war of attrition, which Capo Family has the ammunition to win, be sure. They'll put a cap in ya."

"Ammo. Chicago, bang-bang," the Yak, whose given name was Honza, repeated, verifying.

"Chicago bang-bang," Shirting said.

"What I want to tell is that there is some place for you and your organization, but you must be careful about the place you want," said the Yak. He was trying to be diplomatic with the foreigner.

"Yes, there are those who will not be happy until there is a Capo Family member on every corner," said Shirting grandly.

"They will need a partner," advised the Yak.

"To maintain quality, Capo's does not franchise. Each outlet is owned by the home office."

The Yak wished he had taken his English lessons more seriously. The subtleties of the conversation were getting lost on him. Of course this was all just supposition; there was something entirely ineffectual and comic about the boy. Perhaps he was a new breed of gangster, dandified by the West. Or perhaps he was just another counterfeit—the city was full of them these days. It was getting harder to tell the tourists from the locals—spotting them by the brand of jeans they wore just didn't work like it used to. Either way, the Yak was determined to find out what his game was. It was for that reason that he was perpetually perched at the end of the bar, keeping Shirting in his peripheral vision.

〰〰

John Shirting, for his part, was sensitive to the Yak's surveillance. He was aware that as a germ of the system, as a revolutionary and visionary, he would eventually have to come up against his Cold War correlative. He welcomed the opportunity. No doubt the counteragent was doing his job well. Shirting had seen him countless times with Bunny, meetings he himself was excluded from. How far his influence extended was uncertain, so he was sure to keep his own agenda in the forefront with Bunny. With this in mind he had planned a meeting with his boss that very afternoon and waited patiently behind the bar for Bunny to emerge from his office. In the meantime, Shirting poured the Yak yet another whisky and set about cutting garnishes for the evening rush. Next to him sat Duke, assigned by Shirting to keep an eye on the man.

The turtle had become a strange surrogate to the pills he had until recently indulged in so heavily. Now that they had run out—during Shirting's bathtub binge—Shirting transferred that dependence to his new animal charge. How often Shirting found himself reaching into the pocket to rub the animal's shell, as if it were some charm he drew strength from. The turtle itself didn't seem to mind, though during particularly anxious times it would repel Shirting's attentions with a quick, grouchy snap, raising a V-shaped welt on his owner's finger. Shirting allowed such protestations to go unpunished. Despite his worries, the black bile, which was an ever-threatening presence in his psyche, remained latent. Any time he felt like it was going to erupt and bubble over he clutched the little animal in his hand and whispered encouragements to himself until the feeling passed.

Eventually Gus arrived to relieve Shirting and beckoned him to Bunny's office. Before he went, Shirting mixed a martini, which he garnished with a sweet gherkin. He plucked the turtle from the bar top and replaced him in his jacket pocket, together with crumbs from a pretzel bowl that had become his pet's main source of sustenance alongside an occasional pickled onion or sausage end.

Bunny's office was in the back of the theater in an unused supply room. John gave a quick knock before entering, drink in hand. It was not unusual for Shirting to find him rifling through bales of unconvertible crowns or picking over the merits of whatever he had traded those crowns for. Thus far Shirting had seen a box of hand grenades, a signed letter (allegedly) by Mozart, icons looted from Russian churches, cubist furniture, and an endless stream of Bohemian crystal pass through the office. Where it all came from and where it was dispatched to was outside of Shirting's responsibilities, and he had learned not to pester Bunny about his collectables.

He set the glass on Bunny's desk, leaving a moist circular imprint on an array of five- and ten-crown bills.

"What do we have here?"

"Signature house drink. At first I was thinking of a Prague Grog, but the lack of real citrus proved too daunting. And herring juice is simply uncooperative, no matter what you mix it with"

"Shirting, are you drunk?"

"Tastings were necessary. If I debauch myself with drink, it is all in the quest for a branded product. Or a product worth branding. Which is something I'd like to discuss."

"The gherkin is a nice touch," said Bunny, taking a sip.

"Ham wasn't really working."

"I imagine not."

"It is my belief that this corporation known as the Prop Room has great potential. I see its expansion along

Planet Hollywood's model, only we will feature reams of Communist propaganda as decoration, buy up Lenin statuary to greet customers, and deliver food orders to the kitchen through a secret microphone in the table. Simply *imply* what you want to eat. It's all in the marketing, believe me on this. Real-time nostalgia is what we'll ply them with. I ask you to imagine a Post Prop Room."

"This is one of your jokes, right?"

Shirting gave an uncertain laugh. "I also think you'll find my 'frequent drinkers card' idea particularly savvy, given the climate of *dissipation* that affects this city. Anyway, here's to making us the foremost purveyor behind the entire Iron Curtain."

"But Shirting, the Curtain is lifted."

"Chinese boxes. Matrushka dolls. Dolls inside of dolls," replied Shirting.

"Sure, John."

"Remember, what we're really selling is democracy."

"And beer. Mostly beer, actually," said Bunny, getting up from his seat.

"Yes, democracy and beer. The whole Prop Room experience is based upon that formula."

"John, take a walk with me."

"Okay."

"And grab a stack of those flyers."

"No problem Reg," said Shirting with a brief salute.

"Why are you calling me Reg, John?"

"Reg? Did I call you that? Sorry. Just a little confused lately."

"Okay," said Bunny, stuffing reams of currency into a Čedok flight bag. "Let's go."

As they walked along the Vltava, Shirting picked over his misnomer. It wasn't the first time he had mistakenly believed he was still working at Capo's. The other day, when he had accidentally given a backpacker from Sydney a Staropramen instead of a Pilsner, he had handed them a Capos drink coupon in compensation. He thought back to the training sessions he had taken during Coffee College, the alchemy technique, and wondered if the effects had eternally encoded the mere notion of service with Capo Coffee, if he himself had been somehow branded. He felt his first real pang of bitterness and resentment against the company. Sippy had never responded to a single missive, though Shirting had narrated volumes about the fascinating new city he lived in and the opportunity it represented to Capo Family Coffee. How dare they ignore such a progressive idea, and how dare they turn their collective corporate backs on this population that needed them so. And it didn't stop there, as he had explained to Sippy. They might infiltrate Mother Russia as well. Set up kiosks along the Trans-Siberian Express route, until they penetrate China, the ultimate consumer base. It was a concept of international service he had wanted to implement. In his more caffeinated, euphoric moments he envisioned himself as a sort of Peace Corps worker for free market values.

"Hey Shirting, see that guy over there?" Bunny was pointing to a hulking man that was being followed by a Korean tour group. He wore a T-shirt that read 'Happy Giant Tours,' and he carried a dainty yellow flag with which he directed his charges. "Go give him a flyer."

"Is that really the customer base we want to cultivate?"

"It's a sideshow party, so we need some sideshow." Shirting looked at the flyer. Indeed, it advertised a party at the Prop Room featuring oddities and curiosities, entitling the bearer of the flyer free drinks all night.

"I'm not sure this falls within the mission," said John.

"Hurry, before they get away."

Shirting executed the order, handing the flyer up to the big man, who received it with a bow, and continued on with his tour. It crossed Shirting's mind to tell him that Jolly Giant Tours might be a more resonant name, but this time he let it slide.

After handing flyers to an assortment of Gypsies, a flock of blind children (tapping through the cobblestone streets with their canes, sounding like a giant beetle), various amputees, a man with tribal markings tattooed on his face, and any backpacker they could spot, they retired to an Old Town cellar bar.

〰〰

The Golden Udder was the sort of establishment that was never mentioned in even the most comprehensive of guidebooks. A pub in a landlocked country that labored under the delusion that it was a longshoreman's bar, there was a sad, secondhand seafaring motif that included a greasy, soot- and cobweb-encrusted fishing net hung behind the bar, a life buoy from an unlucky boat called the S.S. Clap adorning the wall, and a taxidermed grouper that looked out over the room with eyes petrified in a permanent expression of humiliation.

In one corner a group of soldiers were passing the day by taking turns at rounding up Gypsies from off the street, who were brought into the Udder and forced to sing. Shirting could see a miserable old woman plucking a mandolin as her captors stomped their feet in merriment. Another table featured a coterie of silent old men who drank from their own personal steins, kept behind the bar; though they sat at the same table, they all appeared to be lone drinkers, roundly ignoring one another. Bunny ordered a pair of Big Goat black beers from the bartender and joined Shirting at the table, where they sat with an old pensioner. Shirting nodded to the solitary man of indiscernible age who was across from them, dressed in a jacket and tie, whose white facial hair seemed to be yellowing before their eyes in the room's thick smoke. The man ignored them, then perked up his ears at the sound of English being spoken. At first he seemed to look at them with an expression of resentment, as if to query just who these people were to come and disrupt his routine with their foreignness, as if rousing his interest presented him with some kind of insurmountable inconvenience; then, after that, a flash of apprehension passed, his expression deflating into one of resignation—it was inevitable, after all. What was there to do but lift glass and drink with the riff-raff?

"What are we doing here, Bunny?"

"Meeting of sorts."

"I think I feel ill. Touch my forehead."

"You're kind of sweaty," Bunny conceded.

"It's in places like this where the plague quenches his thirst and then some. I feel we should depart without delay."

"This place? This is like an institution. Hrabel passed a kidney stone in the bathroom or something. There's a plaque by the pissoir."

Shirting's hand fell into his pocket where the turtle's smooth shell awaited his touch.

"Oh, there he is," Bunny motioned to a dwarf who was being handed down a Becherovka from the bartender. He waved him over.

"Zdeněk, *ahoy*."

"*Ahoy*, friend." Zdeněk hoisted himself onto the bench and rested his shot in front of himself. Shirting was taken aback by the dwarf, though not by his stature; rather, it was his dress that drew his curiosity.

"Is that . . . Union gray?" Shirting ventured in disbelief.

"Yes. There is something like a fight today. But not a real one, you know. Something like a football match."

"Zdeněk is part of a Civil War club," explained Bunny. "You've seen Honza around the bar, right?"

"You mean the Yak?"

"Yeah. He's General Lee. Zdeněk here is General Meade."

"Today we are doing the Gettysburg portion. Being on the North is like playing with the Russians. I am wanting to be on the South team, but Honza is hating me now," said Zdeněk.

"At least you get to win," ventured Shirting, who did not like to see the dwarf so depressed about such a matter. But Zdeněk just shook his head.

"They win," he said.

"Impossible," said Shirting.

"It is true," lamented Zdeněk. "They bought the uniforms. So they win."

"That's treason," countered Shirting.

"Do you know how hard it is to get some American Civil War uniform in such a size? This is even beyond my ability. So, they are winning."

"It's downright un-American if you ask me," said Shirting, his suspicions about the Yak solidifying.

"Yes, this is true," said Zdeněk.

"I've tried to get in on the game, just for kicks, but they won't let me," said Bunny.

"Yes, there are no foreigners allowed at this moment. We have to keep the Czech spirit strong."

"That's messed up."

"You see what I'm saying," said Shirting. "Chinese boxes. Dolls within dolls. Dearest Matrushka, dance with me."

"Okay, but moving on. Did you bring it?" Bunny asked Zdeněk. "The reel?"

"Of course it is real. I do not deal in the fake," said the offended dwarf.

"The film. The reel."

"Ahh. But of course," said Zdeněk. He took the satchel that was hanging from his chair and from it withdrew a black metal box. "You have, I assume . . ." Bunny held up the Čedok bag of currency. "It is all good."

"Let's see it first."

Zdeněk unhinged the buckles of the box and pulled back the lid, revealing an ancient reel of film wound on a rusted spindle.

"See that," Bunny said to Shirting. "That's the first reel to the original *Frankenstein* movie."

"Wouldn't it be easier to just get it on video?"

"No, you don't get it. This is the original silent Lon Chaney version. There's not a single surviving copy. Any usable portion would be a treasure." Bunny made a motion to pick it from its place, and Zdeněk snapped the box closed.

"You must not touch. It will, how do you say, discompose."

"Disintegrate," advised Shirting.

"Yes, this. You must never take it from its place. It is very delicate."

"Then how will I know it's the real thing?"

"I have traded five boys from the Ukraine for this. For their sake, it should better be real."

"If it is so valuable, why are you selling it to me?"

"I am out of the game now. Too much competition from the Russians. I start a souvenir shop and settle down. I make postcards and fake crystal animals. It is where the true money is anyway."

"Fake crystal animals. This is Zdeněk's way of going straight," Bunny said to Shirting.

"It is your choice," said Zdeněk, taking the box from the table and replacing it in the satchel.

"Not so fast," said Bunny. "I'll give you your money. But if this turns out to be a ruse, you'll be hearing from me."

"Are you threatening a member of the Union Army?" said Zdeněk.

"Just hand over that box," said Bunny. He pushed the bag of notes over, and was given the old metal in return.

"No, my friends, I must be flying. I have some activity to perform," said Zdeněk.

"Enjoy the battle," said Bunny.

"In Český -land I take my stand, to live and die in Český. Away, away, way down South in Český," sang Zdeněk, collecting his bag and heading for the door, but not before Shirting could give him a flyer, inviting him to the Sideshow later that week.

HEMINGWAY NEVER DID THIS

GUS BOARDED A TRAM TO HIS APARTMENT IN NUSLE. NEO-beats take public transportation, Gus decided long ago. The *proletariat chariot*. It would inform the themes of restlessness and rootlessness that he was cultivating in his work. He would write the first tram novel and give tram readings. It would be his own little innovation, his gift to the discipline. After a short ride he disembarked and trudged up the hill to his lodgings. He lived in the spare wing of a large, regal apartment that had escaped the eye of the Communists and their apartment-dividing ways, only to be opened up to strangers because now the owner couldn't afford to pay the heating on her own. The place had the feel of an estate sale; the landlady was always unloading one piece of heirloom furniture or another. The twenty-pound, white marble-based phone Gus had bought himself, but left it out for her to use.

When Gus arrived home, he found a plate of cinnamon fingers waiting for him. Eveta, the landlady's granddaugh-ter, was constantly cooking for him—it was not unusual for Gus to come back to find dinners of pork and cabbage set out on an electronic warming tray. She was just sixteen and a homebody; Gus had encouraged her to come out to the Prop

Room one night, then regretted it when she showed up in a formal dress and stood alone in a corner all night sipping the pineapple juice he had bought for her.

The family owned a little dachshund named Matisse, which Gus loathed. The dog was a true xenophobe, targeting Gus with well-placed ankle nips and covert assaults on his clothing when he made the mistake of leaving his door open. It would single out Gus's slippers at the front door (his personal pair, included with the rent) and hide them under the massive couches. Gus made pretense of liking the dog, upon whose assistance he depended from time to time.

Today was one such occasion. On arrival, Gus wolfed down half the plate of cinnamon fingers and leashed Matisse under the pretext of a walk. The dog fought him all the way out the door and down the stairs, barking so violently that Gus could see curtains in the courtyard being drawn back as the building's aged residents poked out their heads. Gus always waved. To date nobody had ever waved back. He muzzled the dog before it could do any real damage.

Though dachshunds seemed to be one of the few breeds that resided in the city, passersby always paused and cooed as though this particular one were the rarest of creatures. As they walked, Matisse made every possible effort to acquaint himself with the coded messages left for him in the excretions of the other neighborhood dogs, but Gus learned that indulging the dog would accrue no goodwill and ruthlessly dragged him from his dogly studies, not pausing until he arrived at the veterinarian's—a basement suite in a nearby tenement.

He always arrived without an appointment, to the ire of the vet's assistant.

"Need to see the doctor," he said in garbled Czech.

The assistant nodded to the waiting room, thick with the effluvium of owners and their pets.

"Emergency," he said to the assistant, who didn't bother to look up from her desk to inspect the dog herself: she knew the score. Nobody protested when Gus was called next into the examination room. Matisse: up on the metal table, shivering with an animal's innate fear of those places.

"And . . . what can I do with you today," the doctor said. His face featured the same disinterest, a free-floating despondency, that Gus had come to expect from the city's professionals. It was a sort of fallen nobility; bartenders at the Prop Room, after all, earned more in a good weekend than doctors did all month.

"I need to shave my dog," Gus said.

The doctor looked at Matisse, but made no move to examine him.

"*Again*?" the doctor said.

"Don't tell me my business," said Gus curtly. He had grown bored of the game. They both knew the outcome, so why do the dance? The doctor looked weary, too, but continued with the interview.

"I should think some ointment would be appropriate, if here is some skin problem. It is some skin problem, yes?"

"The problem is more serious," said Gus.

"More serious?" The doctor looked at Matisse with distaste.

"I will have to shave."

"Shave," said the doctor, "Yes, that is the thing."

Gus nodded his head abstractly and fingered the bruise on his chin. His mind was elsewhere. His poem "Hyena Lover" had been booed off stage by a group of American women the previous night. That wasn't so bad—it gave him a certain notoriety—but one of the women had then accosted him with a pair of brass knuckles at the bar. He had defended himself, saying the poem was merely satire; she rapped him smartly across the chin, claiming the blow was also satirical. A schism had occurred between the expatriated sexes—they had reverted to junior high school students at a dance: boys on one side, girls on the other. Gus had no platonic female friends, and neither he, nor any of his expat coterie dated within their nationality.

"But if there is anything you could do," Gus said, regaining his composure and handing the doctor a hundred-crown note plus a few American dollars to punctuate the deal, "to take away a bit of the discomfort."

"Naturally, we do not want to upset the creature any more," the doctor said, taking the notes. "I will give a recipe something for the pain, if you think it will benefit this creature."

"The creature will be most grateful," said Gus, impatient. The doctor took his time in finding his prescription book.

"You will give him half a medicine before the procedure. After you will give him a medicine every six hours, or as you need it. Is it clear?"

"All clear," said Gus. He pocketed the paper and plucked Matisse from the table.

"And do you know how to properly administrate the peel?"

"The peel?"

"The peel, the peel." The doctor was making Gus work for it. As if there were no other veterinarians in town.

"Ah, the pill, ha-ha. Yes, I know."

"And please do return if the creature is resisting in his problem," the doctor said, adding as a parting shot, "by anointment."

"By anointment," Gus nodded, *sure*. Matisse and Gus garnered a few muted looks of resentment in the waiting room, then were out the door. On the way back home Gus let Matisse piss as reward for his role. They stopped off at the pharmacy to exchange the slip of paper for a small jar of hundred-milligram pills of ketamine. Each pill might fetch ten dollars in a club in New York, but Gus wasn't planning on selling any. Nobody needed to bother with such a niche drug when heroin was so cheap (somebody, somewhere was building a market; the city was, as of only a half a year earlier, awash). Other unknowable forces at work. The pills were his private stash. He liked to take half of one and sit and watch TV with his landlady (watching *Beverly Hills 90210* dubbed into Czech while stoned was something else) or just ride trams the whole day through and work on his poetry.

When they got back to the apartment, Eveta was there waiting for him. Matisse practically flew into her arms.

"You didn't like my biscuit?" That he had eaten only half the plate of cinnamon fingers did Gus no credit. They would be pressed upon him until they were gone.

"Eveta, I have to go now," he said. Gus knew she understood, yet she gave him an uncomprehending look.

"Please, I have something small for your dinner," she said. Indeed there were several plates already set out on the table. It was a tactic he had yet to learn how to repel. She would frequently sabotage him with gargantuan dinners she produced from the kitchen, which lay somewhere off in the warren of hallways and rooms that composed the enormous apartment—Gus had never seen it. Five languages she spoke, yet all she seemed to do was cook. He could not understand her attentions. He was eight years older, purporting to be a writer, yet she had already read (in English) every book he brought home and had even introduced him to the works of Woolf, Hrabal, and Bulgakov. She played the violin, but she would cease practice whenever he arrived home and would never allow him to see her with the instrument. It was her modest life dream to see the Klimts in Vienna.

When Eveta uncovered the first plate, Gus knew he was in trouble. Piled there was a mountainous serving of spaghetti. He had made the mistake of telling her it was his favorite food, the mere thought of North Beach Italian making him crazy with homesickness, without knowing that in Prague the preferred style of eating the pasta was with a bottle of catsup as sauce and covered with grated waxy Edam cheese that never really melted. The disturbing truth was that he had come to enjoy the concoction, and even found himself craving it after a while.

"Please sit," she commanded. Gus felt he had no choice but to comply. He had gained ten pounds since moving in with them. He had visions of growing so fat he might not be able to get out the doorway, forced to wed Eveta and live a life enslaved by never-ending meals and maternal hospitality. But it wasn't the hospitality that got to him, so much as the guilt of accepting it. He was not used to being waited on. He felt some debt was being forced on him, yet they never asked for anything in return, simply that he accept. He had tried padding his rent to compensate for some of the food, but was rebuffed. He had once attempted to reciprocate by buying Eveta an English–Czech dictionary; but when he tried to give it to her she had run crying from the room: he had inadvertently criticized her language skills.

Eveta never ate with him. She liked to stand behind his shoulder, out of his line of vision, and observe. *Like a jailer*, he thought. After he finished the spaghetti she produced a second course: parsleyed potatoes and a fried pork cutlet with a creamy cabbage sauce. (Eveta was a vegetarian, but never chided him for eating meat.) Occasionally the grandmother would walk in, look around, examine his plates, give a generalized nod at the unfolding scenario, and wordlessly return into the bowels of the apartment. After the entree Eveta served him a plate of ruggalach with Turkish coffee. She rarely spoke, and never asked him if he enjoyed the food. Sometimes she would produce a *Time* magazine and ask him to explain what a particular word meant, though she had not done so since the dictionary incident. It still sat on his desk unused, for he was not interested in learning Czech.

It occurred to him during the meal that he had not written all day. He took half a pill during coffee to dispel the anxiety. Eveta noticed this but said nothing (though that night he would find a box of aspirin on his pillow). When he got up to leave, she also remained silent. He only saw her wince when he made the perfunctory gesture of clearing his dirty plates. She whisked them from his hands and scolded him in Czech.

"There is some Dvorak concert on TV tonight," she said, setting the plates back on the table. He knew the dishes would be gone by the time he got home. He wondered if he was being invited or reproached. Always so unfathomable. He tried to remember if he had promised to watch it with her.

"I've got to work tonight," he said, going to the door and putting on his leather trenchcoat. She said nothing, but walked over to him and gave him a kiss on each cheek. Like he was going off to war. But he knew she worried about him after seeing the club. He felt the first rush of euphoria from the pill; he had to get out of this musty, grim place. She was so young, yet so grandmotherly. It aroused entirely unique feelings in him—dodgy, conflicting feelings he only sought to escape. Dvorak: why Dvorak when the rest of the city was listening to Michael Jackson? Five languages, yet she never left the confines of her apartment to talk to somebody. And why didn't they ever turn more lights on?

Even though he had his own keys she let him out, then peeked coquettishly from behind the curtains, watching after him as he descended the stairwell in the courtyard. So pale up there, like she was disintegrating into puzzle pieces behind the white lace. He waved at the bottom step and was off.

〰〰

By the time he boarded the tram, Gus felt his mind and senses had consolidated several feet above his body—a detached sublime feeling. Objective. He was but a puppet, the veterinarian the giant puppeteer pulling his strings. The tram passed under the castle; he felt like he was perpetually passing under that castle. Joseph K. had it wrong—it's not that he couldn't get to the castle, what was disturbing was that he couldn't get away from it. This town had torn up Kafka, so how did Gus himself expect to survive? The ketamine had taken him higher than he had anticipated. He avoided looking at the other passengers, who appeared to have been dipped in beeswax. They moved in slow, determined gestures. Forces at work Gus would never be privy to. Worker bees, a shared consciousness driving them. *Conditions were right*. He took out his notebook, licked the tip of his pencil, and began writing his epic tram poem.

THE SIDE SHOW

BUNNY HAD HUNG A ROPE SWING FROM THE CENTER OF THE room, and a band of drunken dwarves, encouraged by Zdeněk, had lured a well-meaning ESL teacher onto its wooden seat for a ride. At first she enjoyed the attention, so like Snow White and her diminutive attendants. She soon began to panic as they pushed her higher and higher still, refusing to let her off, poking her with long switches or swatting her passing bottom when she screamed for them to stop.

This cruelty was being vicariously enjoyed by Girish Patel, Abe, and Mizen, who had claimed a table early in the evening, though they had yet to receive their drink order from the cocktail waitress who was wise to their tip-dodging ways.

"I'd call that one Drunky, the one that looks like the evil little water fountain ornament," Patel said of Zdeněk, who could be seen tipping his bottle of wine then spitting the contents into the air, the arch crossing the path of the captive teacher, leaving slashes of red across her white blouse.

"And there are Pukey, Scampi, Tardy, and then there's Tipsy and his good buddy Klepto."

"Very *pozor*ful," Mizen said by way of caution.

"And the little one? That's the faithful and cuddly Good Wank. There's pornography in that there scenario."

"How *apropos*," Abe said to Mizen. "Patel has decided to take that job at *Friend Kitty* magazine." Everybody quieted to hear Patel defend himself, but the squat Indian just tipped back his beer and grinned.

"Patel," said Mizen, "always ahead of the curve."

"One can only sit around in cafés so long, my friends. It is time to take the docunovel into the arena of the private sector. Unlike you lust-mongers, I see great creative possibilities in the stroke-mag genre."

"For instance?"

"My first shoot will be a tribute to this legendary city. Imagine if you will a Golem called to service by the Rabbi's wife. Hilarity, pornography ensue. The crazy, green lump of clay just won't quit until the entire ghetto is satisfied. Dig?"

"Girish Patel, the man who put the *lust* back in *lustrace*," Abe quipped.

"Come on Mizen, I'm waiting," Patel said.

"For what?"

"Let's have that anticapitalist Chomskian spiel."

"I find your personal exploitation to be at the very least far less covert than that of the economic system you represent. I am saving my outrage for when I get to view your final product, which, as an academic, I will be given *gratis*, I presume."

"Ah yes . . ." mused Patel. "Even the Reds take a break for some good porn."

"A naked body is a *classless* body," countered Mizen. "That augers well for my spy camera issue, shot entirely with Russian Lomos. The Secret Files of a Soviet Sex Spy. *Apparatchicks*. You pull back the iron curtain, and what do you get but some cheap burlesque—that's what I love about this country."

"I should introduce you to Lenka Number Two. We only used to make love surrounded by a horde of tranquillized cats. It was a weird fetish thing. I've still got some strays hiding around my apartment. Every now and again I take a lid off a pot and there one is, grinning lasciviously up at me."

"Notice how he didn't say whose fetish it was," said Abe.

"Sleeping cats, how very original," Patel said. "Do introduce me to Lenka Number Two, and any other Lenkas you might be keeping from me."

"I have them hidden all over the city. Some are under deep cover; we pass each other on the street and don't say a word, but we both know our common destiny."

"Mizen, you've got the right attitude. Date a foreigner. This city is filled with them."

"Patel," Mizen reproached, "we *are* the foreigners."

"Semantics, college boy. The point is the same. Forget about American women. I want to be taken care of."

"It's called the New Nannyism. I'm writing that down, by the way," Abe said.

"Gus has one."

"That Eveta's a keeper. Good ruggalach."

"Yes, a Hoboken grandmother embodied in a Czech seventeen-year-old. A casserole lover, somebody to grow rotund with," Patel mused. "A succubus in the form of a tempting fried breaded cutlet. I'd be perfectly happy on a little farm raising chickens with such a woman. Take back your aerobicized thighs, for Girish Patel wants them no longer. And keep your gray-flannelled office sirens, with all their portfolios and take-out sushi. Show me the girl who doesn't bring home the bacon, but *slaughters, bleeds,* and *cures* the bacon. Show me the girl not averse to enjoying a pint of beer in the middle of the afternoon. There is no more beautiful sight than that, I tell you. Give me a little belly to show off to my friends. It's the third and most seductive breast in my opinion. I want a blonde, Slavic cherub, legs stout and fatted, in the kitchen cooking dishes of regional and international cuisine. How happily I would look upon the wife who is whipping together the strudel that will send us to an early grave. We will die well-fed, and happy I might add. Girish Patel won't live forever." They all nodded in agreement to that articulated truth.

From their perspective they could see that the teacher had burst into tears, which elicited no sympathy from the dwarves, who only drove her harder. Noticing the trio of expatriates watching him, Zdeněk tipped his bottle in their direction, causing them all to simultaneously look away. Nobody wanted to be singled out as the next victim.

〰️

Shirting had been banned from the bar and bar area. His unending discourse on drink assemblage and mania for service was causing friction with the Czech staff—there was something overly zealous about his attitude that reminded them of the party officials so recently dispensed with. Bunny had assigned Shirting to the door, where, along with a Cameroonian refugee, he was to collect the invitations and the thirty-crown entrance fee that was designed to keep the hoi polloi out.

"Are you hard traveler, or soft traveler?" the Cameroonian asked Shirting, during an interval between guests.

"I don't know," said Shirting.

"I cross the Sahara with nothing but a sack of onions for my food. I sleep under sand and suck water from onions during the day. Then I make a raft and sail from Morocco to Spain."

Shirting felt he should respond in kind. "My in-flight meal was less than satisfactory, the tuna on the alleged tuna melt was but tepid and was served with the most appalling coffee," he said after consideration.

"Ha! I am a hard traveler. You, my friend are a soft traveler. This is why I am called Hard Road, and everybody else is called Soft Road. I am called Hard Road and I will return to England, because I am an Englishman." The Cameroonian crossed his arms in satisfaction, then disappeared into the club, leaving Shirting alone at the post.

The invitations, which entitled the bearer to a free drink, had been much prized, and several counterfeiting operations were attempting to infiltrate the club. Groups of homeless men showed up with the words "free drink" hastily scribbled in Czech across the backs of beer coasters from nearby *pivovars*. Shirting turned them away, but they kept returning with new, more brazen attempts. Several came on their knees, claiming dwarfdom. One offered to maim himself by cutting off his finger, but balked when Shirting called his bluff. "There, you see," the man said, showing the back of his hand, hiding his thumb behind his palm. Eventually Hard Road had to be called back, which immediately struck fear into the hearts of the old tipplers, many of whom had never seen a flesh-and-blood African before in their lives. "Slave trader!" they called out to Shirting, before departing for their regular pivovars, filled with stories of adventure and personal prowess with which to ply the barman.

"Those men are all soft travelers, I am a hard traveler and an Englishman," Hard Road informed him once again. Hard Road collected the cover charge and it was Shirting's task to stamp hands. Hundreds of palms seemed to pass before his eyes: Who were these people, and where did they come from? He heard accents that spoke English in any number of variations. It occurred to him, for the first time, that he had truly been living in his own bubble, that the city was pulsing with currents of life and commerce that he was entirely excluded from. Upon that realization Shirting disappeared one hand into his jacket pocket to keep the mounting disquiet at bay. Nothing: he had left Duke in Bunny's office to feed on bar olives. His next impulse was to stop each person and ask them where they were from and exactly what they were doing in this fine city of Newfangle. That they had all traveled here— somehow it represented a community, and Shirting wanted to be sure he was a visible and involved member.

"Tourists, my little *bon jourists*. Come one and all. Backpackers and backsliders. Tell me your tales of travel and bold border crossings," Shirting called out to the crowd.

Hard Road put a quick stop to that excursion; the line was backing up down the block. And as time passed Shirting ceased giving even the most cursory glance to the revelers in favor of dispatching each person quickly into the club. The stamp was a winking Cheshire cat that Shirting mistook for a lion. For amusement he accompanied each impression of the palm with a pacified roar. Eventually, a palm roared back.

"Don't you remember me?"

Shirting looked over the person outfitted like an old babushka, complete with plastic grocery bag.

"Ah yes," said Shirting. It was that expat artist who kept popping up.

"I'm in costume," she said.

"So be it."

"I'm the Universal Babushka. Ta-daa!"

"I see," responded Shirting.

"Well, maybe I'll catch you inside," she said.

"Perhaps," said Shirting. Though he stayed at the door he allowed his animated self to escort Lila into the club, spin her around the room, then join in a line dance along with the squadron of dwarves, the giant, and Shirting's own turtle.

〜〜〜

As the sand of night slipped away, the chaos at the Prop Room reached an unprecedented level. Gus would later joke that it was actually a party thrown by the city's census bureau to determine just how many foreigners were in their midst. Women danced atop the amplifiers, homoerotic flirtations were cashed out in the men's room. The Ukrainian bathroom attendants were pulling down serious money. To them, and few else, Prague was the West, a symbol of prosperity. They could be recognized by the sweatsuits they wore, products of some distant land where it was still fashionable to decorate clothing with slogans and made-up logos in English. The boys took on nicknames of the misnomers they sported: one was Hop on Pop Club, another was Snow Flake University Athlete, another Anheiser Bulls Freedom Marshall, another Debt Well Water. No matter how many times Hard Road whisked them away, they would return, climbing back into the club through windows, sneaking in under overcoats, springing from the plumbing like sewer rats, as far as he could tell. Anything to ply their trade, to live.

Bunny kept a watchful eye out for the Yak. It was disturbing that he had yet to show. The Yak had been worried about the sideshow theme, dismissing it as overly conceptual. Then again, it was the Yak who had wanted, instead of Mexican food, to install a sausage stand, like the ones all across the city. "If people wanted Mexican food, why weren't there taco stands on every street corner?" he had reasoned. It was the start of a rift between them. The Yak refused to even sample the fare, which mostly consisted of mashed up pinto beans, pita from the Arab market, and Edam cheese. The Yak was convinced that the Czech *párek* were a national treasure and the real money was in exporting them worldwide. It was a nationalistic feud, one only aggravated by the Yak's suspicions about Shirting.

This was one of the reasons Bunny had surrounded himself with brutish sorts, expatriates who had lost teeth in Rugby matches or gotten stamps in the back pages of their passports signifying deportation from other countries. He did not know what falling out of the Yak's favor meant. Earlier that week he had been forced at gunpoint by a masked assailant to buy the very gun he was being held up with. Another bale of crowns for a German Mauser with a gamey trigger. Bunny and Hard Road had searched the building for the stickup man but to no avail. Bunny secretly thought the Yak was behind the incident, but felt unsure about confronting him—the Yak wasn't a good communicator. When he was pleased, he bought Bunny shots of bourbon until he was sick; when he wasn't, he got a strained look on his face and the garbage wouldn't be collected for a week. And Bunny had noticed, on the way in, that the dumpster was overflowing.

Shirting Ferrets One Out

It happened that Hard Road was called into the club by Bunny to try to dissuade the giant from abusing his physical advantage over a backpacker from Philadelphia. The tourist had trailed the large man into the bathroom in an attempt to snap an invasive but altogether unique photo. The American's screams could be heard echoing through the theater, seemingly keeping time with the DJ's groove.

This left the entire responsibility of the door to Shirting, a post he abandoned almost immediately. What caused Shirting to leave the entrance wide open to the stalwart, aged boozing insurgents, who charged the unguarded position without hesitation, was that he saw a tiny, frail figure exiting the club, hatbox that served as her purse slung over her shoulder—Magda Sminkova, whom he hadn't seen since she left him with the keys to his apartment. What sort of operations she had been carrying out in the Prop Room he did not know, but he felt that his duty to find out superseded all else.

He suspected she had not seen him as she left; she slipped past him with a dazed look in her eye and displayed a rather loopy gait as she walked down the street. Shirting followed behind her, noting the ditzy path she took; one moment she favored the right sidewalk, the next she mimicked a tightrope walker stepping foot over foot along the curb. Shirting considered it highly unprofessional of her to make herself such an easy target to follow; he found himself having to browse in front of store windows in order not to overtake her. Once he even bumped into her from behind. He had excused himself and in return been told not to mention it; he was sure his cover was blown but she didn't even turn around. After that Shirting backed off and let her walk several strides ahead, keeping his gaze trained on the round target of her hatbox.

Shirting followed the Sminkova youth onto a tram that departed from the Národní třída junction. Unfortunately for him, she had opted for the back door and had a clear view of the car, leaving Shirting to hide behind a hefty babushka, crouching in front of her glare like a submissive dog. As the tram rollicked and bounced up the street, the backward-riding Shirting began to feel motion sickness, prompting him to turn around and face forward. No sooner had he done so than he felt a tap on his shoulder. The babushka had changed costume and was now brandishing the red armband and official badge of a ticket controller, there to nab freeloaders, tourists, faredodgers like John Shirting.

"I don't speak Czech," he said by way of excuse.

"*Fahrschein*," she said loudly in German, as if for the benefit or entertainment of the other passengers.

"Look," Shirting said, "can't we just keep this between ourselves?" But his foreign tongue only attracted the attention of the passengers in his immediate vicinity, who were confirming their mutual disbelief in the existence of foreign entities who had learned neither Czech nor German. He was suddenly a monster that was being driven out of town by a torch-wielding mob. As they rallied, another babushka took it upon herself to wave a ticket in Shirting's face and explain the finer points of the public transportation system, loudly enunciating each syllable in Czech so that he might understand her; several of her comrades were abridging her instructions, punctuating her diatribe with recommendations of their own, delivered from their seats.

Luckily for Shirting, the crowd that gathered to partake in his humiliation had blocked him from the sight of Magda—who, it can be told, was dozing on her hat box, now used as a makeshift seat. After considerable folly, Shirting was dismissed by the stern controller with the payment of a small fine, though he was not released from the attentions of the second interceding babushka, who was demonstrating to him how to plug the ticket into the stamping contraption that clung to a hand pole and bit into the paper like a hungry bug. The chorus of passengers verified her technique and encouraged Shirting to give it a try himself. Tickets of proper stampage showered down upon him like so much confetti.

It was enough to drive Shirting from the tram. Such was his luck that he would not be wholly interrupted from his mission, as the Sminkova youth had disembarked at the same stop and could be seen wandering away from Shirting, heading for a highway underpass. Shirting sallied on after her.

In time she stopped in front of a bullet-pockmarked tenement building that stood alone between two vacant lots—so unlike the grand architecture of the city center. A shudder played scales down his spine. In such a place like this the secret sharer lurked, having taken up a squatter's residence in some dark, abandoned apartment—enjoying its own private gallows humor.

It took a keen eye to discern which bell she rang; it would be the same bell Shirting would ring, after some deliberation, only to be denied entrance after he was unable to supply the voice on the intercom with a password. Two Gypsy children who were kicking a doll's head back and forth between them stopped to watch Shirting as he contemplated his next move. He figured the apartment was a headquarters for moles such as Magda. The political forces she represented had indeed fallen, having to utilize such a seedy and inconvenient location. But he knew that it was in such places that these factions thrived undetected. No doubt they also sang in chorus with Mizen's jingoistic folksongs.

Shirting was surprised when Magda burst out through the building door, stopping short at the sight of him. At first she seemed not to be able to place him, then gave a gasp of recognition.

"Ah-ha!" Shirting shouted, causing her to jump again. "I am onto your game. You can just forget any plans you might have for toppling the reformative forces at work at the Prop Room." The girl regained her composure and tried to pass Shirting, but he stood his ground.

"I don't have your money," she finally said.

"Those funds have no doubt been put to wicked purposes that I can only imagine."

"Then you know. It is true that this is a small city," she said, strapping her hat box across her back as if to guard it.

"You can deceive your mother and your sainted grandmother, who brings me daily joy with her visits, but you cannot fool me," he said.

"How is my grandmother? Does she have new teeth yet? We come from a family of orthodontists and we can't even afford new teeth for her," Magda said, as though accusing Shirting, as though he were the family breadwinner.

"That you have sold them out for your life of subversion and betrayal and still maintain that you care outrages my sense of fairness and family," said Shirting. Indeed, he did feel quite faint, and his palms were sweating profusely.

The doll's head suddenly appeared between them, rolling so that its one intact eye gazed up at him. Shirting couldn't be sure if the children were inviting them to join their game or if it had simply gone off track. He kicked the head back at one of them.

"You people are crazy," Magda said, "you Americans. You come to here and all you can say is how beautiful the city is but nobody ever stops to look at the people. You live here but you don't really live here, you are still living in your own crazy places, you have just brought some things and tried to make again your own country here."

This moment of candor shocked Shirting. He was unsure how to proceed in the face of such honesty and spleen. Her tactic was good, to be sure. He was suddenly unsure that they were equally matched.

"Well, what did you expect?" he said.

"We expected a superhero from America. A cowboy from the West. But the only cowboy we see is on cigarette ads. We are the refugees camping in your Marlboro country. You are cigarette-smoke ghosts."

"Your claim is legitimate," Shirting ceded; there were so many Marlboro ads that the city sometimes seemed to consist of open plains and rutty canyons instead of medieval architecture. "But I would only ask you to look for the beauty in such messages. It is only propaganda, which you should be immune to at this point, having trained so well in its dissemination. Perhaps it's the price you pay if you want to enter the free market."

"What you call free is like so much occupation from our end, and you are only the blind soldier," Magda said. She spat on the ground at Shirting's feet. She had twenty deka-grams of Afghan heroin in her box, a Faith No More tape in her Walkman, and the tram was just arriving. She left Shirting there to chew on his defeat, which did not last long. After a moment of bewilderment, Shirting's buoyant mood returned. He took out a notepad and wrote the building's address down. It would all be part of the case against her (which he intended to present to the Sminkovas, hoping they would favor him over her, perhaps making him an honorary family member).

∼∼∼∼

By the time Shirting returned to his post at the door, the event had turned into a free-for-all. The insurgent cabal of old men that had gate-crashed were busy appropriating abandoned or unminded drinks. There were few chairs so they stood around in circles, boozily mimicking groups of American women who danced around their purses. Shirting doffed his hat to the old tipplers, then decided immediately that he needed to do a sweep for counteragents. A single one could bring these noble plans to their knees. He pressed his way into the theater, unsure exactly what the infiltrat-ing entities looked like, only quite sure they existed. How did a Communist appear? Certainly his lineaments were more severe than the rest of us. Certainly there was no aura of pleasure or decadence about them. But were they visibly depraved? If only his guidebook had been a bit more spe-cific. He had seen Lenin iconography, so all facial hair was suspicious. Shirting was quick to check the bathroom, as it seemed like the most obvious place for them to congregate. He broke up a tryst in a toilet stall, incurring fury from a Ukrainian teen, who with a threatening pass of his switchblade persuaded Shirting to forestall any further investigation. "Continue with your free market experimentation," decreed John Shirting, then moved on.

Shirting ran into Bunny making his way to the dance floor. "Shirt-Man," Bunny said, "where you been?"

"I can't explain right now," he responded.

"Hey, have you seen Honza?"

"Who?"

"Honza. The Yak."

"No, but I'm on the lookout for his sort."

"If you find him let me know."

"Oh, I shall deliver that communiqué without delay."

The balcony was the realm of the proletariat, so Shirting mounted the steps with an evangelical fervor. Shadowy figures moved about that dark space, Shirting barely able to see in front of himself. He called into the darkness: "Travelers and fellow travelers, I bid you to depart from the premises. This territory is sovereign."

"Hear how he rages," came a voice.

"How he raves," responded the other.

"The beast has returned, I put it to you. Do we need further proof?"

"Proof is in the putting." The Golem hunters unabashedly gazed at Shirting as they consulted a deck of Tarot cards.

"Draw one," the man said, holding out the deck to Shirting.

"What's your angle?" said Shirting.

The man nodded to him, wordlessly indicating he should take the card. Shirting did so.

"Whelp of Retribution," his partner said. Shirting laid it on the table. It was an ornately illustrated card that featured a downtrodden character who was also pulling a card from a deck, upon which was that same such Whelp. The motif continued *ad infinitum*.

"Indeed," said the man. He reshuffled the cards and Shirting chose again. The same card emerged. And a third time. With each instance the woman pronounced the result with increasing urgency, as though winning numbers in a lottery. The man remained cool.

"Draw again," he said.

Shirting suddenly felt a stab of anxiety. He thought of Duke. He had left him in Bunny's office, and without the animal there in his pocket, his mania was reaching an uncontrollable level. He would need to find his sidekick before expelling any more Communists.

"I am sorry, I have no more time for parlor games." With a doff of his imaginary hat, Shirting bid them good-bye.

He took one final look over the balcony's railing out onto the dance floor, admiring the sashaying light the disco ball sent off like fairy fire. He paused to observe the gang of dwarves fall upon a passed-out backpacker behind one of the amps; it was Zdeněk who produced a pocket knife and cut through the boy's clothing like a Caspian fisherman looking for caviar in the belly of a sturgeon, the search yielding the boy's passport (worth far more than his currency on the black market). And so they went down the line, each one scavenging something useful off the body, picking it over like so much carrion, until the only one left was the one dubbed Good Wank, whose share would amount to a sweaty bandanna and a tin of Tiger Balm. Shirting spotted Girish, ingratiating himself into a group of Czech teens; Lila dancing on an amplifier; Mizen, looking sober and handing out pamphlets. Then quite suddenly he caught sight of the Yak. There, in the center of the dance floor, still wearing his overcoat. The man moved stiffly toward the door. Shirting decided to give chase. But by the time he descended the balcony stairs, he had lost sight of him. Shirting scouted the room, then pressed toward the café. There he again caught sight of the Yak, making a quick exit from the premises. Shirting followed him out the door, tailing him to his Mercedes sedan. The Yak got in, started the engine, then pulled out onto the cobblestone street, shooting slush back at Shirting as he peeled away.

~~~~~

It happened without warning. As he walked back toward the Prop Room Shirting could see something had gone terribly amiss inside. The revelers spilled from the entrance covering their faces with their shirts like bandits. The bandits were hacking and blinded. People stumbled from the building, some thrown over the shoulders of others. As he approached the entrance he could smell a thin, noxious odor: the smell of the gas, which reminded Shirting of the fetid water from a vase of flowers whose bloom were long gone. Unmistakably insidious. He needed to find Bunny—he pushed against the current of people, but was repelled by the rushing crowd and by the fumes, which burned his eyes. Allowing the crowd to push him back outside, he waited for Bunny amid the nauseated revelers. Before long an ambulance arrived, shortly followed by several more. Then came a fire truck and, finally, the police. The officers tried to corral the sick and assaulted. They seemed unsure whether to beat or comfort the crowd, though many could not resist the temptation to poke at the debilitated foreigners with the blunt end of their truncheons. Those from the crowd who were well enough snuck away. It was, after all, early; they had expected as much from this part of the world and would not leave disappointed. Some were already sitting on the curb detailing the attack in postcards home. Others tried to bear witness, though most could not speak with the native police. One told of the briefcase that had been placed near the stage and began to emit tear gas.

Finally Shirting saw Bunny tumble from the entrance-way, trailing currency from a garbage bag.

"Sabotage," intoned Shirting, once they found each other.

"Jesus," Bunny said, hacking.

"Trust nobody," advised Shirting, "they're craftier than you can imagine." Seeing Bunny's salvaged booty suddenly reminded Shirting of his own solitary possession. "Did you get Duke?"

"What?"

"Duke! My turtle."

"Sorry John. I grabbed what I could. Even my Franken-stein reel's back in there. Look, maybe you should make yourself scarce. I'll meet you at the Golden Udder later," he said.

"Why can't I stay here?" asked Shirting.

"Do you have a work permit? Residence permit? Anything?" Bunny said. Shirting thought of the sole, lonely stamp on his passport from the airport. "If not, then you don't work here. I don't even work here, okay? Now get lost."

Shirting: abandoned for all his good work. He had made a heroic effort to defend the club from insurgents but had been overpowered, then not even commended for his efforts. It was just like Capo's, he mused on the melancholy path to the Udder, fired when the going got tough. He would wait two hours at the bar, nursing his Big Goat, but Bunny would not show up, only the group of old men, who would huddle together telling each other stories of their own personal prowess during the crisis. (The next day, Shirting would return to the Prop Room only to find it chained shut, a police barricade across the door. In time, he would stop checking—for the club would never open again.)

He decided to walk home to clear his head.

On the Charles Bridge he ran the gauntlet between the soot-black statues. Who wouldn't be paranoid going through that aisle, deserted late at night, the giant saints looking down from their poised places along the stone railing. Shirting felt their judgment; they spoke to him like black-faced cartoon characters pimping their individual canon. He picked up his stride, the ominous fog that haunted the streets during winter, a result of coal heating, chasing him all the way; and the castle looming before him like some anti-Oz. He kept his pace up over Nerudova. It was Friday night and Shirting saw nothing but closed storefronts. But for the occasional *pivovar*, the streets were deserted, as if the gas attack had cleared the entire city. It was all he could do to just get back to the comforts of the Sminkova household. The dogs barked at him on his way up the stairs, but he did not mind; it was a welcome relief to the silence.

BOHEMIAN RHAPSODY

FRIEND KITTY

THE CONDENSATION THAT FORMED ON THE TRAM WINDOWS
had a sooty consistency: the glass never really came clean
when Shirting wiped it with a rag, leaving the view smudged,
impressionistic. That wasn't the worst of their problems—
the whole operation was at risk of degenerating. The girl
(Darina Nováková from Český ráj, Darina Nováková on a
lark) sat shivering in her seat, wrapped in a fur coat made
from some tattered and unrecognizable pelt. Girish Patel,
affecting a pince-nez, wearing a Hefner-style smoking jacket,
sat galled in a beach chair positioned in the center of the aisle.
Abe took notes, trying to act professional, already blushing.
The tram made all the regular stops; they had only been able
to license out the back portion, so passengers were corralled
behind a length of twine that Abe had tied between hand-
rails. Patel hollered at the girl in English, then commanded
Shirting to find her release form. Shirting, palms sweating
and unable to concentrate, shuffled through his attaché case.
It was woefully empty. Gone were the company guidelines
and protocols; he had even left his travel journal at home—it
had not been opened in months. Inside the *Friend Kitty* folder
he found the form "Prague Spring Chicken" scrawled across

the top of a page in magic marker. He handed it to Patel, who immediately thrust it toward Abe.

"Did she check 'full frontal' on the form?" he yelled.

"Oral, aural penetration, bodily fluids, *et cetera, et cetera.* Multiples but no Russians or Gypsies," replied Abe.

"But does it say 'full frontal.' Did she check-off 'full frontal'?" screamed Patel.

"There is no box for 'frontal.' It's inherent in the contract, one would think."

"One would think?"

"'Animals of mammalian variety,' checked. 'Root vegetables,' checked. 'Bulbs, assorted fruit.'"

"Disloyalty, disloyal . . ."

"'Ping-pong balls,' checked. 'Magician's wand,' 'Star Wars action figures' minus Chewbacca, 'frozen fish fingers.'"

"Were you planning a photo shoot or a children's birthday party, might I ask?" snapped Patel.

"Mizen helped," countered Abe, "It sounded reasonable at the time."

"Mizen, great. I'm glad you consulted level minds on this. Do you know how much this photographer is costing? Five hundred crown an hour."

"That's probably a fifth of what you'd pay in the States," said Abe. "It's a good deal, really . . . if you think about it in dollars?"

"Not if she won't take her clothes off, you wankers."

"Language, Patel. Really, that's inappropriate," said Abe. "I'll abridge you later, okay?"

"Wank is inappropriate? Wank happens to be our frigging field derrick. Spooge, our petroleum. I demand maximum strokability from every picture. Our readers deserve no less. Remember, we're on the cutting edge here. Go work for *Playboy* if you want appropriate."

"The clothed subject, let us arrive at and dominate that evolved niche," said Abe. "I call it Corrective Porn."

"You traitor. They've gotten to you, haven't they?"

The tram yawed down the Old Town side along the river, pitching from side to side in seafaring undulations. Patel had hoped to get most of the lead-in shots off so he could shoot the climax with the National Theater in the background, but the girl just wasn't cooperating. She pouted in her seat, refusing to give in to Patel's outrage. It looked like they would have to ride to the end of the line then shoot on the return trip, which would involve repositioning all the lights to the other end of the car. Or they could just ride out the return trip and begin the cycle again, if sunlight allowed. They had already been checked by a controller and the whole entourage had been fined for riding without tickets. Patel had tried to explain that he had paid a hefty sum to the city for the rights to the location, but the controller remained stalwart and was eventually paid off.

Shirting, rubbing his hands together for warmth, hung back. The surreality of the scene—the odd juxtaposition of the daily commuters and the photo shoot—was not the first he had witnessed since going to work for Patel at *Friend Kitty*. (They had invaded centuries-old palaces, debauched monuments, shot gleeful humping where students had once been massacred in sundry uprisings). "We don't live in Russia, yet we satisfy the Russian fetish," Patel had stated. "Weaned on all that smoldering Cold War threat, and now we finally get to peek up Mother Russia's skirt. It gets me excited just thinking about it. Remember, it's not just our job to titillate, but to *demoralize*. Our patriotic duty, if you will." But now, the gothic cityscape, each tram window view a picture postcard, seemed nothing but mundane to Shirting. Sex, it was the last thing to occur to him. In truth, his employment in that position had coincided with a black mood that seemed to have been engendered by the dark and bitter winter the city was enduring. Shirting, made somber by the drifts of coal-laden snow, the season's own black bile secreted through the industrial smog that turned a white shirt gray by nightfall. Shirting was a sooty soldier throughout the monastically short days. He muscled through them, pressing against the seizures of time, the very sludge of minutes that stiffened him at the joints. If only Shirting had no use for money, if he were able to renounce the need for sustenance, or even companionship, for that matter, he would surely spend the days in bed hibernating, only to emerge in the deepest of night when the chill snaps at the skin like a wetted towel corner. The theater of the winter night in Prague, a city that to him seemed faintly enchanted in the darkness—squalid, austere, and cheap in the day. As long as he had been there, half a year now, he made no claim at understanding the city, though he did develop a visceral sympathy for it—there was an organic pulse that seemed to echo his own: Nobody belonged here. Even the Czechs were intrusive mice in its ornate dollhouse. That was the thing.

The happiness he had felt at the Prop Room was gone, that was for sure. Happiness, a foreign feeling anyway, cheap as a cellophane wrapper or Styrofoam box—it was a stranger to Shirting, and he didn't really feel comfortable with it. Nothing but an overplayed pop tune, dumb in its insistence that you like it. What would the happiness personified look like sitting across from his secret self, all adorned with bangles and colored bunting, effortlessly winning at cards? But now that it had been usurped, he feared its replacement. The junta of mood. An uprising of shadowed figures, sneaking about, carrying ladders between them, throwing up climbing ropes, securing rooftops. The execution of synapses. A rekindling of sorts. The entire message encoded within his grandfather's pills erased from history, torn from the books. Censured by great black pens. Shirting, unlike so many other people, it seemed to him, was forced to start all over again, with nothing but his own self—and the flawed architecture of his personality—to depend upon.

"Abe goddamnit," Patel yelled. "Can't you talk to this girl?"

"I've tried."

"Didn't you take eight weeks of Czech lessons? Didn't *Friend Kitty* pay for you to enrich yourself linguistically?"

"Actually, I thought it was very forward thinking of me to opt out of the Czech lessons in favor of Esperanto."

"Esperanto?"

"*Jes.* Language without borders. Much more globally pertinent."

Patel, taking matters into his own sweaty mitts, called into the ring of gaping commuters for an English speaker—*Is there a doctor in the house*—and was rewarded with a babushka who had a grandson living in Canada. The twine was unstrung for the old woman by Abe, who escorted her over to Darina. They conferred together for a few minutes before the old woman announced to the crew that her agent had told her she was going to be in a yogurt ad. The release had been erroneously translated. This threw Patel into a sulk, until, after further conference, it was determined that the girl was agreeable, if the shoot included yogurt, plus a supplementary fee that would be negotiated by the babushka, who knew the value of a dollar. A collection was taken up among the staff, but the babushka proved to be an able representative, making further demands for mineral water, champagne, and an éclair for herself.

"Shirting," said Patel, "here's the *Friend Kitty* bank card. If you hurry, you can get to the square where there's a cash station, and get back by the time the tram has returned." Patel wrote the code down on Shirting's wrist and dispatched him, reminding him to pick up the yogurt and other foodstuffs on the way.

Shirting disembarked from the tram and started at a brisk clip for one of the few working cash stations in the city. As he walked he felt the predatory gaze of the gargoyles that hung from cornices. He brushed past the citizenry, zombified by the cold. Old men in their placards were drunk at noon, standing in the middle of the street, daring the traffic to run them down. Now that Shirting saw life without the protective lenses of the pill, he realized what a melancholic's Wonkaland the city really was. And he was trapped there, stuck in the sheer iciness, feeling that if he stayed much longer he too would frost over, crystallize into a petrified sculpture. He picked up his pace to keep warm and arrived at the cash station to find himself at the back of a long and conspicuous line comprised of tourists and the few Czechs with enough clout to have a foreign account. He braced himself against the air that froze his nostrils closed when he sniffled. In time he found himself at the front of the line and was forced to unglove his hands to insert the card into the slot. He drew back his sleeve and checked the code, then punched it into the machine. Two thousand crowns shot out, which he stuffed into his pocket.

"This is the wrong machine for you," said a voice from behind. He turned to see a man with a ruddy and flushed face, who wore a loden cape and fur hat. He strained to remember where they had met before. The man stepped up to the station, pulled his own sleeve back to reveal a number tattooed on his arm. He punched in the code that he read from his skin, and the machine spat money out.

"The code you have been given is the key to immortality, to Timbuktu, to Xanadu, but the machine you seek is strictly extraterrestrial. There is a city above this one, invisible yet material, where finer variations of our selves dwell. The Celestial Motherland. Only there are these codes truly valid." Shirting then recognized him as the skinhead he had been accosted by the previous summer. Only now he had a prosperous appearance to him, and carried a sleek black briefcase. Shirting reflexively jumped back, but there was no pig in sight.

"I desire none of your high jinks, now I must be going," responded a perplexed Shirting.

"All that has been robbed will be returned with divine interest. Compounded by the heavenly accountant. On another plane, these codes, so brutally etched into our skin, will serve as invitations to the highest empyrean, where we will suckle upon godly colas and nourish ourselves with supreme snack mix," said the skin. "In the meantime, cold cash does suffice. A wistful of dollars." He held the bouquet of cash up to the sky like a sacrifice, then quickly slipped it into his breast pocket.

"None of what you are talking about is real," said Shirting.

"Real? Any so-called knowledge about reality is but a secret, private knowledge, and is a kind of death." Before Shirting could formulate a response, the skin retreated into the crowd.

Shirting contemplated. *A wistful of dollars.* He found it disconcerting; even though the man had spoken pure nonsense, he felt something private had been exposed about himself. *A fistful of dolorous.*

He began to walk slowly toward the tram stop. He reached the rampart and walked up the Old Town side of the river. Perhaps a scenic view would enhance his mood. It was Europe, was it not? Let some Old World charm work its magic. But the frequency with which Shirting passed lovers gazing dumb-faced into each other's eyes only soured him more, and he had to dodge tourist snapshots like sniper fire. (Could evidence of Shirting's existence, in a Muybridge photo sequence, be produced from his role as an extra in snapshots from Korea, Kansas City, and Kuwait? It could; there he is in a Polaroid taken by a backpacker from New Orleans, frozen in a pose that suggests an animal scurrying to get out of the way of oncoming traffic.)

In time he found himself leaning against the embankment railing facing the meditating Ronald McDonald afloat across the river. Its restorative powers worked on Shirting, lent him a bit of centeredness that he was missing. Shirting, in his mind, also sat in a lotus position, mirroring the meditating clown, communing with him. It calmed him, and he stayed that way for untold minutes. But then he noticed the float begin to mutate. Before his eyes Ronald's head was shrinking.

"Jiminy!" cried Shirting as the head began to visibly deflate, an indenture creasing its brow as though the clown had been brained with a divine crow bar. Then the neck buckled, leaving the head bent grotesquely over on its shoulder.

"Assassinated," mumbled the dumbfounded boy. He watched as the body collapsed in on itself, eventually doubling over into the muddy waters of the Vltava. A mocking cheer went up from the crowd who had gathered to watch. The clown's demise clearly entertained the masses. Nobody felt what Shirting felt, that an icon of progress and free-market values had been desecrated. If they had gotten to Ronald, how long would it take before he too was singled out?

"Wanton violence will get you nowhere!" he shouted. "Remember, the eyes of the world are upon you. The eyes of the world!" Silence followed his proclamation. "Stop looking at me," he added, when he realized the eyes were in fact on *him.*

"Shirting, get over here!" He turned to see Abe hanging from the tram window; it had just stopped in front of the National Museum. Shirting started to run for it, but ceased when he realized it was hopeless. The tram, lit-up against the dusk like a cheese display case, closed its doors and continued on its path up the river, carrying away Darina and the fuming Patel. Shirting would have to wait to catch it on its next pass. He stood shivering at the stop, but the feeling of apprehension he was experiencing only grew. He had become an easy target, a sitting duck. The germ of the system had become a cog in the wheel, serving immoral, possibly corrupt ends. The situation demanded recklessness. Drastic measures needed to be taken to release him from the forces with which he had aligned himself and to keep his dark mood at bay. Within that moment he decided to return to the cash station, wait in line, and continue to draw cash until he had milked the machine dry. A discretionary slush fund was needed. Shirting left his vigil and retraced his path back to the square, all the time feeling as though he was being pursued, as though each citizen's gaze were only part of a greater gaze—perhaps that of the city itself— that was compiling evidence against him. After waiting in line again, he was able to get almost five hundred dollars from the account, the day's maximum withdrawal. He took a metro from the square to the main train station, where he bought a ticket to a soon departing train. He needed to lay low for a while, and where better to do it than in a country whose name approximated appetite itself? Shirting: Hungary-bound.

THE DESIGNATED RIDER

THAT HE HAD NO LUGGAGE, NO CHANGE OF CLOTHING, NO PLAN—
that he had just embezzled—did not dampen Shirting's
enthusiasm for the sudden retreat. He turned all responsibility over to the train, which rocked him gently, agitated him
in a lapidary fashion, smoothing away the rough edges. He
sat alone in a compartment, head resting against the window so he could experience the rush of scenery unframed.
As the train came to its first stop in Kolín, a southern suburb
of Prague, he watched the commuters piling into the train
through his compartment door. The car was obviously full,
yet people paused in front of his compartment, inspected
its solo occupant through the glass door, and moved on. It
was Shirting's first clue as to how disheveled he must look.
Indeed, over the past season his suit had gained the atten
tion of a colony of moths that lived in his wardrobe. They
had nibbled at the woolen lapels and exacted quarter-sized
holes from the elbows. The white waffling of his long under-
wear showed through gaping apertures on his knees, and his
shoes had become a mockery of scuffage and wear. He felt
his chin: tender spirals of hair grew there, a scrim of a beard.
When had he stopped shaving completely? He could not say.

The conductor—a young woman who carried with her a cracker, tapping away the crumbs with the tip of her index finger the way one would tap the ashes from a cigarette— collected his ticket then left him to again rest his head against the window. If only train riding were a compensated vocation. In this modest position John Shirting was quite sure he would excel. A designated rider in every cabin, to ensure the train was properly appreciated, and not treated as some mere beast of burden. As the suburban tenements, huge gray ships on treeless sites, industrial parks, and abandoned factories gave way to an almost immediate countryside, the thin forests and widening plains began to smear and dissolve. Concrete bunkerlike houses and muddy shacks. His eyes fluttered, then closed. Perhaps there was something to what the pig-loving skin had said: a city above, in mirrored inversion, where we move without the brute feelings of loneliness and melancholy; where we shed our burdensome somatics in favor of a blazing, incandescent spirit. Ah, to gain a visa to such a place—that was the thing.

The rush of the train propelled him into a half-dream state. There he was, Sunday in his grandfather's apartment, the morning paper eviscerated across the breakfast table. Shirting pressing a flesh-colored ball of Silly Putty onto the Sunday funnies. A fresco of Snoopy peeled back, then pulled into an elongated Snoopy, as viewed through a funhouse mirror, then stretched wide, horribly mutated before being balled up again. The old man in his robe, greeting the morning with a shot of Old Crow.

"Who you playing with today?" he asked.

"*Peanuts,*" Shirting answered.

"Name the living person you are playing with today, then we need not talk about it any more."

"Howard Lundy," the boy replied, after a few moments of consideration. In truth he was planning to bike downtown to the Pin Hole to see a double feature of George Romero zombie movies. They were R-rated and—in at least one case—X-rated, but the Pin Hole never recognized such distinctions when it came to their younger clientele. In this way he had become a precocious fan of *Pink Flamingos, Harold and Maude,* and *Fritz the Cat.* Shirting would pay his dollar-fifty, sit in the balcony, and stay for as many showings as he could stomach. Never mind that he would come back nauseous with fear and unable to sleep—these were atonements he was willing to endure. Such excursions were kept secret from his grandfather, who refused to acknowledge the very existence of the film medium since his own enterprise had been hijacked. Howard Lundy was the name of the high schooler who worked the box office on weekends, so it was only a partial lie. The fallacy also served another purpose—his grandfather, furious that Shirting had nobody to call a friend—had once made him pick a classmate at random from the mimeographed class phone list to call for a play-date. Mercifully, Shirting was able to crib the name of a boy who had died, along with his parents, in a catamaran accident a few months earlier, and verify plans with a prerecorded message from the phone company.

A pair of voices penetrated into his dream state.

"You see he is resting."

"Resting, or planning?"

"He is . . . in repose."

"Quick, take a fiber sample."

"I can't reach."

"Put the slivovitz down, for heaven's sake."

"Quiet now."

Shirting shook himself awake, or he thought he did, but instead of being on the train he was sitting in the front row of the Pin Hole—long closed since the phenomena of the multiplex took over—watching *Dawn of the Dead*, the color sequel to the black and white classic *Night of the Living Dead* that Shirting had sat through so many times before. A pivotal scene was transpiring: it was well into the movie and the heroes were trapped in a shopping mall surrounded by the undead who, in between sating their shopping urges, hunted the live humans for food. Shirting settled back to watch the satisfying images of human dismemberment and cannibalism. It took only a few moments before he realized that the film was not the *Dawn of the Dead* he had grown up loving; though the scenery and story appeared the same, the identities of the characters were altered. In the partially decomposed zombies' faces he recognized Patel and Abe, Magda and Mizen. These were less menacing zombies, more like extras in Michael Jackson's *Thriller* video, yet somehow more disturbing in their familiarity. Shirting checked himself, and had a vague notion that he was lucidly dreaming. The voices came again.

"You see him struggle. Don't doubt that over time the beast has acquired self-consciousness."

"Do you think it is possible?"

"Synergy over alchemy. All is possible."

Shirting turned around in his seat to search for those familiar voices, but the aisles behind him were empty, except for a pair of teenagers necking in the shadowed back rows. He returned his attention to the flickering images of the film. Shirting watched in agitated excitement as the hero, a blonde, nameless actor, wandered through the aisles of a clothing store, ignorant of the security-guard-turned-zombie that was stalking him. Just as the actor was pausing in front of a rack of shirts (even in this apocalyptic landscape he could not ignore his shopping impulses—a sin demanding penance) the more proletariat zombie jumped him from behind, its skin green and decaying and its vacant eyes wide with hunger as it bit into the man. Shirting watched in benumbed horror on realizing that the zombie featured his own likeness. It was his secret self, let loose across celluloid media. Vengeful, furious, in its star turn.

"Maybe one more slivovitz."

"The bottle is empty, dear."

"Come, then. We have nothing but time."

Shirting woke with a start. The dream was so vivid that it took him a few disoriented moments to realize where he was. Locomotion reminded and calmed him. He looked out the window. The sun was falling behind the overcast sky, the bleak color of fogged photographic paper. But Shirting was not alone in the cabin anymore: across from him sat a portly Czech man dressed in workers' blue overalls who was snacking on a párek sausage, sweaty with grease, and drinking from a bottle of pilsner. The man stared at Shirting, as if daring him to find distaste in his noisy supping. Shirting, in a cold sweat, still shaken from his dream, looked away. After such a dream the smell of the meat was so overbearing that it drove Shirting from the compartment. He stood in the train's smoky corridors, looking out at the barren, frozen farmland. The conductor came back down the hall, stopped in front of Shirting, and spoke to him in Czech. There was an urgency in her voice. Shirting nodded at her, somehow afraid to admit to this civil servant that he was a foreigner. Deep cover and deception was his mode. She continued her speech, took another cracker from the package, nibbled a bit off the end, then continued on down the corridor.

It wasn't long before the train came to a halt at Štúrovo, the final stop before crossing into Hungary. What would it be like to break free from this country? To part these clouds, burst from this dour sack of space and blaze southward, glorified and triumphant, if only for a while? What would that be *like*? He watched the grumbling passengers depart from the cabin, so many that the train appeared to be emptying out. Shirting stood in the darkened corridor waiting for that surge forward that heralded the final push to Budapest, each moment pregnant with anticipation. But the train didn't move, and indeed appeared deserted when he walked up and down the corridor peeking into the individual compartments, the smell of the departed passengers and their meals all that remained. Shirting grabbed his bag and took an exploratory step down from the coach. A man who appeared to be waiting in the shadows of the station quickly approached him. He spoke in a hurried Slovak, then recouched his question when it was clear Shirting was a foreigner.

"English, yes? Budapest. Ride. Taxi."

"Train, I take train," said Shirting, appropriating the man's broken English.

"No. Not train. No train Hungary."

"No?"

"No workers Hungary. No workers. No train."

"What sort of sabotage is this?" Shirting demanded.

"No train. Workers gone."

The forces conspiring against him were more organized than he had suspected. He had fallen for their ploy. But they would not lay their hand on him so easily. No, not without a fight. Shirting turned and fled from the man. Surely the border was crossable on foot. He rushed off into the night, into the desolation of countryside, rushing as if pursued, though at the hind of his scampering body the only thing to follow John Shirting was his attaché case.

ŠTÚROVO

By the time he arrived in town, which turned out to be several kilometers from the station, he was half-frozen, panting a misty breath that dusted his beard with frost. It was a small town with hunched, unadorned buildings. He walked briskly through it toward the Danube. But where he had expected to find a bridge, there was only a partial extension, a half smile in the moonlight, the other half disappeared, the road leading to nothing but bitter winds that rushed over the river. At the river's edge a ferry rested bobbing in the current—Shirting looked at the timetable and discovered that no more would cross that night. Again, the country had conspired to trap him, as though Prague had sent a hook out to catch him by the back of his collar and draw him back.

He turned wearily toward the town, and saw that there was an inn not far from where he stood. He would take the ferry in the morning, then perhaps he might find a bus to Budapest. Trudging up the gentle incline, for the first time something occurred to him as he gazed up at the mushroom- and melon-colored huts: he was in a foreign country. It had never seemed as such in Prague. But here he was, isolated and at a disadvantage. How utterly odd. No matter. He would take a single room and establish his own autonomous, sovereign borders. A little country of Shirting.

～～～

He slept well into the next morning. No dreams of zombies or golem trackers had invaded his rest, and he woke ready to tackle the remaining leg of his trip. He checked out of the inn, and descended the hill toward the ferry. He could see that there was already a large crowd of people amassed, waiting for their turn on the small boat. If it was true that the trains were no longer running, all the cross-border traffic would have to pass this way. Shirting joined the bottleneck. Old women with contraband stuffed into their sweaters, vegetable-filled bags, one carrying a live goose under her arm. The tiny ferry's haul, once the automobiles had taken their places, could receive only shavings from the crowd. Shirting waited until afternoon before he was able to hand his passport over to the guard at the boat's plank. The gruff man, younger than Shirting, scrutinized the document. Shirting smiled at him benignly—*you'll get no trouble from this humble wayfarer, sir*—hoping to speed the process along.

"American?" the guard asked, though his nationality was clearly emblazoned on the passport.

"*Ano,*" said Shirting, trotting out one of his few Czech words for the occasion.

"Over there you go," said the guard, pointing to a small patch of frosted turf on which sat a group of people, immediately recognizable to Shirting as American backpackers.

"No. *Prosim.* I have to cross. *Pozor.* I need to get out of here," he said, adding, "I'm not like those people." The guard handed the passport back unstamped.

"Over," he repeated. With no other choice, Shirting complied. He hesitantly stepped from the line and moved over to the group to sit on their periphery.

"Man," one was saying to another. "I bet this is how the Mexicans feel."

"Yeah," said his companion. "The Mexicans at *Disneyland.*"

"Yeah," concurred his friend. "Disneyland."

Shirting was suddenly embarrassed for himself. For not only was he a misfit among the Czechs, he also felt he was losing common ground with his fellow countrymen. At Capo's a comment like that would have simply gone unnoticed, lost in the patchwork of vapid chatter that the place seemed to provoke from people, but now he found it oddly disturbing. His hand went reflexively to his pocket, but found no turtle there. He bowed his head and sent a silent prayer out to the assaulted Duke. But there was something in his pocket: a piece of cardboard, perhaps his train ticket. Shirting withdrew it and found a playing card—no, it was more of the tarot variety—and on it he saw the same illustration he had encountered before, a character not unlike himself peering down into a similar card. *The Whelp of Retribution.* Shirting looked around, but that strange couple was nowhere to be seen. He replaced the card in his pocket, relieved to at least have something there to reach for in moments of anxiety. It should be pointed out that finding the card there in his pocket provoked one such anxious moment—he ran his finger over the worn surface to quell the feeling.

"Hey you."

Shirting checked behind himself: it was that same painter girl in Dickies overalls and an old Russian World War II overcoat. Shirting strained to remember her name.

"Oh," was all Shirting felt capable of contributing. A silence fell between them.

"Do you like the beret?" she said. "It's ironic. 'Cause I'm an artist."

"Yeah, sure. I mean, I don't really get irony, but like the hat."

"But you don't think it's funny?"

"No. I just said I liked it, didn't I?"

"You're not supposed to like it *literally*."

"Fine, I don't like it."

"You're not supposed to dislike it either. You're just supposed to think it's funny."

Shirting emitted a wheezing, appreciative laugh.

"Stop laughing at me," she said. "I really don't get you."

"This is crazy. All I want is to get across, so I can go to Hungary."

"I've been here since six this morning. They're segregating out all the foreigners except Hungarians and Czechs. They say we can go after the locals."

"But there will be trains coming from Prague all day. The line won't ever get any shorter."

"I guess they're not really worried about that," she said. During their exchange she had taken her beret from her head and slipped it into her bag. Her short-cropped hair gave her an undernourished, refugee look.

"Why are you going to Budapest?" she asked him.

"Sick," he replied.

"Really?" She sounded impressed.

"Need treatment only the Hungarians can provide. Hungarians know about these sorts of things, I'm told. Curative preparations of paprika. The doctors and various government entities wanted to keep me in Prague, to pioneer experimental procedures. They pulled all sorts of nasty tricks to get me to stay. I wouldn't be surprised if this was one of their ruses."

"No kidding," she said.

"Yeah. I probably shouldn't be talking about it."

"You look okay to me."

"It's more of an internal thing. Misaligned humors and whatnot."

"Tumors?"

"*Humors*. Like I said, it's complex."

"Contagious?"

"Highly."

"Oh. If it gets much worse I'd like to paint you." She withdrew a sketchbook from her bag and made a few exploratory passes with her pencil.

"Well, I guess I'll be going," said Shirting, getting to his feet.

"Wait. What about the crossing?"

"Oh, I've made other arrangements," he said. "There's a hospital boat up around the bend. I didn't take it before, because that's the first place those wily Czechs will look. But now I see I have no other option."

"Well hey, wait. Maybe I'll see you in Budapest. There are some salami factories I want to check out, but other than that, I'm free."

"I shall look for you at the monument to slaughtered martyrs," he said.

"Okay. Okay. The martyrs monument," she replied, writing it down in her notebook. "Wait, which war?"

"The revolution before the last one," he said.

Shirting doffed an imaginary hat and took his leave, ambling back up the hill toward town. He wasn't sure exactly where he was going, but he knew he could not bear to sit there and be ruthlessly caricaturized by that American girl. As he walked he knew he would have to modify his plan. Evasive tactics were called for. His employment at Capo's had taught him, if nothing else, to think on his feet. He walked the distance back to the station and found a commuter train to the hub town of Břeclav. From there he could easily make it to Vienna, a place more aligned to his political leanings. It was easily enough accomplished, a short ride on a caravanlike commuter train that left hourly—but he discovered that when he arrived in Břeclav, the train that would take him over the Austrian border would not be arriving until later that evening. Time on his hands. With nothing else to do, he left the station to explore the town.

This was his first attempt at tourism, so John Shirting planned to make the most of it. Unfortunately, the town square was easily seen in ten minutes, and after that there was little else but surrounding factories and residential lanes, which, in the biting wind, only made him long for shelter. During his brief excursion he happened across a small *pivovar*, the sign out front depicting in woodcut a painted red devil holding some sort of small animal on a pitchfork. The windows were fogged, but the door was open, so he entered, momentarily blinded until his eyes were able to adjust to the diminished light of the room. The place was empty but for a group of teenagers dressed in black heavy metal sweatshirts, drinking beer. The bartender, a gaunt man with wild, manic hair and a nutmeg-colored beard waxed into a point, looked Shirting over. He gave him a smile that was somehow solicitous and predatory at once. An AC/DC song played on a tape deck from behind the bar, but it wasn't the original version: a singer with a Slavic lilt screamed out the lyrics over a facsimile of the music, some Cold War version of "Highway to Hell." Shirting's first instinct was to retreat, but he felt he had already begun an action that demanded completion, so he took a table by the window and waited for the man to come around from the bar to take his order.

The bartender turned from his new customer and toward the sink. He washed all the glasses, drying each one with his rag, then turned again, surprised to find Shirting still there. He finally sauntered over to take his order.

"*Pivo*," said Shirting, then adding in English, "have you got anything to eat?" The man looked at him quizzically, then maddeningly replied in German.

"Just the beer, then. *Pivo*," said Shirting, too defeated to protest.

"Ahhh," man exclaimed. "Pardon." He held his hands up, imploring Shirting to have patience, then disappeared into a back room. Shirting, unsure what he was in for, looked over to the group of metalheads for guidance, but they seemed wholly uninterested in the foreigner. Over the radio he heard the sound of muffled shouting coming from the back room, which abruptly ceased as suddenly as it had begun. The bartender returned through the door with a wide grin on his face, then went to the bar to pull Shirting his beer from the tap. He lopped the foam off of the top with a ruler-sized instrument, refilled the glass to the top, then set it on the bar. From the back room emerged another person, who made quick, frightened steps toward the bar. She collected the beer from its place and delivered it to the waiting customer. She set the beer down in front of him, then said, "You speaking English?" Shirting looked up. His desideratum, dumbfounded, his pale protégée, forgotten Frogger.

THE FROG WAYFARER

1

THE HALF-GLOBE OF MONIKA'S BELLY PROTRUDED TOWARD HIM. In that swollen world, in that distension of fabric-covered flesh he became momentarily mesmerized, the image of a tiny pixilated frog appearing in space as though conjured by a crystal ball. Frog universes, exploding stars, miasmas of antimatter and ectoplasm existed in that space. An insurgent amphibian was being formed under the cover of his former student. To lead a hopping infantry, an army of frog revolutionaries. Shirting, immediately sympathetic with the infant, let out a brief croak, then became conscious of himself and quieted. If only he could trade places with that unborn child, suspended in that orb of maternal custody.

"You are speaking English," she repeated, breaking the spell. He met her gaze: She looked weathered and aged, her eyes flickering with sly recognition. He had found her, and she respected him for it.

"I am. Are you?" he said.

"I am," she affirmed. He felt a rush of pride for his former pupil.

"Will you sit?"

"I am not," she responded. Shirting looked over to the bartender, who was leering at them. Shirting at once discerned that he had walked into a complicated situation.

"Food?" she asked. "Please, food."

"Yes," he said.

She wrote something down on the chit of paper in front of him and started for the back room.

"Caviar Egg," the bartender yelled after her. She turned and said something in protest, but he raised his fist and repeated his order. After she disappeared the bartender looked over at Shirting, then made a pantomime gesture, shaping an imaginary belly. "*Velký*," he said, then followed with similar gesture describing the breasts. "*Malý*," he added, inviting Shirting to share a licentious joke with him. Shirting gave a curt smile, then turned his attentions to his beer. But the bartender would not leave him alone. In a moment he was towering over his table, smelling of garlic and alcohol. He pulled a chair back and invited himself to sit.

"*Malý*," he repeated, once again describing two breasts with his hands, then pinched his imaginary nipples, making a hissing sound. "*Mléko*," he said. He roared with laughter this time. "*Káva*," he wheezed. "*Mléko*." He paused, then looked very seriously, if not longingly into Shirting's eyes. "*Jsem* Devil. I am Devil," he said.

Shirting: stroking the card in his pocket as though trying to rub it through. If only he were still armed by the pill's protective shield. No matter: He recruited his animated self to manhandle the Devil. The battle was fought with roundhouse jujitsu kicks and searing laser vision. The Devil favored fireballs and a lightning-dispensing pitchfork. In the end, the Devil was knocked unconscious, miniature demons in red long johns dancing around his battered head. Shirting would go on to take possession of the establishment and rename it The Triumphant Frog, eking out a living behind the bar while Monika raised the child. Peasant blouses and goulash for life.

But this was not to be. When Monika delivered the food, a hard-boiled egg with the yolk removed, filled with frozen whip cream and speckled with red fish roe, the Devil grabbed her by the wrist and pulled her onto his lap. He restrained her and gave her a mock bite on the neck, which she struggled to evade half laughing, half shrieking. Shirting looked her over: she was far along in her pregnancy—she shouldn't have been working like she did. The Devil grinned wide-eyed at Shirting.

"*Anglicky*," he demanded.

"*Ne.* No. It is not so good," she pleaded.

"*Anglicky*," he repeated, then whispered into her ear.

"Caviar egg," she said to Shirting. "Please, good appetite."

Shirting looked at the lone egg on a bed of pickled cabbage. He held it to his mouth, then took a tentative bite, which sent the Devil into a fit of laughter. When he had laughed himself out, he dispatched Monika to the kitchen again, where she duly returned with a plate loaded with a pork cutlet, more caraway-spiced cabbage, and doughy boiled bread dumplings.

Though his appetite had left him, Shirting numbly dispatched with the food. The Devil had disappeared behind the bar again and was trying to impress him with his selection of Western hits. He produced an original Johnny Cash tape, following it up with another cover album, featuring Simon & Garfunkel songs with lounge music backing. One of the drunken teens made a loud protest, then found himself with his sweatshirt hood forcefully twisted around his neck, being ejected from the bar by the Devil. Another beer was then sent Shirting's way along with a shot of Becherovka.

Monika had seated herself across the room, around the corner from the bar where the Devil could not see her, but within full view of Shirting. She looked wearily at him one time only, then turned her attention to an emery board with which she began to manicure herself. He ate without relish. While slicing through a piece of gristle, he discovered on his plate, hidden beneath the slice of pork, a note, spotted and nearly translucent with grease. Shirting was able to discern the handwriting as Monika's, though the ink was smudged. He discretely extracted it from its place, folded it into a napkin, and put it into his pocket. The Devil, already getting bored of his foreign guest, began to drink alone behind the bar and mumble along to the lyrics. Shirting finished his drink and asked for his tab. The egg was surprisingly expensive, and the Devil had already tacked on a "cover charge" that Shirting paid without protest. He looked back at Monika as he turned to leave, but she had disappeared once again into the back room.

Shirting missed his train. He had quite purposefully allowed it to happen. He would be forced to take a room at the town's only hotel, a concrete tower on the main square, paid in cash from the *Friend Kitty* fund. As he wandered the deserted hallways in search of his room it occurred to him that he was probably the only guest, and the silence around him confirmed the suspicion. Once in his room, he took the note from his pocket, unfolded it onto the desk and tried again to understand its message. In time, after much extrapolation and speculation, he discerned that she had slipped him some sort of homework assignment. The hieroglyphs of congealed gunk were pored over by the traveler, the boy looking for a clue to their mutual destiny. But, in the end, it was not a love note at all. Did it represent some kind of unstated invitation—or, when all was said and done—was he simply supposed to correct her mistakes?

Shirting refolded the paper, took an envelope from the hotel stationery, and sealed the missive inside. He put the envelope into his attaché case, then turned in for the night.

2

THIS PARTICULAR NIGHT SOMETHING WAS EATING AT HIM. During those dark hours some vandal was leaving graffiti on the whitewashed walls of his mind. Black spray painted slogans scrawled in some inscrutable language. He awoke during the night, sat bolt upright in his bed. Shirting was sure he was not alone in the room, but when he flicked on the bedside lamp—nobody. He turned the light out again, lay back down, and was suddenly embraced by a pair of human arms that gripped him tight. Cold, cadaverous skin, pulling itself against his body. The being radiated sorrow, sorrow that passed into him in waves. Shirting moaned. *Suddenly sadness.* The black bile had caught up with him; as quickly as he had fled, it had pursued. Jumped by his secret sharer.

"Miss me?"

"Get away from me, you useless bastard."

"Sorry, is that the talking cure, or just the cure talking?"

"Can't you just leave me alone?"

"Don't be a pill."

"Cheap," said Shirting. "Cheap and futile."

"You need me, fucker," replied the apparition, clutching him tighter. Shirting wrestled, extricated himself, swatted around blindly for the lamp, then flicked its switch. All alone. Next to him a gray hazy contour like a shadow, or vapor, or something burned away. The matter disintegrated and fell into soot on the pillow. Shirting left the light on and slept no more that night.

~~~~

The following morning Shirting resolved to return to the Devil's for breakfast. He needed to see Monika once more. The weather had settled a bit, the air hardly stirred as he strode across town then down the quiet side-lane, only to find the establishment locked. He peered through the window; the room was empty. He rang the bell. No answer. Standing there, he pondered what to do next. Just then the light inside the Devil's flicked on. Shirting again peeked in the window and saw the Devil making his way slowly toward him. He wore a bathrobe and was carrying a green unlabeled bottle. The man opened the door to Shirting, looked at him as though he was a complete stranger, then began to gesticulate wildly. It was a madman that Shirting was confronting, an unintelligible cipher of the forces of chaos corralled behind the skin of a drunk bearded Czech. From the room there came a foul smell.

Shirting did his best to follow the pantomime. The Devil made the motions of a person in a state of defecation: He described a swollen belly, then pushed it flat, making a crude flatulent sound. It was then that Shirting realized it was indeed the act of birth the Devil was trying to communicate.

The Devil followed this by cradling a small baby in his arms, using the bottle as a stand in, rocking it in a touchingly gentle fashion and singing a muted lullaby. Then he let the bottle fall and shatter, yelled out a redundant crashing sound to accompany that of the shattering glass. He looked helplessly at Shirting, drew a line across his own throat, reached out and shook Shirting's hand, then slammed the door in his face.

Shirting stood momentarily dumbfounded in front of the door. Suddenly the wind bore down on him, buffeting his face until he wore an expression winced in discomfort, a chiaroscuro of morning sadness around his mouth. Then the message hit him: Monika had given birth last night, and something had gone wrong. He turned from the door and began back to the hotel, the realization that she was no longer alive becoming clear. The speculation, the mere notion, froze his circuitry solid. The homework assignment would be her final dispatch.

〜〜〜

Shirting arrived back at the hotel, packed his bag, then checked out. He had given up on his idea to travel to Vienna. He craved Prague now, was nostalgic for it. The city had cast out some sort of hook and was reeling him back in. He would not fight it. It represented grief to him, and it was grief he desired. But he would be forced to spend one more day in Břeclav, for the train did not depart until later that evening. He purchased his ticket and spent the day wandering the outskirts of town. There was no mourning on that walk, just cold, placid acceptance. Here, in the forest where he walked, there were trees bare of leaves, a dead landscape frozen into a state of suspended animation, with the sun trapped, well-contained behind the raw woolly blanket of cloud. It seemed enough, a natural projection of his internal panorama. If only his mere perception could be rendered art, if only appreciating such a droll scene were a pliable talent. He would be renowned, a connoisseur of chilly and scentless places, where the trimmings of time are devoured by whatever feral, exiled spirits reside there.

Eventually he came upon a deserted orchard. Pear trees, denuded of their fruit, dangled their branches into the wind as though peasants passing time fishing in a dead river. Shirting wandered amid their trunks, already thinking fondly of Prague. Nebulous Newfangle. The hoarfrost on the forest floor caused him to lose his footing more than once, so he walked with his eyes leveled at the ground to prevent further such ambushes. There, something caught his eye. Perfectly yellow, and spotted with brown freckles, a pear rested at his feet. He picked it up, it was real and tender as if he had taken it from a fruit-seller's crate. He looked up at the tree from which it had fallen and saw that it was filled with similar fruit, beautiful ripe fruit, ready to drop. A cluster of blackbirds called cheerfully to each other as they gorged on its flesh. Laughing to himself, for it was pure lunacy to come across such a spectacle, he picked several and stuffed them into his pockets, making lunch from one without delay. As he gnawed on the fruit, which was succulent to the core, with juice that ran warm as blood, John Shirting continued on his way, leaving that miraculous tree behind him.

He suddenly became unsure just how long he had spent wandering. The sun, blocked from sight, divulged no information. The light had a liquid, gray quality that seemed corrosive and but for the pears left everything drained of color, as if it were all scenery from an old movie filmed on silver nitrate. He started down the path by which he believed he had come, jumping over roots that surfaced then arched in mid-air and retreated back into the soil. Shirting picked up his pace, for he did not want to spend another night in the deserted, expensive hotel. He felt that if he stayed in Břeclav much longer he would be rejoined by various abandoned emotive lives of others, discarded, orphaned sadnesses that had nowhere else to go but search for accommodation in vessels such as his. That he would become a tenement for such needy spirits.

Up ahead he spotted movement. He was not alone after all, thank heavens. His state was such that another person could make all the difference. The shape appeared to be childlike, a little boy playing with his white-coated puppy. He strode steadily on toward the figure, but as Shirting approached he realized that it was not boy at all, but a young woman, and it was not a dog, but an albino piglet, which she led on a leash. Once he was almost upon her, viewing her from behind the cover of skeletal branches, she turned toward him: it was Monika. If she saw him, too, he could not tell. Her skin was ashen, her stomach flattened. She appeared younger than he remembered her from yesterday, and her hair sat flat against her head even in the coursing wind, as if she existing in a less turbulent place. She suddenly looked straight at him, smiled, and released the piglet from its leash. It came, darting quick as a cat, toward Shirting. He could see its red eyes glowing with zeal. Shirting turned and bolted. He tripped and tumbled through the undergrowth in the direction of the path. He could hear the patter of tiny hooves behind him and the frenzied squeal in pursuit. Shirting was no runner, but he carried his heft skillfully, and was soon striding down the hill behind the town, his attaché case bobbing behind him.

When he was finally within reach of habitation, he turned to see that he was indeed still being pursued, only not by the piglet. It was the small white dog he had originally seen. It came bounding up to him, licking at his hands and playing around his legs, gave an excited yelp, then turned and ran back in the direction from which it had come.

Shirting made haste across town and was able to jump onto his train just as it was pulling away.

THINGS THAT FLUTTER

1

GRANDMOTHER SMINKOVA HAD DRIFTED DOWN TO THE CELLAR.
It took the very last of her weight to do it, but there she was
amid the abandoned wine casks, rusted gardening tools, and
jars of stewed fruit, expanding and diminishing her own
form like a bellows, in a pantomime of breath. It was there
that she discovered the wayward child, the Infant of Prague
(the very one), who had fled his place and was taking refuge
in various subterranean hideouts. Grandmother Sminkova
found him drinking Lipton tea and chain-smoking Sparta
cigarettes. She begged him to return to his exalted seat at
Saint Janos Church—*think of the tourists*, after all. She would
accompany him there herself, carry him in her vegetable bag
like contraband. The infant merely took a drag off his smoldering cigarette and said, "Sorry Sister, I gotta grow."

The Infant was convinced that such a feat was possible,
what with the intervention of modern science and democracy.
He had been held back too long, restrained, kept from his true
calling, which might just involve a jazz quartet and the Black
Madonna, though she shouldn't hold him to that. "Too many

tears have been cried over me already. It's Chinese water torture, believe me on that count," he complained. Grandmother
Sminkova wanted to take him by the ear—give it a good twist—
then perhaps treat him to some cocoa, but she felt her energy
was already departing. "Don't worry Sister, they'll get over it:
I'm easily replaced. Auditions will be held. I happen to know
personally several impresarios, not to mention human traffick-
ers, who will take up the task. For now, I'm staying right here."

Grandmother Sminkova felt herself drifting. Skyward,
the least complicated direction. She left the Infant with her
shawl, which he wore toga style, snapping his fingers to
some bluesy rhythm that played inside his head. She floated
upward, rising, as though on a cola bubble—effervescent—
past the pot of cabbage (sad earthbound cabbage, boiling like
a sick person's laundry), then momentarily dissipating in the
steam, riding on the smell, intermingling with the particles,
collecting their nutrition, then reforming as she traveled up
into the lodger's room.

The poor American, were they all so bedraggled and
lost? There in bed, going on noon.

"Pathetic, isn't it?" The voice came from within the wardrobe. The door swayed open, and Grandmother Sminkova
beheld the strangest of sights: A man as old as her—though
not exactly a man—his human head poked out from the
awkward body of a turtle. He was set upright, his amber and
muddy brown underbelly facing her. His webbed feet featured dull claws over which he seemed to have no control,
claws grabbing at air and pulling shirts from their hangers.

"Youth today have no concept of work. I'm sure you will
agree." Grandmother Sminkova thought of her own lost,
drug-addled granddaughter. Those memories were worn
and filled with holes and uncertainties, as though the same

colony of moths that flew around the lodger's garments had invaded her mind and fed on her dreams.

"Yes, it is true," she conceded. She was able to surmise that despite his harsh words he still cared for the boy, as she did, and was waiting to fully abandon this world when his grandson's soul was settled.

"He has been lying there like that for days now. I go and ruffle his hair but he only shoos me away. This is what thanks I get. I have traveled far, and I am tired." The old man suddenly withdrew his head into his shell. After a few moments Grandmother Sminkova could hear a muffled snoring coming from the orifice. *Old dotard*. She gave him a powerful kick in his shell's midsection and the head sprang out like a shot.

"What was that? Who? Oh. You old stinker you." After his outburst, the old man appeared to relax, then without warning began to flicker like an image from a reel of old film. "Disintegration is a talent," he said, "that I am still learning." His head disappeared back in his shell as quickly as it had sprang forth.

"I will come with you," Grandmother Sminkova told him. "When the time is right. I said, I will come with you!" She tapped the shell again but he gave no response. She could now see the flickering coming from within the shell, as though he had a black-and-white TV in there and was hibernating in front of it. She searched her apron and found, in its folds, the fresh sturgeon she had hidden in case she should go hungry on the journey. She dangled it above the black hole of the elder Benda's shell. He emerged again and snapped at it with viperlike speed, tearing the tender flesh from bone with his teeth. She held it there for him and he went about, all manners forsaken, sating himself, keeping one eye rolled back and observant of other predators. In his state of feeding, he appeared momentarily content, but the pleasure was all Grandmother Sminkova's.

2

When Shirting woke it was well into the afternoon, and the sun had already set. Four days now since its rays had alighted upon his being. Since his return from Moravia he had once again become a night-dwelling creature. The news that Grandmother Sminkova was in the hospital with a poor prognosis, coupled with Monika's sudden appearance and departure, had sent him into an unqualified funk. The cold rotating blade of the season was trimming its charges down to a more manageable number. Shirting was constantly feeling his own forehead to make sure that this winter-induced plague had not stowed away on his own person. Any feeling of faintness sent him scrambling for his bed. He hydrated himself with a procession of bottles of curative mineral water, punctuated with lone shots of Becherovka, which he poured from a bottle he kept icily cold in between his window panes.

But this was not a time to ruminate—the season demanded contrition, and Shirting was prepared to submit. On his bedside table was the *Friend Kitty* cash card and whatever monies were left from his journey. It was time to make amends and reclaim his place within the gears of the machine that was transforming the city at such an accelerated rate. To sally forth, to do battle with the very night if need be, if only to return those stolen goods. He jumped from bed and made his way over to the wardrobe. He swung open the door to reveal his sharkskin suit, pressed crisp by Hanna. That wardrobe had figured heavily in his dreams recently, and in truth he was a bit afraid of it. In the middle of the night, of its on accord, it occasionally opened hungrily as though it wanted to devour him whole; other times it gave a grand yawn, leaving traces of Old Crow fumes in the night air.

Shirting dressed, threw on his overcoat, and headed into the dark of the hallway. At his door he observed the breakfast that had, in recent days, replaced his traditional homemade offering, an Amway Breakfast Bar decorated by a garter belt of whipped cream. Shirting's morning meal was now a dolled up piece of product. He casually kicked it over to Mizen's door. He paused in the corridor and listened. From within his neighbor's abode he heard a low-pitched growling, followed by a shriek and then what sounded like the snapping of several mouse traps. Shirting cringed, imagining the debauchery transpiring in his neighbor's rooms. He hustled down the stairs and out the door. Instead of waiting for the tram, he opted for a brisk walk. His route took him over the castle hill, under the path where, during one lost time, those out of favor with the court were dangled aloft inside cages and meant to suffer the ridicule and harassment of the public. He circumvented the more touristed streets and found himself at the top of the hill of Strahovska Park, where he paused to appreciate the lights of the city that lay before him. It was a board of circuits, flashing with warning and kinetic energy. The smell of ozone and charcoal. He could see Wenceslas Square, its row of bright light twinkling like some neon caterpillar making its way across the cityscape. The city was conspiring, a tension in the air. In his heart Shirting knew something was afoot. The night was arming itself with frozen air, sending out preemptive strikes in the form of piercing winds. The night, a deep and impenetrable moat around that invisible city in the sky.

Shirting had planned to go directly to *Friend Kitty*'s offices, but the pang of hunger in his stomach demanded attention. So, in search of nutrition, if not companionship, he strode quickly down Nerudova. Before long he was crossing the Charles Bridge and making his way toward the square, where he knew he might purchase a quarter of a roasted chicken along with some brown beer. At a red light somebody stopped next to him to ask him directions in Czech. He threw his arms up in confusion. Shirting: being mistaken for a local.

Down Celetná ulice Shirting walked in zombified fashion, numbed to the activity around him. Soon a chorus of chanting voices penetrated the bubble of solitude in which he moved. Exactly what they were chanting he was unsure, as they persisted in using their native tongue. He stepped aside and stood next to a bench to watch the crowd approach. They appeared to be a group of children and attractive teenagers waving pickets like battle-axes, holding placards and handing out flyers. Shirting had to jump back into an archway just to get out of their path. Their fervor was unmistakable.

"Revolution," Shirting thought, "has finally come. The real revolution, not this sham socialist mother-love. The revolution that favored a person's finer qualities. The revolution of the rarefied." Then from above came one explosion, followed by another. Shirting quickly took cover under a bench. *Violent revolution*, the only real kind. *The blood of our oppressors shall run in the streets like wine*. From his place he shouted out—imploring the crowd not to continue in the direction that they were—straight into the epicenter of the battle, where the missiles surely sought their targets with precision. But nobody heeded his pleas. Indeed, they appeared to by hurrying toward the commotion as quickly as they could.

"Hey, fireworks," he heard a tourist shout out.

"What's it, the Fourth of July?" the other joked.

Shirting refused to believe the ruse. But he needed to confirm it with his own eyes. Everything else was just hysteria. He snuck from his place and joined in with the crowd, rushing along the side streets toward Wenceslas Square. A witness of international stripe was needed to verify, if not testify later in front of international tribunals, and Shirting planned on fulfilling that role. Witnesses were no doubt treated well, fed three times a day, if not held in a certain esteem.

But once he reached the square, Shirting became confused. The crowd seemed to be congregating beneath the dramatic pyrotechnic display, in front of a brand new branch of the White Swan shopping center. A stage had been set up and decorated with bunting and colored lights. He had arrived just in time to catch the celebratory show. It wasn't revolution, after all, just the opening of another department store. Shirting should have been desensitized to it by now, for there had been store openings throughout the autumn, each employing a fireworks display to punctuate its alignment with American values. Shirting felt crestfallen, let down. He sighed in disappointment: revolutions were such lazy, unpredictable things. He wished they'd get their act together.

Shirting purchased a Nescafé from a sidewalk vendor and waited with the rest of the crowd. Before long he saw the demonstrating teenagers once again parading toward them. The crowd surged back in excitement, and Shirting was almost knocked from his feet, caught up in the history of the moment. He kept his eye on the rogue faction. It was only then that he noticed some of the signs had been lettered in fashionable English and stamped by the White Swan trademark. *Down With Your Mother's Kitchen—Shop Swan; Down with Your Father's Tool Chest—Shop Swan*, they read. The crowd seemed to enjoy it, many chanting along. A sort of collective desire spurred them on, demonstrating in favor of nonstick crock pots, in favor of automatic mulchers. The energy from the attractive youngsters was such that they incited ancillary demonstrations. "Down with my Noisy Neighbor," one faction had elected to make its slogan, while another took the opportunity to decry late-arriving trams, singling out the number 19 line as being particularly tardy. It was a tricky sort of marketing they practiced; Shirting did not fully understand it but doffed his imaginary hat to them anyway. Nor was Shirting innocent of voicing his own desires, "*Down with Black Bile,*" he chanted under his breath.

While he was there, he felt obliged to take a sneak preview of the store. It occupied an entire five-story building. The limestone had been sandblasted into gleaming newness, standing out on the block like a single polished tooth in a mouth filled with rotten ones. Shirting followed the denizens inside. Though nothing was yet for sale, the goods were set out under glass or behind ropes like an art gallery exhibit; people gawked, scandalized at first by their mere availability and then afterward by the prices. The sales girls—who, resembling game show models, wore formal gowns—moved them along. Shirting clocked John Deere lawn mowers (though he had yet to see a lawn worth mowing during his entire stay), endless arrays of Dutch-made cookware, Black & Decker tool kits, juicers, food processors, display cases of Waterman, Mont Blanc, and Parker pens. There was a stand featuring chocolate bonbons; they were giving away free samples and the line stretched out the door. There was also a display stocked with high-end imported liqueurs and French wines. An old man had mistaken it for a bar and was bitterly complaining that all he wanted was a pilsner and he couldn't even get service. *"No way to run a business,"* he offered sagely in English. In the clothing section Shirting noticed, along with the omnipresent Nike Levi's, so many brands that lauded themselves as American fashion (Big Cowboy jeans, Rough and Rinsed jeans, A-wear-ica shirts) though he had never once seen any such products advertised in his native country.

The newness of the store helped Shirting see just how depleted he had become. The former, pill-popping Shirting would have felt right at home among the merchandise, a person comfortable with the hand-sell. But now he felt only ostracized from it, just another gawker. What looked like a security guard, a man dressed in a well-cut black suit, trailed behind him, tail him. But Shirting had no interest in shoplifting goods of any sort. Who was behind this most elaborate of deceptions—that was the real question. It was a monumental sham, no doubt intended to snare those with capitalistic leanings. Like a giant piece of glimmering bait. A huge bug light set out in the wintry darkness. The sales girls were almost certainly highly trained agents, prepared to abduct Shirting at any point, disappear him into a bare, poorly lit back room and inflict all sorts of torture and bodily aggravations on his person. He immediately dispatched his animated self to submit to their persuasions, almost tripping over a babushka's heels as he became lost in his own imaginings.

Shirting decided he had seen enough. But when he turned back, he discovered that White Swan featured one more vendor, one that would throw his mood into pure bedlam: in front of him, occupying a small kiosk with its telltale black and green coloration, was a Capo Family Coffee stand, Magda working the register, while at the helm of the espresso maker was Jason Bunny Shoup.

JOHN SHIRTING AND THE VERY SILENT PARTNERS

"OH, HEY," BUNNY SAID CASUALLY. "I WAS WONDERING WHEN you'd roll around."

"What kind of chicanery are you pulling here?" Shirting said.

"It's pretty incredible, isn't it? All that time you were talking about Capo's at the Prop Room, and now here they are. Pretty fantastic, huh?"

"You can try to counterfeit the look, but the philosophy behind the product is impossible to duplicate."

"Counterfeit? This is the real thing, John." Bunny handed a freshly pulled shot of espresso over the bar in a trademark Capo cup. "Bang for a buck?" Shirting tasted it—at once it brought back those pleasant days on Wells Street, a simpler time when Shirting had a clearly delineated purpose, when he was an accepted and invested partner. It was indeed the patented deep roast used by Capo's. The very sound of that hissing espresso machine, coupled with the aroma of the thick espresso it discharged, was sending him into a bout of nostalgia and longing that he previously would have thought himself incapable of.

"Nice *crema*," Shirting commented grudgingly. "But for my money I like the shot timed to a perfect twenty-one-second pull."

"Hey, cut me some slack. I'm still trying to get the tamp right. I tend to pack a bit too tight."

"A common mistake. Like pinball it takes a *supple wrist*."

Bunny acknowledged Shirting's advice and turned from him to catch up with a few orders. Shirting observed and mentally checked the mistakes his old boss was making in his rush. The thermometer in the milk read ten degrees above the accepted level: practically burnt. Bunny didn't wipe down the steaming wand after each drink, and his cupping system was a shambles. A desecration of the temple Shirting had once maintained. Bunny double-cupped a large Capone'cino and turned his attention back to Shirting.

"We worked out a deal with White Swans all across Europe. And this is only the beginning. I'm helping engineer the building of the flagship store in the old Prop Room building. It's going to be the corporate headquarters for Eastern European expansion. Then into Russia. We hope to follow the route of the Trans-Siberian railway down through Mongolia until we hit Beijing. China, the grail of any corporate expansion. Sounds amazing, doesn't it?"

"But that, all that, was my idea," said Shirting. "The Semi-Secret Service."

"Implemented," said Bunny. "But I don't think you can chalk those ideas up to just one person. I think they're really just in the air."

"Oh."

"The individual has little place here. This isn't about ideas or personalities. You know we all have a shared vision," countered Bunny, as he topped off a *panne cotta* for

216

an old pensioner. He had been well-indoctrinated. "This is bigger than just us."

"That is true. But that said, what about *me*?"

"We looked for you. The *Friend Kitty* guys are pretty pissed, as I'm sure you can imagine."

"You stole my job," said Shirting, the realization dawning on him. "That is my position."

"Hey, don't get hot," said Bunny.

"Quisling! I call quisling!" Shirting shouted. "Benedict Arnold at best."

"This guy giving you trouble?" Shirting hadn't noticed the man in the black suit that had come up behind him. An American, wearing sunglasses. Standing behind him was a true Capo Coffee Family Made Man. Shirting should have recognized the corporate uniform before, but out of context he just looked like some sundry spy or Mafioso.

"No, he's okay."

Out of habit, Shirting was quick to pull from his attaché case his Perks & Percolations card. He handed it over to the man, who studied it closely as a border guard would a passport.

"This has expired," he said, handing it back to Shirting.

"I know, I know. I just wanted to make a point," he said.

"Which is?"

"I'm one of you."

The Made Man looked Shirting over. He noted the waxy hair, the whiskered face and swollen eyes.

"Are you drunk?" he asked Shirting.

"No," said Shirting. "If I have partaken in an afternoon shot of Becherovka, it is only in the celebratory spirit of the occasion. Or you can chalk it up to cultural exploration, if you like."

"I would recommend the double Lucky Latte'ano for such occasions," said the man. Shirting immediately realized he was being dismissed, that the Made Man was hand-selling him product. "It's twice the espresso, but we can make it half-caf, if that is more to your tastes."

"I know what a Lucky Latte'ano is!" yelled Shirting. "I practically invented it. And don't insult me with your half-caf condescension. I can handle twice the caf as a ruffian like you."

The Made Man and Bunny exchanged glances. Shirting knew he was in trouble. Speaking in such a tone to a Made Man like that in Chicago might have resulted in a broken finger at the very minimum.

"You are damaging the atmosphere we have tried so very hard to create," said the Made Man. "You see customers calmly sipping their coffee and other coffee products. You see them connecting with their spirit. Individual *and* collective spirit. You wouldn't want their first impression of Capo Coffee Family to be one of discomfort and perhaps violence, would you?"

"Come on Shirting, give it a rest, you know?" chimed in Bunny.

"You dirty rat, you," said Shirting to Bunny. He felt a grip around the back of his neck.

"Stop," said Bunny, interceding. "He's cool. Just let me talk to him for a minute." Shirting felt the hand release. Bunny waved him over behind the bar. "Listen," he began, "I feel bad about this. The thing is, they've got a file on you, and it doesn't look good. But maybe tomorrow you could come by the headquarters and we'll have a talk. Perhaps we can work out some sort of freelance position.

"Freelance? We both know such things just aren't possible. You're either *in* or *out*."

"Let me work on that, okay? As point man I'm in sort of a unique position here."

"Okay," agreed Shirting.

"Now get out of here before we both get in hot water."

"A shot for the road, perchance?"

Bunny pulled another shot, timing it to a precise twenty-one seconds, and handed it over to Shirting, who carried the cup from the kiosk in both hands as though he were cradling a small bird.

~~~~

Shirting carried the cup all the way home, savoring each cautious sip, until there was nothing left but a brown dampness that clung to the cup's wax coating, which he mopped out with the tip of his tongue. He did not dispose of that cup; instead he tucked it into his attaché case, imagining it on his desk as a sort of hood ornament to the new life that he saw unfolding in front of him. As a germ of the system, he was suddenly sort of successful.

On arriving home, Shirting found another reason to celebrate: as he approached the top landing, he discovered his neighbor's door open, and a quick peek inside revealed the disheveled scene of somebody packing up. Boxes were stacked in the anteroom and he could hear Mizen giving directions to an unseen partner.

"Dear Herbivore," Shirting called out. "Are you there?" Mizen poked his head out from his sitting room.

"Oh, it's you," he said. "Come in if you must." Shirting did so.

"I see you have officially declared defeat."

"Nothing of the sort. My animal companion and I are making an exploratory excursion down to the Balkans. We're going to do some shows in Serbia to try to get them to rethink their abusive strategies, then it's over to Romania as part to the Ceausescu Reformation Party. The apartment is simply too expensive to keep."

"Lenka, I presume?" Shirting said to the girl who had poked her head out from behind the corner.

"Jitka," she said modestly.

"Jitka?"

"Indeed," said Mizen. "That whole Lenka scene was beat. I don't know what I was thinking. Hey, you want some peanut butter? We'll call it a peace offering."

"Sure," said Shirting. Mizen sent Jitka into the kitchen, where she retrieved a jar of crunchy Jif.

"It's not as exotic as it used to be. Most supermarkets are stocking it now."

"Nonetheless," said Shirting, accepting the gift.

Mizen topped his box off with a few Chomsky paperbacks, then taped it up.

"So what's it going to be with you, Shirting? You're not learning Czech, so I can't imagine you're going to stay here. This city is going to hell."

"I hope it does not offend you, but unlike your plans, mine are only just beginning to take shape. Now that Capo's is in town, it is only a matter of time before the true revolution is instigated."

"Capo's, I heard about that. Really sad," said Mizen, shaking his head. "Shirting, you and your revolutions."

"Not just any revolution, but that in which we are led by our better selves. Imagine, if you will, our governing body is like an espresso machine. . . ."

"Come on now," Mizen pleaded.

"Seriously. I've been thinking a lot about this lately. A perfectly calibrated machine distills what is best in the bean.

One that is too forceful leaves the bean's subtle, hidden qualities underutilized. But one whose pressure is too lax will allow the fine grounds to steep too long. Never leave a bean idle, Dear Herbivore. Bitterness is the unfortunate result. But the perfectly calibrated machine allows the individual characteristics to arise, to come to the fore and shine like a bit of distilled sunlight. Every color of the rainbow lies within, you know."

"More corporate propaganda. Shirting, when will you ever learn?"

"Old friend, my objectives are being achieved as we speak."

"Shirting, the only worthwhile revolution is the one within—you can believe that or not. Otherwise, if you insist on taking part in this cultural imperialism, then I suppose you are in the right place, after all. This city is filled with drones who lack only a queen bee to tell them what to do. What is there to fill that huge void left by the demise of communism? Contrary to my best efforts, it appears it is MTV and pornography. A principality of the worst that our country has to offer."

"While I am sorry to see you disappointed, I must beg to differ."

"Okay, I'm not going to argue anymore," said Mizen. "I'll be gone in the morning. Got to wake up early to keep one step ahead of the likes of you Capo Coffee folks."

"Very well, I bid you *adieu*," said Shirting, giving Mizen a doff of an imaginary hat. He waved to Jitka, who surprised him by stepping up close and kissing him on the cheek. It was the first human affection Shirting had experienced in a long time. He felt a tear begin to well up in the corner of his eye and had to hastily retreat before the solitary drop wet his cheek. *I am the Boy. That can't enjoy. Invisibly.*

In Which Shirting Returns
to the Frothy Fold

Shirting showed up at the Prop Room building early the next morning. He had done his best to smooth out his appearance, bathing in his tub's lukewarm water and shaving the night before. He had even, with great ceremony, taken his Capo's apron and visor from their storage space in the wardrobe and tried them on in front of the mirror. He admired himself and went through a few practice maneuvers behind an imaginary espresso machine, loosening up the wrists, getting back some *Zen*. It felt utterly comfortable, and the uniform still suited him; were it not for fear of wrinklage, he might have slept with it on. On the morning tram he could not resist wearing the apron over his sharkskin suit, drawing any number of curious looks. And there, on that tram, on the route into the city, passing under the magnificent palace and St. Vitus Cathedral, amid the smell of freshly fallen snow, Shirting was touched by the first rays of sun that morning. The fresh light had a purging quality. Oh how he had missed the sun.

There was nothing on the facade of the building to indicate that it had been appropriated by Capo Coffee Family. From the outside it looked much as it had in the days of the club—an abandoned, degenerated space. But once Shirting walked through the front door, the change was apparent. Within the flurry of activity, a refurbishment was underway. The chaos of the start-up office, not to mention Shirting's authentic Capo uniform, allowed him to move through the building unfettered. Shirting recognized a number of Bunny's former bouncers and bartenders dressed in Capo's T-shirts, a few donning the shoulder-padded suits of the operation's muscle. Made Men in training. Shirting noted Hard Road hunched over a computer monitor, typing frantically. The three Czech bartenders, Darina, Eveta, and Suzannah, were there too, performing a taste test, taking turns at sipping from a flight of French press pots. An office had been set up in the café, and Shirting could smell the vacuum-packed whole beans from the storage room in the back. Capo Coffee Family posters hung on the walls with the familiar old slogans. It was obvious to him that Bunny was not exaggerating about the proposed expansion: this was not the support system for a solitary kiosk.

"Hey, Shirt-man." It was Bunny, rounding the corner with a twenty-pound bag of beans thrown over his shoulder like a dead body. Despite the vacuum packing, the roasted bean smell was all over.

"Reporting for duty," said Shirting, saluting. "Just set me up with a rag and I'm ready to take that honored position behind old steamy."

"Yeah, um. Listen, let's have a seat in the office and talk about that."

"No need to ply me with coffee. I'll take mine at my post. Naturally it will take me a few drink assemblages to get back in the swing of things, but I assure you each and every customer's expectations will be duly exceeded." Bunny took him silently by the shoulder and led him into the office, shutting the door behind them.

"Look, Shirting, I can't let you on the machine," he said.

"Like *fun* you can't," replied Shirting.

"No, it's true. Your file. It has you marked as a mole. I don't know what you did in Chicago, but the higher-ups won't allow it."

Shirting looked down at the apron: the gangster on the Capo insignia appeared to be sneering at him. Changeable little gangster that it was. He stood up and untied the apron from behind.

"No need for that. Like I said, I've worked something out. I know that this isn't exactly what you're looking for, but I have arranged for a position for you. And I believe that if you stick to it long enough, the higher-ups might be convinced that your intentions are true. A penance of sorts."

"What sort of position?"

"I don't want you to be offended."

Shirting merely nodded and prepared for the worst. From a stack in the corner, Bunny pulled a sign with the insignia painted on the front. It was made of heavy cardboard with lamination, and had two shoulder straps. Shirting: recruited as a walking billboard. He looked at the offering dumbly.

"So, this is how it's going to be?"

"Look," said Bunny, "the worst of winter is over. It's getting warmer every day. By spring, I'm sure I can talk them into letting you back behind the machine. There should be at least five new outlets open by then, and we have a real shortage of talent over here."

Shirting took the sign, examined it, then hoisted it over his shoulders. He felt like a human playing card with it on. *Whelp Help.*

"What if the police stop me?"

"We've got it all worked out with them, don't worry."

"I'm sure you do."

"And I paid off the *Friend Kitty* guys. I do feel partially responsible, so we'll consider it a signing bonus."

"For that I am grateful."

"So here's the deal. Just work daylight hours. Try to keep to the Charles Bridge area and the Old Town, where the tourists congregate. They're going to be our primary market until the Czechs get the hang of it. And feel free to stop in the White Swan anytime to recharge your batteries, on the house naturally. All you can drink."

"I haven't taken the job just yet," said Shirting.

"No? I don't get it. What's the hang-up?"

"No hang-up," said Shirting, pausing, the mechanisms in his mind churning. "Just one question."

"Yeah, what's that?" said Bunny.

"Who was it who gassed the Prop Room?"

"I can't talk about that."

"It was the Capo's people, wasn't it?"

"Don't go there, Shirt-man. Dangerous territory. I think you know that."

"Just how long have you been working for them?"

"Come on, you know I can't answer that."

"Uh-huh."

"Well. Are you saying you're not taking the job?"

"I'd like a cup of java before I head out. It's going to be cold today."

"That's what I want to hear. Let me pour you one. It's from a new product, the K.G. Bean Blend. Super dark. Impenetrable. Secret ingredients and whatnot. Packs a punch. They're not really into subtlety in this part of the world, are they?"

"Thanks," said Shirting, accepting the cup.

"Well, I've got to head out and relieve Gus at the stand. Don't be a stranger."

"I won't."

〜〜〜

With that, Shirting headed out into the city, signboard strapped over his shoulder, weighted down by the sign, disposable coffee cup warming his hands. He began to amble toward the Charles Bridge, feeling utterly conspicuous. Where he had once tried to pass as invisible, he now stood out in any crowd, people looking on him at first with curiosity then with a touch of repulsion, as if he were an untouchable, having sold out his very body to corporate interests. It was understandable, for the men who plied his trade were all lost men, saddled with billboards advertising everything from souvenir shops to McDonald's. Shirting soon found he had an affinity for these people and exchanged quiet, empathetic nods with all those who passed, much like bus drivers do with one another. Professional courtesy. A secret society of the dispossessed, the unaccepted.

He also discovered that the sign made him an easy target for snowball-throwing children. Shirting: hunted like a beast. But other than that occasional hazard, the work was easy. There was nothing for Shirting to do but walk, and give occasional directions to lost tourists. And walk he did. He found, after several days on the job, he could set his body on automatic pilot; walk himself into a trancelike state, a meditative meander. An artist of the solitary stroll. He found it neither pleasurable nor uncomfortable, this mode of life. It was simple transport, an extended in between moment that he was living in. A peripheral zone, where time collapsed upon itself, the days passing unnoticed. His feet had become accustomed to the cobblestones; he no longer clip-clopped like a horse. When his legs got tired, he sat on a bench to rest; when his energy waned, he stepped into the White Swan and replenished himself with a series of espresso shots. *Put a cap in himself.* At first it was just Bunny working behind the bar, but eventually Suzannah and Eveta took his place. Shirting relished the breaks that he took with them, and even though they were younger than him, they assumed a maternal disposition when handing over his drinks.

〰〰

Things carried on like that for the rest of the winter and into the spring. Where others prepared the new outlets, Shirting walked. Where Czechs younger than himself were taken under the wing of the giant corporation, Shirting walked. Where new hires ruled at the espresso machine, Shirting walked. He had given up asking Bunny when he was going to be allowed to resume that post, for he had already been put off so many times. Indeed, the black bile had risen to the surface, after all. He offered no defenses. Shirting, but a gull caught in the oil slick of that dark humor. He, in short, tasted the familiar, not unfriendly flavor of despair. He was now resigned to it, however; it was a comfortable feeling, and not entirely unwelcome, for it was preferable to emptiness. Had it not molded him, throughout his life, like a third parent? Right there, without even thinking about it, Shirting accepted that this insurgent emotion had reclaimed its authority, and its will would be exercised. Happiness, a word of convenience under the best of circumstances, was only a parasite that had lived within him, one that demanded constant feeding—but the sorrow, *oh the simple sorrow*—demanded nothing but complicity.

Shirting took solace with the other dispossessed human billboards, whose experiences had left them with no shortage of disappointment to commiserate with. In time, their friendly nods had turned into brief conversations, which were better acquitted over a pint of beer. On such occasions, they retreated, on the clock, to the warmth of the smoky cellar that housed the Golden Udder. The place had become a sort of clubhouse to the walking billboards. Shirting, owing to his national birthright, was something of a celebrity with the men. He was asked to produce his passport on numerous occasions to prove he was indeed an American sign carrier, and not some scab Romanian or Ukrainian.

In this way he lived a purgatorial existence. Days buzzed on coffee and beer, never intoxicated, but always under the influence. It was a half-life, a divestment of ambition and hope, leaving a husk of a person. It was obvious that, despite Bunny's reassurances, Shirting was never going to be allowed to pull shots again, at least not under the auspices of Capo's. They had him where they wanted him: demoralized, contained.

Grandmother Sminkova had died in late winter. Shirting attended the funeral with Hanna, and then took her to the Sugar Shop, where they partook in a ceremonial cream pastry.

On that somber day Hanna had asked Shirting if he didn't want to move into Mizen's vacant apartment, but Shirting declined the offer. He felt attached somehow to the bare, drafty room he inhabited, as if he, like Capo Coffee, had sentenced himself to an atonement.

≈≈≈

"It's the plague," Shirting explained to Janos, the white-haired human billboard for a souvenir shop on Karlova. "It has inhabited my body. Did you ever see *Night of the Living Dead*? I have been possessed by an otherworldly disease, which has rendered me spiritless. I walk. It is what I know." Janos nodded empathetically, though he understood nothing of what Shirting said. They were drinking beer together, that was communication enough. "See this beer. *Pivo*? If there is anything that can provoke my spirit, it is this. So with that said, while we are still among the living, please allow me to purchase one more round." Janos's eyes beamed. Shirting raised his hand, but the bartender had anticipated him and set two more beers down before he could rest his own empty stein on the table. Shirting and Janos both quaffed heavily. Shirting: chasing the liquid dose.

Already tipsy during this second beer, having desperate thoughts during a lull in conversation, he began to see possibilities in the dingy basement pub, possibilities he had never seen before. One could capitalize on the uniformity of such *pivovars*. McDonald's, after all, sold not much else than a kind of consistency. Just add a little marketing, and there might be Golden Udders all across the city. He envisioned a Golden Udder brand beer—subsidiary deals with Čedok and the national airline. There could be a little Golden Udder kiosks at the airport, one in each metro station; ideal places for the dank feel already cultivated by the original Udder. Shirting sent a silent *Nazdraví* to the tiny catalyst Germ within, still alive and kicking after so much brutalization. He explained it all to Janos, who, readying himself for his third beer, rubbed his hands together and agreed enthusiastically.

Shirting ordered the next round with authority. The bartender practically worked for him, after all. He sent a round to a distant table of old men as well. "One day I shall break up your little tribe and send you each as a representative to a new franchise, in order to instill the proper mood," he informed them from across the room. If they only understood, how they would respect him. Shirting settled into his drink, giddy with his new plan, a whole new stage of his life unfolding before him. He didn't need Capo's, didn't need Bunny Shoup either. And as for the pill, well, the beer was as fortifying, it just took him in another, yet equally legitimate direction. Shirting was open to exploration.

"I'd like to see a little pamphlet explaining the particular qualities of your brew, you know, really educating people about beer. Make them comfortable with the *mere idea* of beer. Exploit the lore behind the drink. This is just for starters." So Shirting told Janos. "Create a mascot. A cuddly cow, wacky yet wise to the ways of the market. And cool, too—sunglasses are a must. Cool always sells, and nothing says cool like sunglasses. Really make him into a crafty personality. We'll name him Brewster. Divine Bovine. Bovinity Divinity. Golden Udder insignias on all the steins. My kingdom for a cow costume. With Brewster at our side we move on to world domination. You, my dear friend, shall wear the Brewster suit. Nobody else can be trusted. You exclusively. Your days as a wandering advertisement are over. My dear

Janos. My dear, dear man. You shall graduate to a wandering cow. Bring out your thespian qualities. We'll give those old Americans a taste of their own medicine. Stampede, I cry! Why shouldn't we?" Janos smiled at Shirting and toasted him through his missing front teeth.

Shirting became quite suddenly morose. In truth, he was not used to so much beer and had not taken breakfast that morning. "The question is this: Is it not good to be a cog in a machine if the machine is effective and seemingly indestructible? Eat or be eaten? Die standing or live kneeling? With that quandary in mind, I am off to hand in my billboard. I call it quits on this Capo-wear. No, don't try to stop me, dear Janos, our day will come." Shirting paid the tab, giving the bartender a firm handshake. How they would embrace the glorious newness that Shirting proposed. All submitted to newness in the end. *Wall fall down. All fall down.*

〜〜〜

Shirting made his way through the day's grayness with a renewed directive. The Golden Udder was not far from The White Swan, where Shirting knew Bunny was relieving Suzannah on her day off. Citizenry parted to let the rectangular boy past. But when he arrived at the department store, he was greeted with an unexpected sight: the kiosk stood unmanned and a short line was forming, growing in length, at the right of the register. Darina, still uncertified at the machine, looked helplessly at the crowd. It was a disgrace to the company's own guidelines, if not their very mission statement. Not a Made Man in sight. Shirting immediately forgot the resentment he had accrued toward Capo's, for he instinctively knew it was time to step up to the plate. His moment had come, and his mood was such that action was demanded. As he trotted toward the post, Shirting stripped off the billboard, letting it fall to the ground behind him. Luckily he had yet to discard his apron: he still wore it to work in hope he would be called up to the major leagues. Shirting made sure the strings were tied tight, then assumed his place behind the espresso machine.

LUCKYBELLY STRIKES BACK

OH GLORIOUS STEAM PRESSURE! THE VERY HISS WAS A COMFORT.
Miraculous milk, running velvety white over the wand,
churning into drifts and peaks of foam. Cumulus clouds of
cream. The bean grinder buzzing like a bee hive. Pulverized
into purity. Had the city ever known such freshness? Such
awesome aroma? Had the espresso ever run so abundantly,
with such a honeyed consistency? Crema layering the top of
each perfectly pulled shot, the color of a well-toasted marsh-
mallow. But all this was secondary, for there was a task to
tackle. Here we had a snaking line of homesick Americans
waiting for their fix. A skeptical Italian, a brash Brit. Curious
Czechs hovering around in the periphery. Shirting, brave
barista, would serve them all.

"Never fear Darina, I'm Coffee College certified," he told
the suspicious Czech who was managing the cash register. She
nodded in agreement, for who was she to turn away cold, hard
cash. Cash in such abundance. Super-abundance. An hour's
wage for a cup of milk and coffee. It was obscene, really.

Shirting quickly improvised a cupping system and went
to work. His hands flew—he became the Hindu god Ganesh
behind the bar—six arms exacting the assemblage of each drink

variation, coaxing the espresso from the machine with firmness and love; with the reverence of an immunologist extracting venom from a snake. Lucky Latte'anos, Capone'cinos of all stripe. *Con Pannes, dopios.* Darina handled the long coffee. They had come on this unthawed spring day to be treated to inexpensive luxury and to be momentarily part of the Capo's clan, and they were not disappointed. It was a sight to behold, and Shirting was rewarded with a round of applause by the satisfied crowd. But the attention only provoked more orders. Word was spreading on the street. Shirting, with flashing fingers, took them all on. His apron flying out behind him as though blown by the wind. For just a few moments, genius had been attained at that post.

What Shirting didn't know was that there were Made Men who had gone undercover. One such representative was checking out kitchenware when the disruption occurred. With a barista in the bathroom, he should not have been admiring his own visage in the galvanized bottom of a double-boiler. The Made Man, clad in a lime-green track suit, advanced from his place amid the crockery, approached Shirting from behind, beheld the awesome power of the insurgent barista, was momentarily breathtaken, then recovered and swiftly clobbered him over the head with the meaty bottom side of his fist.

Shirting, at once floorbound. Blackness. A pause. A loop-d-loop in time. Shirting divested of bodily constraints, free to let his mind's eye open wide, color rushing in kaleidoscopic swirls. A new mode of perception took over. Sudden stimulation; a confluence of his animated self and the heightened reality he was experiencing. Shirting, overthrowing Shirting. Usurping. Shirting becoming the super-Shirting, puffing out of his clothing, muscular, deft, and righteous. Indeed, an uppercase "L" ornamented his tee.

"Ladies and Gentlemen," he announced grandly to the now animated crowd, "there is an avenging entity in town, and his name is Luckybelly."

"Ker Pow!" exclaimed the bubble above the Made Man's head as Shirting sent him sprawling with an uppercut. His flexing muscle was enough to keep any other comers at bay. He quickly prepared himself a triple Lucky Latte'ano, which he drank straight from the milk pitcher. Avenging was *thirsty business.* Having outgrown his place behind the espresso machine, he jumped over its hissing machinery, sending the gathered crowd scampering for cover.

"Do not fear, citizens of Newfangle, though I am absolutely avid, I declare myself a benevolent force in your midst. But do not come too close, that is my only request." With that pronouncement Luckybelly strode from the department store and out onto the square. Quite suddenly he was all alone. He looked from one end of the square to the other, but the city before him was deserted. Not only that, but the blustery cold had relinquished its grip as a warm spring breeze blew, almost tenderly, across his path. And gone were the cigarette billboards and neon signs; nothing blocked the austere beauty of the pastel-colored buildings. Graffiti had been scrubbed away, and no French fry wrappers polluted the macadam walkways. It was a Prague of the mind, a pure Prague. A cut gemstone under glass, unsullied by daily business and human traffic. Indeed, above the skyline there appeared to be a long pane of glass covering the strange altered city. He moved down the street—a latent, potential energy permeating the air he breathed. The smell of electronic fumes and something familiar that he immediately recognized as the musk of Slot Dogs red hots.

Two glowing figures approached him from down the block—as they got closer Shirting could discern that they were accompanied by a bleeping noise—the pixelated images of Girish and Abe—adopting the form of the zombified minions from the Luckybelly game—his natural enemy. As they approached, Shirting withdrew his pen from his attaché case, twirled it in between his fingers and prepared for the confrontation. Patel set upon Shirting without warning, jaws open and hungry for flesh. Even his graphic self appeared to have a sweaty brow. "I dispel you from the dolomite of my doldrums, the humus of my humors," exclaimed Shirting, by way of battle cry. It took little more than a dexterous tap flourish with the pen to obliterate his enemy; Patel, disappeared in a puff of smoke, accompanied by an explosive sound effect. Abe, agile with his own pen, put up more of a fight, but was soon overcome by Shirting's wizardry. The American cowered beneath Shirting's superior gaming acumen.

"Be gone you, young pretender. I dispatch you to disseminate my message to the masses. I want you to spread the word. Tell them there is an Avenging Entity in town. Tell them of my offended sense of justice, tell them of my undisclosed woes. Tell all who have hurt me or done me wrong. Tell all those who have ignored or misjudged me. Tell them I am here and will right the wrong they perpetrated." Abe consented and scuttled away, emitting a contrite beeping sound as he went. Luckybelly looked around for more enemies to dispel, or any other avenging dirty work that needed to be done. Suddenly before him appeared two uniformed policemen, one male, one female. They approached him cautiously, but without apparent hostility.

"Passport," said the man. Shirting thought he recognized them.

"Avenging Entities are excluded from such protocols," he replied.

"Not here. I'm sorry," the man responded. Shirting realized they were the Golem trackers, only the man had totally lost his optical affliction and the woman's skin was clear and faintly tanned. "You are subject to the same laws that the rest of the citizens here are. And a valid stamp of passage is one."

"What citizens? This is a ghost town as far as I can tell," said Shirting, puffing up his chest dramatically, in hopes of intimidating the duo.

"There is no need for that," said Dobromilla.

"Please, don't embarrass yourself," said Dobromil. "It only proves that you are not ready to reside here."

"I don't understand," said Shirting, who, upon exhalation, had unwittingly shrunk back to his normal size, superhero no longer.

"Look," said the man, pointing toward the sky. He looked through the great pane of glass that covered the city like a dome, and off into the faint galaxy beyond. It was not a window but a screen. The outline of a spectral face in the darkness beyond. A familiar face, sweating over the Luckybelly game he was trapped in, moving Shirting, controlling his actions with an unseen joystick, the sinister satellite Shirting, eyes squinting in concentration.

"You see the problem."

"Yes."

"It has ceased to be an emotive state. We can't have this."

"Wait," said the woman. "We're forgetting something."

"What?"

"The charmed letter," she said.

"Oh, of course."

"It's a matter of form, you see."

Dobromil took the attaché case from Shirting, opened it, and shook it out. From its mouth fell his mission statement. Without ceremony, Dobromil slashed the card from the air with his cane, the action setting it ablaze, its plastic giving off a stench as it blistered, then withered under the flame. As it disintegrated, Shirting too felt something unidentifiable disintegrate within himself. If he could name it, it might not have felt so bad, but he was without employable expression, it was undeniably a quality particular to himself that distinguished him from the rest of the world. He felt pain, sorrow, and grief all at once, but he would be hard pressed to qualify it as bad; to him it felt only real, unmistakably alive. Life rushed him, in fact it surged through his veins. Life blew the circuit within him.

And then there he was, inhabiting the same skin as his Secret Self, staring down at the Luckybelly game. Luckybelly had met his demise amid a vicious riot of zombies. The "Game Over" graphic flashed, accompanied by the beeping sound-track.

"No more replays," said the voice, Kodadek going over the day's receipts. Shirting looked back at the man, the squirrel-red moustache dominating his face so much that it became his sole characteristic. A pale, stout man hidden behind the veil of that moustache. Shirting remaining at the machine, only wanting to play one more.

"I almost got high score that time."

"You're champ, kid," said Kodadek, packing up for the day. Shirting too, his self consciousness momentarily eradicated by the excitement of the game. He grabbed his book bag and accompanied Kodadek to the front of the store, where the older man turned the games off one by one. At the door Kodadek gave him a friendly, companionable pat on the back of the head. "See ya 'round," he said. Shirting said nothing. He only looked after the older man as he got into his Nova and drove off. Shirting unlocked his Mongoose and rode down North Sheridan toward home, jumping freshly tarred-over potholes along the way—skimming through the air with each effort.

His grandfather was there at the kitchen table, head slumped upon his crossed arms, asleep with a bottle of Old Crow in front of him. Next to him a book on turtle care lay splayed, the spine cracked. Shirting closed the book. His Grandfather emitted a wheezing snore—his beaklike nose trembling with some dreadful dream. The old man began to flicker in front of Shirting's eyes. Electrostatic sparks flew from his body, circling in the air like fireflies. Shirting lifted the vibrating body into his arms. The elder Shirting was light as a balloon, hollowed out somehow. Shirting carried him to his bed and laid him down. By this time his flickering had accelerated, he had diminished into a formless mass of static confusion that hovered above the sheets. He gave one final flicker, a vain attempt to reclaim human form, then disappeared, leaving behind only the smell of ozone and bourbon. Shirting, too, went to bed, pulling the sheets up over his eyes.

~~~

John Shirting woke up alone, with a sore head. *Otherwise okay.* On his bedside table he found a brief note from Bunny informing that he had once again been excommunicated from the Capo Coffee Family organization. Whoever had taken him home had removed his apron, and his visor was nowhere to be seen. From outside his window he could hear the blackbird emit several consecutive calls and then go quiet.

Shirting thought of Mizen, missing him already. He sprang from bed, feeling oddly refreshed, then he washed and put on his sharkskin suit. Looking out the window revealed that spring had catalyzed in the city: tender green shoots poked up through in the Sminkovas' garden, and the white petals of an apple tree fluttered in the breeze like tiny fans. Shirting prepared to leave his room. To rebirth himself into that city. Out the door he went.

But as he descended the stairs, he could hear somebody else huffing and puffing on their way up. On the Sminkovas' landing, to the tune of barking poodles he met Lila, canvases strapped to her back like expansive wings.

"Oh, hey, I heard that there was another American living here, I didn't know it was you," she said.

Shirting helped her up the stairs to the apartment.

"It's a great space, no? The nicest young Czech girl rented it to me. She's off to Heidelberg, I guess. I hope I'm not going to get kicked out of this one anytime soon. Sometimes I just don't think it's worth it living in this city." Shirting kept quiet on that point, and followed her into the room.

"Here, I'm glad we met. I've got something to show you," Lila said, flipping through the canvases until she came to one in particular. She withdrew it from the stack and slid it across the floor to him as though dealing him an enormous card.

"It's my first non-meat-based picture. It's going to be the start of a whole new series." Shirting could see the outline of his portrait looking back at him, the flesh tones done in bright pink, Shirting frozen in time.

"It's not finished," she apologized. "but if you want to sit we can get it done in no time."

"I don't mind," said he—John Shirting—who had always preferred acquaintances to friends.

ALSO AVAILABLE FROM
NEW EUROPE BOOKS

A page-turning dystopian classic that stands alongside
Brave New World and *Gulliver's Travels*

978-0-9825781-2-4

"Massively entertaining. . . .
Make room for the new
Gulliver!"
—**Gregory Maguire, author of**
Wicked **and** *Out of Oz*

"[A] dystopian cult classic."
—*Publishers Weekly*

"Highly entertaining."
—*Booklist*

"As if Bradbury and Orwell
had been mixed with fresh
wild berries."
—**Miklos Vámos, author of**
The Book of Fathers

New Europe Books
Williamstown, Massachusetts

Find our titles wherever books are sold, or visit
www.NewEuropeBooks.com
for order information.

ABOUT THE AUTHOR

M. Henderson Ellis lived in Prague for two years in the 1990s and there taught English and tended bar. A Chicago-area native and graduate of Bennington College, he has lived in Budapest, Hungary, since 2001. In 2004 he founded the English-language literary review *Pilvax*, which he edits to this day. He makes his living as a writer and freelance editor at wordpillediting.com.